THE WAGES OF SIN?

When Ancilla Martin encountered Lord Devin Langley by chance at a country inn, she little expected what would happen. She had known Devin as a friend of her late husband—but never dreamed of him as her lover.

Her lover he proved to be—in a night of romantic folly that swept both of them off their feet . . . or so it seemed.

But now morning had come—and Ancilla awoke to find Devin gone. All the lord had left behind were five crisp ten-pound notes to show what he had coldly calculated the evening to be worth.

Flushed with anger, Ancilla crumpled the banknotes in her white-knuckled hand—and passionately vowed that Lord Devin Langley had only just begun to pay for his night of pleasure and her night of shame. . . .

A SPORTING PROPOSITION

A SPORTING PROPOSITION

by
Elizabeth Hewitt

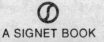
A SIGNET BOOK

NEW AMERICAN LIBRARY

A DIVISION OF PENGUIN BOOKS USA INC.

SIGNET TRADEMARK REG. U.S. PAT. OFF. AND FOREIGN COUNTRIES
REGISTERED TRADEMARK—MARCA REGISTRADA
HECHO EN DRESDEN, TN, U.S.A.

SIGNET, SIGNET CLASSIC, MENTOR, ONYX, PLUME, MERIDIAN
and NAL BOOKS are published by New American Library, a division of
Penguin Books USA Inc., 1633 Broadway, New York, New York 10019

First Printing, July, 1983

4   5   6   7   8   9   10   11   12

PRINTED IN THE UNITED STATES OF AMERICA

1

Devin Langley ducked his head to pass through the low doorframe of the sprawling farmhouse and stepped into the stableyard behind it. He filled his lungs with the brisk early-spring air and let it out again forcefully. A tall, athletically built man, he had felt cramped by the narrow back room his host used as an office, and now, outside, he unconsciously flexed the muscles of his back and shoulders as though he had been physically confined.

A shorter, more heavily built man came out of the house behind him, puffing forcefully on an old-fashioned long-stemmed pipe to which he held a piece of lit kindling from the kitchen fire. He took the stem out of his mouth and turned the pipe toward him to glare suspiciously at the contents of the bowl. "It's a damn shame, my lord, a damn shame," he said to the taller man. "You shouldn't have had to put off your plans and go out of your way like this, and for nothing more than a hoax. Still, it could have been worse, could have been worse." He put the pipe back in his mouth and sucked at it vigorously.

"I suppose," agreed Lord Langley shortly but not unkindly. He was suffering from a severe sense of ill usage at the disappointment he had just received, but he liked and respected Nathaniel Hoby and could not justly blame him for his troubles.

Having at last made the embers inside his pipe glow to his satisfaction, Hoby threw the much-reduced piece of kindling onto the grass and crushed it. "Aye," he repeated, "it could have been worse. If you hadn't met Emmet Folkstone in town and heard from him that I was here instead of with my brother in Cheshire like you'd been told, you'd have had a long journey with no more at the end of it for you than you do now."

"Every cloud has a silver lining," Devin said dryly.

Hoby followed Lord Langley's gaze to a nearby paddock, where a dark chestnut stallion, his fine breeding evident in every line and graceful motion, grazed peacefully. The farmer nodded his head sadly; he understood what his guest was feeling. Someone, a friend of Langley's, perhaps, with the bent of a practical jokester, had persuaded a bloodstock agent to inform his lordship that the great thoroughbred champion, Hoby's own Spanish Coin, now at stud, could be added to Langley's own stud for a price. Langley had arrived at his doorstep two hours ago, expecting what amounted to the fulfillment of a dream, and it had been Hoby's sorry task to dash his hopes.

The worst of it, Hoby thought, was that these young ones were always so sincere and took everything so seriously. A greater tempering of years or a less earnest desire to possess the thing he coveted might have made Langley more suspicious of the offer, for Hoby himself had once told him that only the direst financial circumstances would ever persuade him to part with the stallion. He stole another glance at his guest, who still stared at the horses in the paddock, too preoccupied with his thoughts to notice the silence that had fallen between them.

When the news had gone around five years ago that the fourth Baron Langley and his lady had been killed in a coaching accident not far from their home in Essex, it had caused a considerable stir. Not only was there talk of the loss to the horseracing world of one of its premier breeders and owners, but since Lord Langley's only son had attained his majority only the week before his parents' death, there was intense speculation as to what he would do with the reins that had been handed to him.

Devin Langley had at that time been on the town for three years, and he had already gained the reputation of a self-contained young man who took no more than a cursory interest in his father's passion for fine horseflesh. Many were the trainers and breeders who waited with keen anticipation for the news that the renowned Fairfeld Stud, begun in the previous century by the third baron, was to be broken up and put up for auction. But Devin had surprised everyone, even those closest to him, by abandoning the carefree pursuits of town life to take up the charge of the extensive estate he had inherited, and the Fairfeld Stud was now considered by those most knowledgeable to be one of the finest studs in the kingdom. The acquisition of Spanish Coin, with his fine bloodlines and proven record at stud, would have made its prestige formidable.

Both men still stared at the horse, Devin Langley with a mixture of chagrin and annoyance, Hoby with possessiveness and sympathy. A self-made man, Hoby knew that jealousy caused his lordship's competitors to claim that it was nothing more than the judicious use of the vast Langley fortune that had built the stud into what it had become. He himself had started with nothing more than an aging brood mare, five hundred pounds, and a burning desire to succeed, and he knew that success in this very competitive business took a great deal more than money. It took talent, dedication, intelligence, and, especially, hard work.

If money were the sole consideration of a breeder, Spanish Coin would long since have graced the stables at Fairfeld Park, the principal seat of the Langley family. The sum that his lordship had offered Hoby for the privilege of owning the chestnut was enough to have sent most men rushing out to their stables for a halter and lead, but a genuine love for the horse and the pride of ownership were more important to the farmer than money, and no sum would have been princely enough to have made Hoby part with Spanish Coin. Hoping in some way to ease the younger man's disappointment, Hoby tried to explain this to him.

"Of course, I quite understand," Devin replied in an offhand way.

"The thing of it is," Hoby said, "I just plain like looking at him. I don't think I'd care for the feeling I'd have waking up in the morning knowing he belonged to someone else."

A smile that reached his dark green eyes softened the somber cast of Langley's features. "I know," he said, nodding understanding. "I don't like the feeling myself."

Lord Langley's curricle, for which they had been waiting, was at last led toward them from the stables, and, smiling at Devin's words, Hoby extended his hand. "I'm sorry matters didn't come to pass as you'd hoped, my lord, but if it will give you any comfort, if ever I do decide to sell Spanish Coin, you are the one man I'd sell him to."

Devin took his hand. "I thank you for that. But promise me one thing, Nate. If you do so, write me in your own hand or come to see me yourself. I won't so easily let my eagerness get in the way of my sense a second time."

"Well, as to that," said Hoby, "there's few of us as will question an offer for something we want badly enough. I don't see that sense need come into it." But, being a scrupulous man, he added, "It does surprise me, though, that you accepted Henry Lippcott's story so readily. I know I don't have to tell you that his reputation as a bloodstock agent is none of the best."

"No," Devin agreed. "In fact, it did puzzle me a bit that you would use him as your agent in such a transaction, but there are those who still do employ him."

"Aye, those who don't wish to pay a fair rate of commission or who want no questions asked," Hoby said dryly. "But from what you told me, he made it sound as if I did want the thing kept quiet."

The carriage arrived and Devin took the reins from the groom and climbed into it. "Oh, he was very convincing. I've always admired you for your straight dealing, Nate, and I did wonder that you would set such stringent terms of secrecy on the sale, but that only proves what you have said, doesn't it? I wanted your horse too badly to look deeply into any conditions you might insist upon." He paused to gather his pair together and then added, "I think that the thing that allayed my suspicions was that he wanted nothing from me. If he had come to me seeking a commission to arrange the sale, I would have found him less credible. But he assured me that you had taken care of everything, and was so knowledgeable about the details of my previous offers to you that I never truly doubted him."

Hoby's pipe had gone out and he banged the contents out of the bowl against the wide wheel of the curricle, chipping the yellow paint with which the black wheels were picked out. "As to that," he said, glancing up briefly at Langley as he removed a leather tobacco pouch from the pocket of his old-fashioned skirted coat, "when you reach Fairfeld you'll no doubt find it's as I've said. One of your friends wished to play a joke on you. He's very likely regaling your other guests at Fairfeld this very minute with the tale of how you'll miss seeing your horses run on your own course because you're so busy running after a horse yourself." Hoby chuckled slightly at his own wit.

Devin smiled, but the smile did not reach his eyes. "I trust I am not without a sense of humor, but I don't think I shall do much laughing if that proves to be the case."

"No blame to you in that. It's a cruel sort of joke that lures a man away from his responsibilities."

Without meaning to, Hoby had touched a tender spot. Devin looked away from him and toward the northeast, the direction in which he was to travel. The sky there was perceptibly darker than it was above them and, perversely, it suited him to be heading that way. He turned back to his host. "I'm rather ashamed of myself for that," he said candidly. "It was entirely my idea to expand our race meetings at Fairfeld to two this season, and then I run off to chase after a horse, as you've said, leaving everything to Geoff to manage."

"You've nothing to worry you there," said Hoby, sucking on his refilled but unlit pipe. "Geoff Drake is the best there is."

"I know. But as steward of Fairfeld he has a great many duties to occupy him without having mine cast upon his shoulders as well. I fear I am becoming too single-minded."

Hoby smiled broadly at this. "It's the way of the sport, my lord," he said, patting the bay wheeler affectionately on the rump. "Once it's in your blood, these beasts become more demanding than any mistress a man could have."

"At this moment, if it were a woman," said Devin with more seriousness than his tone implied, "I'd buy her an emerald the size of an egg and bid her a fond farewell."

"I doubt it would answer," Hoby said, laughing. "You've married this one, my lord." He then repeated an earlier offer to put Langley up for the night, which Devin again politely declined. Expressing a desire to reach Colechester before he became benighted, Devin took his leave of Hoby and steered his horses out of the yard.

When he had turned onto the main road, he dropped his hands, and his pair, perfectly matched not only in color but in gait for the smoothest possible action, broke into an easy canter. Though the brightening rays of the sun were absent, there was about the day a brittle

crispness, such as can be found only in early spring,
which gave the new-leaved trees and fresh shoots of
grass the beauty and grace of the untouched. Though not
indifferent to nature's beauties, Devin noticed nothing of
the day's loveliness or freshness. A nonphysical malaise
that had been creeping up on him for some time per-
vaded his soul and made him oblivious of everything but
his own disquieting thoughts.

He did feel like a married man, one who found himself
in a relationship that, although still passionate, had become almost burdensome.

It had not been a love match in the beginning. But
Nathaniel Hoby was not the only one who had heard the
whispers and innuendos. In the beginning it had been
pride that had driven him to carry on his father's work
with that man's dedication, but the sport was in his
blood and blood will tell. Every promise that he had
made to himself had been honored, ultimately not through
pride but through love.

This vague discontent that troubled him had begun, as
near as he could remember, more than a twelvemonth
ago, at the time when his younger sister, Lucina, after a
triumphant first season, had married a young man with
diplomatic aspirations and gone to live with him in
Ireland, where he had been posted. It was not as if their
parting had left him bereft of her company, for since
their parents' death, she had lived much of the time with
their maternal aunt in Bath, nor did he feel envious of
Lucina for the love match she had made.

Perhaps the problem, he thought as he mechanically
slowed the pace of his carriage when the open road narrowed to become the main street of a village, was that
the success of the Fairfeld Stud mattered too much to
him. For its sake he had neglected more than his sister;
he felt as if he had in some way neglected his own life.

His sister had found joy and a sense of completeness in
the love she had with her husband, but he doubted the
solution to his discontent was that simple. A number of
women had touched his life, in both platonic and more
intimate ways, but inevitably as they had come into his
life they had gone out of it again and yet he was heart
whole. There were women he liked and considered his
friends; there were women he desired. But if love was the
great thunderclap that the novelists and poets claimed it

to be, then it was a feeling that had yet to touch him. He supposed he would marry one day—his name carried that obligation—but if he were not to be touched by the grand passion that had been the answer for his sister, then the usual sort of dynastic marriage some years in the future would do well enough for him.

The spatters of rain that had been falling from time to time for the last half mile or so began to increase in amount and intensity; reluctantly breaking out of his self-indulgent reverie, he finally pulled over to the side of the road to raise the hood of the carriage. This was not the easiest thing to accomplish alone, since he had to keep his horses steady as he pulled up and secured the hood. One of the conditions for the sale of Spanish Coin, he had been told, was that he see Hoby unattended, and even after his meeting with Mr. Folkstone in London had made him suspicious, he had still followed the instructions. Now he cursed himself for a fool for this and for anything else he could think of to find wrong with his life. But finally the task was completed and he was again on his way toward Fairfeld, his humor not much improved by the effort expended.

"We'll end in the ditch, I just know it," said Sally Beade in a voice that had the catch of a sob in it.

The carriage gave a lurch and a roll, seemingly on the brink of fulfilling her prophecy, then suddenly righted itself again and continued its slow, tortuous progress along the rutted road.

Ancilla Martin, sitting beside her in the stuffy post chaise, gave vent to an exasperated sigh. "Nonsense, Sally," she said bracingly. "We shall do no such thing. We are in far more danger, I should think, of ending up at a complete standstill in the mud."

Unconvinced, Sally shook her head and blew her nose into her handkerchief. "I've never seen it rain so hard, Miss Cilla," she said. "Coachman can't possibly see a foot ahead of him. We should have stayed at Littlelands until we could be certain of the weather."

Her sense of the absurd well defined, Ancilla laughed. "If everyone in England delayed travel until they could be certain of the weather, no one would ever go anywhere."

But Sally was not to be teased into good humor. She had believed that their journey was ill conceived from

the start, and with the familiarity born of many years
and trials shared together, she had not hesitated to make
her view known to her mistress.

"Poor Mr. Jack," she said morosely. "He must be rollin'
in his grave at these goin's on. He never would have
guessed that his own brother would try to put his widow
out of her rightful home. But if you ask me, Miss Cilla,
it's all of a piece. Mr. George is and ever has been
nothing but a bully. Always out to take what he could
from anyone who wasn't stronger than him. Was as a
boy, same as a man."

Ancilla could not deny that her brother-in-law had
been an unpleasant child; she herself had been his victim
more than once; but it was not now conducive to her
peace of mind to believe that his childish mischief had
come to fruition as adult cruelty. "I wish you wouldn't
carry on so, Sally," she said in a tone that made it clear
that she had said so many times before. "You know that
this is just a misunderstanding. When I spoke to George
about the deed to Littlelands Cottage at Mr. Sedgewick's
memorial service for Jack, he didn't try to deny that
Jack had purchased it from him when we were first
married. He said it was an oversight that it had never
been drawn up, because of the informality of the transaction, but that he would take care of the matter."

"Aye," said Sally, "and that was near all of two years
ago, and never a word nor a sight of him since."

"You know George despises the country. Littlelands
Manor has been shut up since before Jack and I were
married, and George was never much of a correspondent
even when Jack was alive."

"Well, that Mr. Grogan person, callin' himself Mr.
George's man of business, didn't wait to put pen to paper,"
Sally said through her handkerchief. "Tellin' you that
your own property was to be sold as part of the estate
and that you should pack your bags and get out like you
was of no account."

Ancilla had to admit that Sally's point was well taken.
When the letter from Mr. Grogan had arrived more than
a fortnight ago, there had been no mention of her right
to the property on which she lived; in fact, Mr. Grogan
had made it clear that she was regarded as a burden to
the estate and could not reasonably expect to continue as
such when a purchaser was found. He suggested, quite

bluntly, that she make Other Arrangements. The angry reply she had drafted at once had brought her only a brief note stating that no record existed of the sale to her husband, and a reproachful letter to her brother-in-law had received no reply at all.

"Well, that is why we are going to London," she said patiently. "I shall talk to George and he and I will settle the matter. We will go together to Mr. Grogan and see to it that a proper deed is drawn up at once."

"You hope."

Ancilla put her head back against the squabs, but the bumpiness of the ride made this position considerably less comfortable than it should have been, and she sat up straight again. "I wish you would do what you could to improve your humor, Sally," she said, a note of annoyance coming into her voice for the first time. "I know how very difficult it must be to have to travel when one is suffering from a head cold, but this is the first time either of us has traveled farther from Littlelands than Colechester, and we should be looking forward to our first visit to London with something other than pessimism."

"You know it ain't the head cold, Miss Cilla. It's no good thing that you should have to go beggin' after Mr. George for your rights. And spendin' money you don't have to do it, too."

"By which you mean that you think I am behaving on impulse," Ancilla said with a dry laugh. "Perhaps you are right. But letters haven't served and I don't much care for the prospect of waiting until a new owner of Littlelands has the constable put us out by force. Besides, I have a very good feeling about this journey, Sally. I think that everything is going to work out very well for us."

"I'm sure and I hope it does," Sally said, but without conviction. "But I'm wishin' we were goin' for a better reason. Like Mary Delfries, who went for a month to visit her aunt and caught that baronet from up north."

Ancilla smiled at her maid indulgently. "Do you think I should apply my time in town toward finding a husband? No doubt I shall find one waiting at the Golden Cross when we arrive, ready to be snatched up."

"If Mr. George was to do the right thing by you, he'd have invited you to come to town to take your proper place in the world long before now."

"George is only my brother-in-law," Ancilla pointed out. "He has no such obligation toward me, and in any event, it would be most improper for me to stay in the home of a man who was not a blood relative."

"There's that sister of his," Sally insisted. "She could have had you to stay when she was still living in town, but she's worse than Mr. George. Married herself to that rich old man and never come back to Littlelands from that day to this. Heard he didn't leave her so much when he died, either. Serves her right for bein' so stuck up and too good for the place she was born in."

"You should not say so, Sally," Ancilla said with gentle reproach. "Mr. Martin was a very difficult, hard man, and it is not surprising that his children should have no love for the home they were raised in. There is no reason at all for Vera to invite me to stay with her. I have not even seen or spoken to her since I was a schoolgirl, and there was so great a difference in our ages that I never knew her very well."

Sally bent to get a clean handkerchief from the cloakbag at her feet. She was subdued by the reproof but not put down. "I know I shouldn't talk so about your relatives, Miss Cilla," she admitted, "but I've known the Martins as long as you have—longer, as I'm older—and the only one worth tuppence was Mr. Jack. You'd have had a different sort of life if he hadn't been so taken with soldierin'. But so it always is; men will have their hobby horses. Your poor dear father, as good a man as ever there was, he was always one for his dogs and his horses, and your sweet mother left on her own so much while he was off huntin'. Seems to me it's always the woman who pays for a man's hankerin's."

Sally always said exactly what she thought and Ancilla knew from many years' experience that there was little point in trying to correct her ways. She was very far from being a proper lady's maid, but Sally had been with Ancilla since the days when she was a very young nursery maid, and Ancilla wouldn't have traded her for the dresser of a duchess.

She reached over to touch Sally's hand with affection. "And you want me to marry again? Suppose this time I met a man who had a passion for balloon ascensions? I would live in hourly expectation of being in black again."

Sally did not respond in kind but sighed sadly. "It's

just that it's not right, Miss Cilla. A pretty woman like you *ought* to have a doting husband, a fillin' nursery, and a fine house. Even Sir Waldo says it's a waste you livin' in a little cottage forever pinchin' pennies and with only me for company."

"Yes, and he would marry me off to his friend Mr. Beecham so he could say he had done his duty by me," Ancilla said, acid coming into her voice, as it was wont to do whenever she spoke of her cousin Sir Waldo Crosby. "Never mind, Sally. I am quite content the way that I am. When we reach London you will have a hot brick for your bed and a nice posset, and tomorrow the sun will be shining and everything won't look quite so bleak."

"*If* we get to London," Sally said pessimistically as the carriage continued to sway from side to side, in and out of the muddy ruts.

Their pace since they had started out that morning had been erratic, gauged to the conditions of the road and the quality of the horseflesh, which Ancilla, who had all but been raised in her father's hunting stables, considered deplorable. For a while they had been moving along at a brisk trot, but now once again they were reduced to a walk. Ancilla stifled a vexed exclamation lest she add fuel to her maid's pessimism, but in fact she too was beginning to become concerned that they would not reach London by nightfall. Normally the distance to London from their home in Essex near the coast did not require more than one full day of travel, and she had made no plans for them to stop a night on the road. She had no idea how close they were to their destination now, but, given their inability to achieve any speed, she could not persuade herself that their progress had been good.

There was the sound of branches scraping against the side of the carriage and Sally moaned dramatically. "We're goin' into the ditch, Miss Cilla. I knew it would happen."

"Don't be foolish, Sally, we are doing no such thing. We are still moving."

Ancilla wiped the misty film from the window on her side of the carriage to see what had caused them to come so close to the edge of the road, and as she did so a hooded curricle streaked past them at a reckless pace. Its wide wheels cast mud up against her window so sharply that she started backward as if the dirt could penetrate the glass. She started to turn to Sally to comment on the foolishness of the curricle's driver, but before she could begin, the carriage began to list alarmingly and then gave a sideways lurch so sudden that Ancilla was thrown to her knees on the floor of the carriage.

This sudden movement made Ancilla feel giddy, but she picked herself up and eased herself back onto her seat as best she could. The carriage was not completely on its side, but resting against and held up by the thick brush alongside the road.

"We *are* overturned," Sally wailed. "Oh, I knew it. I knew it."

The frightened horses plunged and strained against their leaden burden, a dangerous threat to the precariously tilted carriage. Ancilla was forced to grab at the strap on her side to keep from being tossed out of her seat again. She turned her attention to her maid, who was making a low, keening sound, and Ancilla saw that she was genuinely afraid.

"It's all right, Sally," Ancilla said gently, attempting to keep her own concern out of her voice. "We are not overturned, but have merely slid into the ditch. If we remain calm and quiet, the coachman will have us pulled out in a very little while." But the continued rocking of the carriage belied her words, and the fear that the accident had injured the coachman and guard, making them unable to attend to the horses, began to overtake her.

Staying in the carriage, batted about and uncertain of their fate, was foolishness to her mind, and, ignoring Sally's wails that she was sure to be killed if she tried to get out, Ancilla reached for the handle. The door swung open before she touched it. The guard, miniature waterfalls cascading from his nose and chin, thrust his head inside.

"We be in the ditch, ma'am," he said, stating the obvious.

The rocking stopped and Ancilla was able to relax her hold on the strap a bit; she asked if he or the coachman had been injured or if the horses had gone down, and, receiving negative replies, she then inquired if it would be possible for them to pull the carriage out of the ditch.

"Aye," the guard replied, "but not with weight in it. We passed an inn about a half mile back. It ain't for the carriage trade, but it be respectablelike." He held out his hand to Ancilla to assist her to the ground. "I'll be takin' you ladies there now and then I'll come back and help coachman."

Ancilla hesitated to take his hand, deploring the delay going back to the inn would cause. "If you could find us anything approaching shelter under the trees, it would probably be better for us to wait there rather than walk through the rain and mud."

The guard shook his head, sending little drops of water about the chaise. "The trees are so heavy with water they'd be worse than no shelter at all, and we won't be goin' on again tonight anyway, ma'am."

"But we must reach London tonight," Ancilla insisted.

"Coachman can't hardly see his hand afore his face," the guard said patiently. "And it'll be dark early this night. We'll never make it to London afore then, and we might not be so lucky when the time comes to have a place to stop convenient."

"We can't be that far from London," Ancilla said, hoping it was so.

"We be some miles south of Chelmsford."

Ancilla was not precisely sure of the distance from Chelmsford to London, but she gathered from the guard's tone that it was not close enough. She glanced back into the chaise. Sally was sitting quietly huddled in her corner; she looked frightened and miserable.

It was more than just inconvenient for them to be delayed another day on their journey, but Ancilla did not feel she could justly argue the point any further. She turned to Sally and told her that they would have to walk back to the inn they had passed and would have to spend the night there.

Sally brightened. "I'd as soon walk twenty miles, Miss Cilla, as end up laid out in the bushes, which we'll do for sure if we go on."

So the die was cast. Ancilla gave her hand to the guard and with only minor difficulty was assisted to the ground. The road surface was like porridge; thick mud oozed into her shoes and crept up the hem of her skirt, and the road was not only soupy but very slippery. More than once during their trek to the inn, one or the other of them nearly came to grief in the mud.

The interior of the inn consisted of one large common room, with a great open hearth, a few long tables and chairs scattered about, a tap, and doors behind it that most likely led to the kitchen and the apartments of the landlord.

The guard saw them safely inside and then left to return to the coachman. Drawing her damp wool cloak more tightly about her, Sally went over to a chair near the fire, and Ancilla approached the tap just as the landlord, an angular man with a cheerful face, came out of the kitchen wiping his hand on an apron.

"Shocking day, miss," he said in the tone of voice someone else might have used to comment on the day's beauty. "Weren't expecting no custom today."

"To be honest, I wasn't expecting to be anyone's custom," Ancilla said candidly, returning his infectious smile. She then launched into an account of the difficulties they had encountered.

The landlord, whose name was Matchem, shook his head and clucked with sympathy at their plight, and all the while carefully scrutinized her to assess her ability to pay for the things she would no doubt require.

The appearance of the young woman who stood before him was drab enough. Her dark blond hair was pulled back severely from her face and her blue-gray eyes added only a little color to her fair complexion. The dress she wore was a nondescript brown and her plain merino cloak was a similar shade.

Mrs. Martin had the voice and manner of a lady even if she did look more like a country mouse, but the thing that tipped the balance in her favor was the fact that Ancilla, for all her lack of plumage, was a very pretty woman, and Matchem was always fond of a pretty woman. He decided that she would do.

"Mrs. Matchem will see to your dinner," he said kindly, "and I'll take you upstairs. You'll be needing a room apart for your maid, with her feeling so poorly. The beds aren't large and two in one wouldn't be any great comfort."

"Of course my maid shall have the bed in her condition," said Ancilla and, with economy in mind, added, "But you may put a cot or even a pallet in the same room and I shall make do with that."

Matchem managed to shake his head sadly while still smiling cheerfully. It seemed to be his constant expression. "The rooms be small, Mrs. Martin. A cot or even a pallet wouldn't fit at all."

Ancilla sighed as she mentally calculated the coins

remaining in her purse and decided that this was no time to start regretting extravangances. She agreed to the two rooms and she and Sally followed the landlord up the stairs.

"I'm surprised you made it this far, Mrs. Martin," said Matchem as they climbed. "The bridge between here and Chelmsford is usually out by this time in a rain like this, and it's as well that you were stuck when you were. A few miles south of here there's a great hollow in the road, and it's probably under a foot of water by now. Always happens in a great rain. We end up a little island by ourselves. In '09 it rained like this for nearly a week and it was a fortnight before we saw anything pass on the road except a village cart or wagon."

Ancilla suppressed a shudder of alarm at the utter financial ruin that such a thing happening at this time would visit on her, and she firmly put such thoughts out of her mind.

The rooms to which Matchem took them were very small indeed, though Ancilla only glanced in hers and then went with Sally to her room to see that the maid was made comfortable. The landlord's daughter, Meg, came up to them shortly afterward to make up the fires, and she told them that her mother was already brewing a posset, which had considerable local repute for the treatment of head colds.

When the carriage with their baggage arrived at the inn, Ancilla helped Sally out of her wet things and into bed and then went to her own room to change. Her room was as small as the one that Sally was in, and a narrow bed, a small dressing table and stool, and a chair in the corner by the door took up almost all of the floor space. With her trunk placed between the bed and the chair there was barely room to turn about, and though she was not used to thinking of the rooms in her cottage as large, in comparison to this they might have been apartments of state. But the room did boast a small hearth, and it was a warm and dry place to spend the night, and for this Ancilla knew, she must be grateful.

Ancilla threw her damp cloak over the chair and went over to her trunk. The key turned easily enough in the lock but the latch refused to budge. She picked and pulled at it to no avail and finally, in frustration, dealt it a sharp blow that did the trick. Feeling that she had at

least overcome one obstacle that day, she smiled trium-
phantly and reached into the trunk for another dress.
She pulled out the first thing that came to hand, a dark
gray cotton round dress that was sadly out of fashion and
had seen better years. It was not the most disreputable
item in her wardrobe; an income that consisted of only a
token pension from the horse guards and a small annuity
left to her by her mother did not leave room for the
luxuries of feminine frills.

In fact, this journey was the one luxury she had permitted herself in a very long time. It was true that she
believed that the only way she could settle her problem
would be to speak to her brother-in-law in person, but
there had been more to her decision to go to London.

Though the daughter of a baronet of ancient lineage,
she had never taken her proper place in the world. The
marriage of her parents had been childless for many
years, and she had been given to them late in their lives.
Her mother had now been dead ten years; her father,
five. She had no family except her cousin Waldo, who
had inherited both the title and the entailed estate. Because of this she had no fortune except for her dowry,
which had been set aside and which had not been large.

At seventeen, instead of the excitement of coming-out
balls and decorous flirtations with dashing young men
that might have led to an (it was hoped) advantageous
marriage, Ancilla had found herself just a poor relation
in the house of her birth, resented as a troublesome
burden by its new occupants.

Her marriage to Jack Martin, shortly afterward, had
been only in part expediency, for she had held him in
deep affection since their days together as childhood
playmates. But he had not thought it proper for her to
follow the drum with him at so tender an age, and he
had purchased the cottage for her from his brother for
her to live in with Sally for company.

Ancilla had gained some independence, and was no
longer under the reluctant care of her cousin, but her life
did not change substantially, nor was there any expan-
sion of the world she had always known. At nearly three
and twenty, she thought it was time that there was.

Ancilla finished dressing and spread her cloak over the
trunk to dry. She went to the dressing table and freed
her hair from its tight restriction. It fell over her shoul-

ders in a thick cloud of dark gold curls and waves. She smiled a little at her reflection. Jack had always loved her with her hair down. He was used to tell her that the natural crimps in her hair made her look like a wild thing come in from the forest.

They had had so little time together. In the three and a half years they had been married, they had spent little more than as many months actually living together. Jack had been such a kind, gentle man, the sort who always focused on the best qualities of the people he knew and made excuses for them when their behavior was less than admirable. She knew he would not have assumed that George was now trying to cheat her and neither did she wish to think that way, but she would have been much easier in her mind if only George had answered her letter.

But the realization that the post would not answer in dealing with him had not really been unwelcome. Once the idea had struck her as necessary, she had not hesitated to take advantage of it to see a little more of the world. She had managed, with the strictest economy, to put away a bit of money from time to time against some unforeseen emergency, and certainly the threatened loss of her home was as good an emergency as any.

She hoped that after conducting her business with George, she would be able to remain in town for a day or two to see the sights of London and to shop for a few things at the famed Pantheon Bazaar, where she had heard incredible bargains were to be had.

She tucked the last straying tendril of hair into the tight knot into which she had again bound her hair, and, determined to think positively, she found a piece of paper and a small pencil in her reticule and began to make a list of the small items she wanted to purchase in town. But when she was done she read it over, then threw it on the dressing table. Silk stockings, doeskin gloves, and new satin ribbons to dress up her old bonnets and gowns now seemed wasteful luxury next to the unexpected expenses she would have because of this wretched weather. She sighed and consoled herself that even a day in London to see the sights was something.

She picked up her shawl off the bed, where she had tossed it, and walked toward the door, but she was arrested by the sound of a vehicle driving onto the muddy cobbles of the courtyard. Her room was at the front of the inn and the small window beside the bed overlooked the courtyard. Curious whether this was simply a local resident or another traveler seeking shelter from the weather, she knelt on the bed and looked out the window. The outside light was nearly gone now, but she saw the carriage clearly. It was a curricle, its hood raised, pulled by a pair of bays. She saw a man, an ostler or manservant most likely, come from the back of the inn to take the horses. A taller man, his face not discernible, got down from the carriage, spoke a few words to the servant, and then went into the inn.

Ancilla continued to stare out the window until the carriage was led away, but she was not really paying attention. She had not given the curricle that had forced them to the side of the road any thought since the event, for she saw no point in upsetting herself over the carelessness of someone she would likely never see again. But she remembered now Matchem's words about the swollen creek that had probably put out the bridge near Chelmsford. She thought it unlikely in the extreme that two such similar carriages would be passing on this road on such an abominable day, and she had a strong suspicion that the driver of this curricle and the man who had been the cause of their trouble were one and the same.

Without hesitation, she left her room and went quickly down the stairs, intent only on seeing the man before he could have any opportunity to bury himself in his room, intending to give him, in no uncertain terms, her opinion of his abilities, his character, and his intelligence.

She kept her eyes down as she descended the stairs, careful not to let her skirts trip her, but when she reached the common room she looked up and came to an abrupt halt, as if she had walked into an invisible wall.

The man stood next to the tap talking to Matchem, his long, caped driving coat dripping small puddles onto the broad-planked floor. His face was turned away from her and she was presented only with a view of his dark auburn hair clinging damply to his head. But she knew this man. She knew the set of his shoulders; his stance was familiar to her. Her heart began to beat rapidly and she had a sudden, craven desire to run back up the stairs.

The man shrugged himself out of his rain-darkened,

drab driving coat as he continued to discuss with Matchem the arrangements he wished made for his comfort that evening. He threw the coat over his arm and, in a pause in the conversation, turned slightly in Ancilla's direction to toss it and his hat on a table behind him. As he did so, he caught sight of her peripherally and he glanced upward. He too stood for a moment as if frozen, and Ancilla found herself gazing into his dark green eyes.

The extra few minutes' knowledge of his presence enabled her to recover from her surprise first. She did not know what to say to him, so she said the first thing that came into her mind, returning to her original purpose. "I might have guessed it would be you, my lord."

Devin Langley turned more to face her and completed the act of putting his things on the table. "Did you?" he asked, his amiable tone a contrast to her manner. "I must confess that finding you here surprises me quite a bit. I did not suppose I would meet anyone I knew here. Certainly not you."

"I suppose I may travel when and where I will," she said coolly.

He blinked at the sharpness in her tone. He had not expected her to make any effort to be especially pleasant to him, but neither had he expected outright hostility. "Of course," he said quietly and without inflection. "The roads are free to those who would use them."

"I am surprised to hear you say so, my lord," she said bitingly. "I would have thought that it would be your philosophy that they are freer to some than to others."

Not understanding, he looked at her questioningly. She raised the corners of her mouth in a slight sneer. "Yours is the best, the most magnificent sort of arrogance— one that is not even aware of the damage it causes to the person and sensibilities of others."

Devin lowered his head, sighed, and raised it again to look at her. "I am almost afraid to ask," he said, "but what exactly are we speaking of, Ancilla?"

"If you did not expect to meet me here, my lord, I can only say that I did not expect to find myself here." She paused for effect. "However, due to the recklessness, the arrogance of one who considers no needs or rights but his own, this is where I find myself and at no little cost."

"May I safely substitute my name for that of 'one'?" he asked, his voice becoming cooler.

"You may," she snapped.

"I am sure I beg your pardon if I have been the cause of any inconvenience to you," he said, managing a credible sneer of his own, "but as it is all of six months since we have set eyes on each other, I fail to see how that can possibly be."

"No doubt you also failed to see my carriage as you passed it on the road a short while ago?"

He did not answer at once, going over in his mind the vehicles he had passed before coming to the White Hawk. "There are not many carriages to pass on a day such as this," he began slowly, "but I do remember passing one not far from here before I had to turn around at the bridge, which was washed out. If that was yours, I certainly had no idea of it, nor do I understand why that should so excite your temper toward me."

"No, it would not matter to you whom you pushed into the ditch," she said waspishly. "Friend and foe alike are fair game to you, my lord."

It had been far from his intention when he had first seen her to argue with her, but his own humor was less than complaisant. In addition to his earlier disappointment, he had not been able to avoid a wetting in his open carriage, and the washed-out bridge had prevented him from reaching the carriage inn at Chelmsford, which he knew to be excellent and where he had planned to put up for the night.

He regarded her somewhat balefully. The last thing he needed to top off this less-than-perfect day was to spend the evening arguing with a woman who was determined to view him in a bad light. "If your carriage did go into the ditch," he said evenly, "I am sorry for it. But it was certainly still on the road when I passed it, and I acknowledge no personal blame for the deficiencies of your coachman's driving."

"Of course you do not," Ancilla said sweetly. "It is your style, is it not, to force others into untenable positions and then adopt a posture of innocence?"

Devin's eyes took on a hard quality and his features set. "Is it our carriages passing today that we are discussing, Ancilla, or another matter entirely? I wish you would tell me. I could manage the thing better if I knew whether it was my driving or my character that I was defending."

Two spots of color appeared in her cheeks. "A gentleman would not behave in any way, especially to a lady, that would give him cause to *have* to defend himself."

He made her a small, ironic bow. "I must thank you, madam, for reminding me of what my obligations must be toward *any* member of your sex," he said insolently.

At this point, Matchem, who had been following their conversation with gaping interest, became concerned that his two guests' discussion was about to degenerate into heated battle. He was a peace-loving man, and arguments, even those that did not directly involve him, distressed him. He intervened to inform his lordship that he was ready to take him to his room if his lordship so desired.

Devin turned his attention to the landlord, glanced briefly again at Ancilla, and then followed Matchem out of the room and up the stairs without exchanging another word with her.

Left alone in the common room, Ancilla sank into the nearest chair, shaken by the encounter. When she had recognized Devin she had not meant to speak to him so, but the cutting words had come to her lips and she had spoken them.

Crosby Hall, like the Martin estate of Littlelands, stood in the shadow of the great estate of Fairfeld Park, and although she had been acquainted with Devin for as long as she had known Jack—that is to say, all her life—she had never been close to him as a child as she had been to her husband; in fact, she had come to know him well only after her marriage. He and Jack were of an age, and their boyhood friendship had deepened when they were at Eton together. After the wedding they had been frequent guests at Fairfeld, and Devin had visited them often at the cottage. When Jack had been called back to his regiment, she and Devin had continued as friends in their own right. They had discovered in each other an empathy, a commonality of thought, and a delight in many shared interests. They had spent much time together when he was in residence, and the short way between Fairfeld and the cottage, which passed through the old, unused Littlelands stableyard, was much traversed. When his sister, Lucina, was at Fairfeld she had joined them, and a friendship had developed between the two young women as well.

These were happy times for Ancilla during her long periods of loneliness when her husband was away, and their intimacy might have gone on to this day but for the fact that the summer before her husband's death, in a freak accident to a store of ammunition at Almeida, Devin had decided to expand and improve the Fairfeld Stud.

He was aware that she had spent much of her time after

26

her mother's death in the company of her father and had assisted him in the stewardship of his stables, and understanding how she must feel at the loss of an activity that had given her so much pleasure, he had very flatteringly asked for her assistance and advice. He had remained the entire summer at Fairfeld, and Ancilla had been with him for at least some part of each of those days.

She had ignored the hints that Alanetta, Sir Waldo's wife, had dropped to her that their being so much together was causing gossip in the neighborhood; Ancilla decided the woman was small-minded, and perhaps a bit jealous of her easy entrée to Fairfeld. When Lady Crosby had gone further, suggesting that it might be unhealthy for her to spend so much time with a man who was not her husband, Ancilla, infuriated, had spoken so sharply to her cousin's wife that it had caused a permanent coolness between her and the occupants of Crosby Hall. But Alanetta, picayune as her intention had been, had touched nearer to the truth than she had guessed.

Ancilla closed her eyes and immediately a scene began to take shape in her mind. She saw herself standing under a leafy canopy of trees that were just beginning to turn with the onset of autumn. She was looking out over the vast, rolling parkland of Fairfeld, and in the distance she saw the thatched roofs of the many stable buildings. She turned to face Devin, who was standing very close to her. His dark head was bent slightly to catch her words; she saw him smile, heard the light baritone of his laughter. A leaf floated down to land on her shoulder and he reached over to brush it away, but his hand remained on her shoulder and then moved gently down her back. He brought her closer to him and she put one hand against his chest as if to push him away, but she did not. As his lips touched hers she deliberately banished the image by opening her eyes.

It had happened less than a sennight before she had had word of Jack's death, and the timing, as much as the emotions aroused in her and the words they had exchanged afterward, had led her to feelings of guilt. She had avoided Devin's company as much as possible from that time on.

It had not gone beyond that single kiss, but, shocked at her own momentary response and at his daring to make love to her, she had recoiled from him. As he attempted to apologize for his behavior, she had refused to hear him. She had attacked his character and his morals with unflinching brutality and ultimately had succeeded in backing him into a defensive posture. They had parted from each other in cold anger, but that night, alone and wakeful, she had examined her heart and realized that his angry accusation—that she had encouraged him to believe that her feelings for him were similar—was not entirely untrue. She felt as if her desires, however unintended and unrecognized, had nearly led her to betray not only her husband but her own values, and she was deeply ashamed.

But time had dulled her grief for Jack and her feelings of guilt, and she had often of late wished that she might renew their friendship, for she missed the easy companionship and understanding they had shared. She had even from time to time indulged herself in the memory of that September afternoon, and in wondering what her life would now be like if she had not been a married woman at the time but free to follow her heart.

She felt reservations about these dreams, but she convinced herself that it was only harmless fantasy, for after the completeness of her rejection of him, she could not suppose that he would ever renew his advances even though the circumstances were changed. She also successfully convinced herself that she did not wish him to do so, that friendship was all that she wished from him.

She supposed it was the shock of seeing him so unexpectedly that had caused her to retreat into defensive attack, and she wished now that she had not spoken so harshly to him. This might have been the perfect opportunity for them to have begun again to be on easier terms and she wished she could unsay her words, but she did not know how. Her sense of justice was well defined and she knew that she had goaded him into anger. His temper was generally equable, his manner always agreeable, but to take this for granted was a mistake. There could be sharp teeth in his ready smile.

The White Hawk possessed no private parlors and she did not care for the prospect of eating her meal in the cramped confines of her room, so she had planned to eat in the common room. Now she envisioned an unpleasant evening, which would consist of either a war of words or a stony, uncomfortable silence punctuated by occasional glares.

Hoping to avoid his company as much as possible, she returned to her room to fetch some needlework that she had brought with her. She took a minute to look in on Sally, who was sleeping peacefully, and then returned downstairs and met Mrs. Matchem setting out places for dinner at a long table near the fire. Mrs. Matchem proved to be a jolly woman, a fit companion for her husband, and Ancilla found herself liking her very much and therefore unwilling to ask her to go to the trouble of dividing the serving dishes so that dinner might be served at separate tables. She supposed she could sit with him for the length of time it took to eat dinner. After all, if she found him excessively unpleasant, she could always move elsewhere later.

The landlady informed her that dinner would be ready shortly and returned to her kitchen. Devin had still not come down, and Ancilla placed herself on a bench in a corner and began to ply her needle. It was not long afterward that she heard a sound on the stairs.

She heard him enter the room and walk over to the table on which the covers had been set. There was a pause and then his footsteps resumed again, coming toward her. She continued with her needlework, not looking up even when he had stopped beside her.

He stood silently for a moment and then spoke. "I am sorry if I said anything to discomfit you, Ancilla." She went on with her work as if he hadn't spoken and he added, "We have been rather successful of late at avoiding each other, but in a place like this it is impossible. Can't we put aside our differences for tonight and share each other's company? I think the evening will pass far more enjoyably for both of us if we do."

She put down her work and looked up at him, and he sat down next to her. "I have apologized to you the best way I know how for what happened between us," he said quietly. "If I could go back to that day and change it, I would. I admit that it was I who misunderstood our relationship. What you offered to me in friendship I regarded as something else. I'm sorry for that and for the things that I said to you afterward, which were the result of my hurt pride. Perhaps we were just too much together that summer."

Ancilla gave him a tentative smile. "And I am sorry

for the things I said to you tonight. I would like it if we could be friends again."

Devin's expression became a delighted grin. "I'm glad, Cilla. I've missed our conversations. There are not many women of my acquaintance with whom I can talk about my horses and be both understood and appreciated."

"Is that good or bad?" Ancilla inquired with a brief laugh. "I doubt that is the usual topic of conversation between a man and a woman in fashionable drawing rooms."

"Perhaps not," he agreed, "but I think it is good. It is certainly very comfortable. I value your friendship, Cilla, and I deeply regret the loss of it."

"What you regret, Devin Langley," she said with mock censure, "is the loss of what you call my 'witches' brew.' "

"That's true enough," he admitted. "We had a problem with Golddigger at the end of last season and I was very nearly tempted to come to you for one of your poultices. You are very much your father's daughter."

"I don't aim for such heights," she said. "There was no one who knew or understood horses like Papa. That is not too surprising. Papa not only bred the finest hunters in England, he cared for each one of them as if it was his child. Though it was his business to sell his stock, he would be sad for a fortnight whenever he sold one of his horses. I'm afraid Papa was not much of a businessman."

"His other qualities more than made up for any deficiency in that area."

"You would not think so, to hear my cousin Waldo speak," Ancilla said dryly.

"I think Sir Waldo believes that breeding or owning horses for any purpose other than the most practical is wasteful frippery."

"I'll wager he has never said so to *you*." Ancilla laughed.

"No," said Devin, smiling. "Being the lord of the manor has its advantages."

"Why didn't you come to me for the poultice?" Ancilla asked abruptly. "I wouldn't have refused to make it up for you."

Devin hesitated a moment before answering. "Would I have been welcome?"

"Yes," she said quietly. "I have always liked you very much, Devin. It was just . . ." She halted, not sure how to go on.

He saw Mrs. Matchem and Meg come out of the kitchen bearing platters, and he rose and held out a hand to Ancilla. "Dinner is being laid," he said. "We have been going on quite well. Let's just enjoy it."

Ancilla went with him to the table, and they sat down to a simple but delicious and plentiful meal of roast mutton, early-spring vegetables, and bread pudding.

"Since this is to be our day for apologizing to each other, I, too, am sorry for the way that I spoke to you before," Devin said as he seated himself. "It has been an unfortunate day for me and I fear my temper is sadly out of sorts."

"Whose would not be, with this dreadful weather?" Ancilla said sympathetically.

"Oh, it isn't just the weather," he said, then told her of the hoax that had been played on him.

"That is despicable," Ancilla exclaimed when he had finished. "And quite cruel, too, for I know how much it would have meant to you to have added Spanish Coin to your stud."

"It is doubtful that this man acted on his own," Devin said, accepting a plate of new potatoes from her. "He knew things that must have been told to him by someone well acquainted with me. In any case, he would have no reason for doing the thing. We never had any business together, but since it is known that he would do most anything for a price, it is logical to assume that someone paid him to come to me."

"But who would do such a thing?"

Devin shrugged. "Hoby thinks a friend of mine wished to play a joke on me."

"I should not care to have that sort of friend," Ancilla averred.

"Nor do I care for it," Devin agreed. "Now you have heard my tale of woe. It's your turn to tell me what brings you here, tactfully leaving out the part about when your carriage went into the ditch. I am sorry, Cilla, if I caused that. I truly had no idea."

"It probably was my coachman's fault," she said, glibly casting aside that man's reputation. Now that they were in charity with each other again, she felt completely relaxed in his company and willing to forget any unpleasantness that had ever come between them. She laid down her fork and told him her story. Devin knew, of course, that Jack had purchased the cottage from his brother and he became quite concerned, for he, too, knew George well, and he placed no reliance on there having been any mistake. He did not say so aloud, lest he give her unnecessary fears, but he wrote the name of his solicitor in town on the back of one of his visiting cards and gave it to her. He also made a mental note to look into the matter himself as soon as he could.

After dinner she remained with him discussing mutual friends and interests, and the evening passed far more agreeably than Ancilla would have thought possible just a few hours earlier. When he told her that Lucina had had to put off a visit she and her husband had planned to make to Fairfeld and London because the latter had come down with a bad cold, Ancilla realized that she had not had a thought for Sally since before dinner. She felt quite guilty and almost at once excused herself to go up and look in on her. Since the hour was advanced, and she had hopes of rising early to resume her journey, she also bid him good night and agreed to his request that they share breakfast in the morning.

She found Sally awake but feeling too poorly even to enjoy being read to, so Ancilla merely gave her a brief, expurgated account of Devin's arrival at the inn and their dinner conversation, then told her that the breach that had come between them—though she had never confided in Sally the true reason for it—had been healed. Ancilla then advised her to get as much rest as possible so that she would feel better tomorrow, and went to her own room.

While undressing for bed Ancilla felt very pleased with herself. After such an unpropitious beginning everything had certainly gone very well. She caught sight of herself in the mirror and saw that she was smiling broadly. Well, why not? she thought. She was very happy, lighter of heart than she had been in a long time. It was not that she did not have other friends, but her relationship with Devin had been special, and she, too, had missed it. She felt rather silly now that she had turned what was after all nothing more than one brief, stolen kiss into a Cheltenham tragedy. Now they would be friends again, and the misunderstanding put behind them and forgotten. She got between the sheets to dream, both awake and asleep, of a happy future ahead.

The morning, though, proved no more suited to travel than had the day before. It was still raining, though not so heavily as yesterday. Ancilla awoke early, and when she saw the panes of the window rain-spattered, she groaned aloud and buried herself deeper beneath the sheets, but she was completely awake, and after a short while she got up and dressed. She went directly to Sally's room and found her maid awake and the picture of gloom.

"It's still rainin', Miss Cilla," Sally said unhappily. "We'll be here for days, just as Matchem said."

"Don't be such a widgeon, Sally," Ancilla said in a light, rallying tone. "This is hardly going to be the second Flood." She pulled back the sheer curtain on the window. "See, the rain is much lighter this morning and will no doubt soon stop and then we may go on."

Sally sniffed, determined in her pessimism. "Meg Matchem says there's lots of shallows hereabouts. Like as not, we'd get just far enough away from here to make the walk back uncomfortable before we'd end up stuck in the mud or back in the ditch again."

"Or we might just make it through without any difficulties and find ourselves at the Golden Cross in London before the day is out."

Sally pulled a face and drew back the sheets with a flourish. "Well, if you mean to go on, Miss Cilla, I'd best get ready for it. I'm not sayin' you're not in the right of it, but I'm thinkin' I'll put on all of my petticoats just to be safe."

Ancilla half sighed and half laughed. "I do love you, Sally," she said, her voice unsteady. She leaned over and gently pushed Sally back against her pillows. "But there is no need for you to get up just yet. You still sound far from well, and the best thing would be for you to stay in bed until I can discover just what our plans will be."

Sally's protests that she was well enough and should be up and seeing to her mistress's things, especially if there would be packing to do, were feeble and easily overridden. In truth, her cold had not yet broken, and she was glad enough to take Ancilla's advice. Ancilla promised to return to her as soon as she had had her breakfast to tell her what had been decided and to read to her for a time to break the monotony of being bedridden.

But as Ancilla made her way downstairs her thoughts were more troubled than she had let on. Every day spent

at the inn, every meal they ate—not to mention the
expenses of the coachman and the guard, which were
also her responsibility—made the finances of their journey more and more perilous. As it was, the time she had
hoped to spend in town was now reduced, and a return to
Littlelands on the common stage a necessity.

Fearing that Sally's penchant for gloom was beginning
to affect her, Ancilla determined to put these thoughts
away, but when she reached the bottom of the stairs, the
sight that greeted her was depressing.

The door into the courtyard was standing open and
Devin stood silhouetted in its frame. Beyond him Ancilla
could see into the courtyard and the view was not
encouraging. The rain, which had seemed light only minutes before, was now as heavy as it had been a day
earlier. But the thing that truly brought down her spirits
was that the cobbles of the courtyard were covered in a
sea of churning mud, when they could be seen at all.
Great puddles, like miniature lakes, dotted most of the
visible ground, and this boded ill for the hope that the
roads would be clear enough to travel.

"Oh, dear," Ancilla said, and the simple words managed to convey every shade of her feelings.

"Oh, dear, indeed," Devin echoed, and turned part way
to face her. "No good will come of our pulling Friday
faces, though. We are at the mercy of the elements, and
wishing we weren't won't make it so."

He spoke in a light, bantering tone, but Ancilla did not
reply in kind. "No," she agreed sadly. She walked over to
stand beside him in the doorway. "And wishing ten shil-
lings were thirty won't make them so, either," she said,
more to herself than to him.

Devin regarded her in thoughtful silence for a moment,
and then said carefully, "Is there a difficulty, Cilla? If I
could help—"

"Oh, there is no difficulty," she interrupted, speaking a
little too quickly. She knew that he would have helped
unquestioningly and with whatever she might need, but
her one experience of accepting the charity of others had
left a bad taste in her mouth and a pride in her independence, and only the most dire circumstance would have
caused her to seek his assistance. Devin understood something of this and allowed the matter to drop, though he
remained concerned for her.

They discussed only trivialities at breakfast, and when Meg had cleared away the last of the dishes, Ancilla asked him bluntly, "You don't think we will be able to go on today, do you?"

"It's unlikely," he replied honestly. "Even if the rain were to stop in a few hours, it would probably be several hours more before the roads were passable again and by then it would be too close to dark to set out."

"Then I suppose I had better tell Sally that we will be here another day," she said resignedly. "I should spend some time with her as well. It is so tedious to be bedridden, and I expect that this is going to be a long day."

"It is certainly likely to be a cheerless one as far as the weather is concerned. Fortunately I have some documents that need attending to that I brought with me from town, so I shall have some occupation." He picked up a dark brown leather pouch of the sort in which legal papers were often kept and put it on the table. He drew papers out of it and, shuffling through them, selected one and handed it to Ancilla.

On the page was a line drawing of a horse, front and side views. Characteristic markings had been drawn on the figure, and at the bottom of the page was the horse's name and a written description.

"Do you remember this horse?" he asked.

Ancilla's brow creased with concentration as she studied the sheet. The name on it was Nimbus, and the description told her that he stood fifteen hands high, that he had a thin white blaze on his face, and that his coat was "true black, mottled throughout with fine white hairs."

"I'm not sure," she said. "Blue roan is not a usual color for a thoroughbred and the name does seem familiar, but I cannot say that I recall him."

"I thought you might, though he was just a yearling the last time you saw him," said Devin. "It was Jack who named him, the last time he was home at Littlelands. He saw him running about in the pasture after his mother and said that the foal reminded him of a dense raincloud scudding across the sky."

"And he said you should call him Nimbus," Ancilla added, now recalling the day.

"Yes. He has become a beautiful horse with a lovely, graceful motion that is quite effortless." He took the page, which she had handed back to him. "I think he's going to be something quite out of the ordinary."

"Do you plan to begin racing him soon?"

"As soon as may be," he responded, smiling. "There will be five races on the first day of the meeting—the usual match races and sweepstakes. But to the last race we have presented a cup named for Fairfeld, which we hope will become a tradition and attract the best horses. I'm running Nimbus in that. It wasn't my intention to do so, but his gallops have been so superior that I really believe he has a chance at it."

"And that will be his maiden race?"

"Yes. Am I being overly ambitious, do you think?"

"No," said Ancilla honestly. "If you think he is good enough to challenge proven horses, I am sure he must be. You have rather a knack for knowing which horses will be champions."

Devin laughed. "Lucina claims I dabble in black magic, but that is your forte, is it not? I admit I have had a great deal of luck."

"You know it is more than luck," she said reprovingly.

"You will think it is arrogance when I tell you that Pomfret has entered his Blue in the race," he said with mock gravity.

That *was* arrogance, or else he thought Nimbus an outstanding horse. For the past four years, Ancilla knew, Bolting Blue, owned and bred by Lord Pomfret, a rival breeder with an estate convenient to Newmarket, had been unbeaten in matches and stakes against all horses of all ages. It was the consensus that, could the gallant horse but maintain this record another year or so, his name would go into the annals of horseracing beside the great ones of Highflyer and Eclipse.

"You must think a great deal of this horse, or else you have private information that the Blue will come down with a sudden colic." She looked at him questioningly.

He shook his head, smiling. "Not at all. I'm not the only one with the opinion that the Blue, if you will pardon the pun, has shot his bolt. He is still winning, but by less of a distance and with a greater effort. I think he can be beaten now by the right horse."

"And now, because of this dreadful weather, you will probably miss seeing your colt run," Ancilla said with genuine regret for him.

"Perhaps not. It may yet stop raining today, and the

roads be clear by tomorrow. If I can start out early enough, I'll reach Fairfeld in time."

"I do hope it stops today," Ancilla concurred, "and not just for your sake." And, lest he should gain the wrong impression from her words, she quickly added, "That is, I wish to get this business with George over with as quickly as possible, for I cannot be easy while my affairs are so unsettled. But that sounds very selfish of me, doesn't it? I do hope that you will reach Fairfeld tomorrow in time for the race."

"I wish we could both be there for it."

This was said with genuine warmth and Ancilla felt suddenly exhilarated. "So do I," she said sincerely. "Race week at Fairfeld is always so gay and exciting. I was jealous of every carriage that passed the road to the cottage last year on the way to the meeting."

"Your banishment was of your own choosing," he reminded her gently.

Disconcerted, for she had not thought of what she was saying, Ancilla dropped her eyes. To keep an uncomfortable silence from falling between them, she said the first thing that came to her. "I wish some generous sprite would transport some of Fairfeld's festivities here for us tonight."

"Do you still believe in sprites, Cilla? Or do you conjure them, fair sorceress? But we might do something out of the ordinary tonight," he added thoughtfully. "Even you can't conjure up a large company of musicians to play for us, but perhaps Mrs. Matchem might be persuaded to whip a syllabub for us. The wine last night was suprisingly good. I think I could convince Matchem to part with a few bottles of his best, which I am sure he does not usually serve to his customers."

"And shall we dress for dinner as if it were quite formal, in the state dining room of Fairfeld?" Ancilla asked with a teasing smile.

"Why not? I know it isn't much, but you must admit that our resources are rather limited. We shall play piquet after dinner, and if you entertain me sufficiently I shall let you win."

"You mean you will try if you can," Ancilla said caustically. "The last time we played together I won three rubbers of five."

"I distinctly remember being very tired and dull-minded

that day," he bandied absently; it was obvious that he
was concentrating on another thought. "Flowers," he said
suddenly and succinctly.

"Flowers?"

"If we had flowers it would add just the right touch,
don't you think?"

"It might," she admitted. "But I doubt the Matchems
have a glasshouse for rare blooms."

He ignored this sally. "There should be some primroses
about, at least, though I suppose they might be a bit
soggy."

"Are you going to volunteer to go out in the rain and
pick them?" she wanted to know.

"There's little worth having that is obtained without
work and sacrifice," he said piously. "And in any case, I
don't mind a little rain and the air will do me good."

"You are more likely to drown," Ancilla told him flatly.
"But if you intend to exert yourself to such lengths, the
very least I can do is see if Mrs. Matchem has any
hummingbird tongues in her larder."

Humming happily to herself, Ancilla went into the
kitchen to speak with the landlady. After a bit of coaxing
Mrs. Matchem allowed as how she had worked as an
undercook in the kitchens of a local squire before she had
wed Matchem, and that a syllabub was not beyond her
art. Further conversation with the landlady revealed that
she had learned not only to cook but to read and write
while in the squire's employ, and she shyly but proudly
showed Ancilla her small collection of cookery books. In
addition to Mrs. Raffald's *The Experienced English House-
Keeper,* she also possessed a recent edition of Mrs.
Rundell's *A New System of Domestic Cookery* and a few
other time-honored volumes. She and Ancilla spent a
delightful hour together poring over the recipes and advice for the proper management of any household, "small
or great," and finally came to the decision to add à la
mode beef from Mrs. Raffald and apple čharolette from
Domestic Cookery to the promised syllabub for dinner
that evening.

3

Her business with the landlady concluded, Ancilla went
to tell Sally the news that they would be remaining at
the White Hawk for another night. Sally evinced no
surprise at this, but she thought it very odd that her
mistress, far from being downcast or troubled by this
setback in their plans, was in a very cheerful and light-
hearted mood. But when she tried to question Ancilla
about it, Ancilla only laughed and said that it was foolish to mope about what could not be helped.

Ancilla dutifully spent the rest of the day keeping
Sally company. She engaged her in light conversation
designed to keep her maid from falling into the dismals,
while she herself took up her needlework; then, when
Sally began to tire, she read to her until, late in the
afternoon, the maid finally drifted off to sleep.

Leaving Sally to her rest, Ancilla thought of returning
downstairs to Devin, who had told her that he planned to
work on the papers he had brought from town during the
afternoon, but then she decided against this. She rang
for Meg and persuaded the girl to help her to dress her
hair in a more becoming style.

There were no curling tongs to be had, but Ancilla's
dark gold hair had enough natural curl to make this no
hardship. They pinned up her hair first one way and
then another, and Ancilla finally decided on a style that
drew her hair high on top of her head in a smooth coil
that had a cascade of curls pouring from the center of it.
She then gently pulled out several tendrils to frame her
face artfully, and was very pleased with the result. Ancilla had brought no cosmetics because she seldom wore
any, but now she wished for a rouge pot, at the least, and
knew she would have to be satisfied with pinching her
cheeks and biting her lips for color.

She had no real choice of a gown; she had only one

39

good dress, a simply designed amber silk, which she had packed on the chance that she would dine with George in town. It was high waisted with a bodice that was a bit narrower than was now considered fashionable, but the color of the dress brought out a golden warmth in her natural fairness and emphasized the blue in her eyes. The skirt fell in straight, graceful folds that accentuated and complemented her height and carriage, and as she stood back and pirouetted in front of the mirror for a better view, she felt the confidence of knowing that she looked well.

She told herself that she had taken such pains with her appearance ostensibly because the idea to dress formally had been hers, but she knew that it was at least in part because of Devin. In fact, she was looking forward to this evening with him as if it were indeed a very special occasion.

Realizing that the hour was advancing, and not wishing to keep him waiting, she went to her trunk to find her stole of white silk shot with gold threads, which Jack had brought her from Portugal and which perfectly complemented the gown.

The stole was not where she expected it to be, and she hastily began tossing her things about the trunk in an effort to find it. It turned up at last in a corner at the very bottom. She surveyed the mess she had made of her clothes, which she had never fully unpacked, and decided that she would not take the time now to refold them but would do so before going to bed. She closed the lid of the trunk, picked up her reticule, and left the room.

The stairway seemed less well lighted than she remembered it from the previous night, and when she walked into the common room she saw why. Th wall sconces and the oil lamps on the mantel had not been lit, and the only light in the room came from the flickering flames in branches set on the table by the fire. Between them sat a bowl of greenery liberally laced with the fragile blooms of primroses, their pale petals glowing golden in the candlelight.

Devin was in the room, standing by the tap speaking to Matchem. When he heard her step he looked up, and the admiration Ancilla saw in his eyes brought a warmth to her cheeks that no rouge pot or any amount of pinching could have duplicated. He took her hand and led her to the table, and she accepted his compliments with more composure than she felt. It was not considered proper for a lady to comment equally on a gentleman's appearance, but Ancilla wished that she might. She had almost forgotten how well he could look in evening clothes. His long-tailed black coat and silk breeches were a credit to his tailor's skill and fit him to perfection, showing to advantage his well-made form.

"I didn't believe you were entirely serious about the flowers," she told him as he assisted her into her chair.

"Well, I have a confession to make," he admitted, seating himself across from her. "I did have help from Meg. I asked her if she knew where any might be had and she directed me to a spot not far from here."

"They are lovely," Ancilla said sincerely. If they had been the rarest of orchids, she could not have been more pleased that he had taken the trouble to find them for her. "Are you certain that Meg's assistance didn't run to picking them for you?"

He pretended to be hurt and regaled her with a humorous account of his harrowing experience of being drenched to the skin just to find a fair lady a few posies. Their banter continued along these lines until Mrs. Matchem herself arrived with the first course, a clear consommé.

The dinner was a great success and when the last covers were removed and brandy brought for Devin, who did not care for port, and a light sherry for Ancilla, they complimented and thanked Mrs. Matchem profusely, which made the landlady blush with pleasure.

With the table completely cleared, Devin produced the piquet decks as he had promised, and they settled down to play. Ancilla drew an eight for the deal, but lost it when he drew a seven. He reshuffled the cards of the first deck and dealt them.

The declarations began with little conversation in between; Ancilla knew from having played with him before that he was skillful at the game and chose to forgo speech in favor of concentration. He won the first two deals easily, but she took the third and fifth, primarily on the fortunes of her cards. When she held the last deal she realized that she was in danger of being rubiconned and risked everything on the discard. It proved less of a successful gambit than she had hoped, but all hope was not dashed until the last trick, which, though she took it, brought her score to only ninety-six.

"Rubiconned," she said with self-disgust. "If we had been playing for guinea points I should be quite ruined."

"If we had been playing for guinea points you would have been repiqued on the last deal as well."

"Are you going to say that you *were* trying to let me win?" she said suspiciously. "I won't believe you. I know I am not *that* bad an opponent."

He gave her an enigmatic smile for an answer. "I'll give you your revenge if you wish."

Ancilla accepted and they played another rubber, which he also won, but not with the ease of the first time. She refused his offer of a third game, saying, "I fear I am sadly out of practice. Another loss would be too depressing to my spirits."

"Should I have let you win?" he asked with an anxiety that was not entirely put on. "I meant tonight to be nothing but pleasant for you."

"And for yourself, too, I hope. Even with our best efforts expended this must be a sad comedown from the way you had expected to spend your evening at Fairfeld."

"Doing the pretty to a lot of bores who must be asked to Fairfeld for appearance's sake," he said dryly. "I would far rather be with you tonight."

"For we have been so gay that time has had wings," she said with mild sarcasm. "Are you flirting with me, Devin?"

He favored her with a slow smile. "A little. Do you mind?"

"I might not if you did not do so by telling me such great bouncers," she answered lightly. "My head is not so easily turned."

"I meant it," he assured her. "When I was forced to turn back at the bridge that was washed out, I cursed my fate. When I met you here, I feared that my evening would be as unpleasant as my day had been. But I wasn't at all displeased. I knew that if nothing else, I would not be dull."

Ancilla laughed. "That should be published as a maxim for all females. 'Berate a man if you will, but at your peril never permit him to be dull.' "

"You may laugh if you wish, but of the two, I prefer conflict. It is at least stimulating."

"Well, I prefer to find my stimulation in a less disquieting way."

"So do I," he agreed, "if I have the choice. I am very glad that we have been sensible and settled our differences. I hope it is not just convenience and isolation that have made it so."

"No. I, too, wish us to be friends again. In fact"—she let her eyes drop—"I feel rather foolish now about the way that I have behaved toward you. It was a small incident and I made rather a lot of it."

"Not without reason," he said softly. She glanced up at him and their eyes met and she understood him. It need not have been a small incident at all. For the first time since they had made their peace, she felt a bit uncomfortable with him, not in a bad way but certainly in a discomfiting one.

The rain had stopped, to their mutually expressed delight, while they were having dinner, and there was definite hope that they would be able to leave the White Hawk in the morning. She used this as her excuse now to bid him good night. "This time I really do hope for an early start," she said, smiling as she rose. "I did have a very lovely evening, Devin. Thank you."

He stood as well, and came around the table to take her hand. "Good night, Cilla," he said, and instead of simply bowing over her hand in the prescribed custom, he brought it to his lips. "I hope this is just the beginning of many happy times that we may share."

The place where his lips had touched her hand felt uncommonly warm and she felt the rhythm of her pulse quicken. She wished him good night again, knowing that she sounded breathless, and, taking a bed candle from the shelf near the stairs, she went up quickly.

Inside her room, she closed the door and leaned against it, listening to the rapid, foolish beating of her heart. You are absurd, she told herself, and went over to the dressing table to remove the pins from her hair. She no longer looked forward to visiting London, but wished that she were returning at once to Littlelands. Her one consolation was that if she could conclude her business with George quickly, she would be able to return almost at once, secure again that she was permanently situated there.

She stared at her reflection in the mirror and a faint

smile lifted the corners of her mouth. She knew that she did need rest for tomorrow, but she did not feel in the least tired; she felt ebullient. She took out the last pin and let her hair tumble down to her shoulders. For no particular reason, she swayed and danced a brief twirling step in the narrow space of her room. Two evenings and a day did not make a romance, she knew, but it was significant to her that after her treatment of him for nearly two years his interest was so easily rekindled. She knew that there had been nothing in his behavior beyond friendship, but there had been more once, and she knew instinctively that it would be so again if she encouraged him. And she meant to do so. This time she was heart whole and free to follow where her heart might take her.

She stood in the middle of the room, hugging herself against the chill brought on by the damped-down fire, allowing her imagination to take leaps into the future. She saw herself back at Littlelands, with Devin again a frequent caller at the cottage. She saw them riding together at Fairfeld, walking through the lovely rose garden, which would soon be in full bloom. Then she moved further into time and saw herself moving about the elegant rooms of Fairfeld, not as a visitor but as one who truly belonged there.

She was a little startled when she opened her eyes to the bare trappings of her small room, so real had her dream seemed. She greeted reality with a wistful sigh and began to undo the small buttons at the back of her dress, deciding that she could just as easily indulge her imagination while in bed and warm. She looked at her trunk with distaste. The mess she had made still had to be put to rights if she were not to arrive in town with her garments full of creases. She attempted to lift the top of the trunk, but it refused to move. Realizing that the latch had stuck again, she uttered an unladylike oath. She had not willfully relatched it, but in her haste earlier in the evening, no doubt she had closed it with too much force and it had done so of itself. She tried striking it again, but all she received for her trouble was a bruised hand. An attempt to open it with a hairpin was equally unsuccessful. She stood with her hands on her hips and viewed the offending object with acute dislike. She had no wish to spend the night in her dress and decided she would need help to open the trunk.

Rather than redo the buttons of her gown, she snatched up the stole from a chair and wrapped it about her tightly. She went out into the hall, but the inn appeared to be in total darkness.

Lost in her thoughts and fantasies, she had not heard Devin come up to his room, but since there was no light below, she supposed he must be there now. His room was across from Sally's, and Ancilla peered beneath his door closely to see if there was any light. It could not have been long since he had come up, but she hesitated to knock on his door to ask for his help. She stood irresolutely in the dim shaft of light that came from her own room and then, with a sudden burst of resolution, she knocked sharply on his door. She determined that if he did not answer at once she would return to her room and sleep in her dress if necessary, but she had barely brought her hand from the panel when the door swung open to reveal Devin silhouetted against the light of the bed candle standing on the dressing table behind him.

He had not yet completely undressed, but he had removed his coat and cravat and now stood before her in his shirt sleeves, the high, starched collar of his shirt sloping gently onto his shoulders.

Ancilla was aware that her color was high and felt foolish at being embarrassed to make her request. "I . . . I am sorry to disturb you, Devin," she said haltingly. "The latch on my trunk is stuck and I can't get it open."

"You aren't disturbing me," he said with a reassuring smile. "We'll see if I can contrive to open it." He took his candle from the dressing table and followed her to her room.

He knelt before her trunk to examine it, and, to make more room in the limited space, Ancilla sat down on the bed.

"I can't think how I can have been so stupid," she said by way of an apology. "I knew the thing was broken, but I shut it before dinner without thinking."

"Why should you have?" he said over his shoulder. "Your sole concern then was to become as beautiful as possible. I hope that was at least in part for my benefit, by the way, and if it was, this is small enough repayment." He paused and returned his attention to the latch. "I think the trouble is that the top and bottom are out of line with each other," he said presently. "Do you think you could push the top toward me while I hold the bottom steady?"

Ancilla brought her legs up on the bed and drew herself over to the trunk. She did as he instructed and the latch sprang open with unexpected force, striking his hand. Stifling a curse, he jumped back and stood up, putting a finger to his mouth. Ancilla scrambled off the bed and went over to him.

"You're bleeding," she said with concern. "And it is *my fault*. I have something in my dressing case to put on it." In her distress for him, she forgot to hold the stole carefully in place, and as she bent over the dressing case it slid from her shoulders unheeded. She returned to him with a small jar of ointment and a piece of sticking plaster, and efficiently ministered to his wound. "That should stop the bleeding, but I'll give you another piece to put on it in case it seeps through again. Does it hurt very much?"

He didn't answer and she looked up at him from her work. All at once she became conscious of her dishabille and, looking away from him, she moved to reach for the stole, but he caught her arm and turned her back to face him.

"Are you afraid to look at me, Cilla?" he asked softly.

"No, of course not," she said, startled by his question. She made herself meet his eyes and then wished she had not.

"Are you embarrassed to be alone with me like this?" he asked with a quizzical lift to his brows.

She smiled uncertainly. "Well, yes, I am. I know it is foolish, for we have been alone since we have been here."

He said nothing; he gently cupped his hand against the side of her face and caressed her cheek with his forefinger. A silence fell between them and what she saw in his eyes stripped away all the pretense. The harmless fantasies had not been harmless at all. She stood perfectly still under his touch. Her heart felt like a drum in her ears; every muscle was taut as if for flight, but she stood perfectly still.

He broke the silence at last, speaking very quietly and almost in a monotone. "It was very difficult for me tonight to talk to you of commonplaces when those were not the things I wished to say to you. I want you, Cilla. I wanted you that day at Fairfeld, and months before that. You were not the only one who felt guilt. I haven't the makeup of a man who can easily and without conscience make love to the wife of his closest friend. Yet I would have if you hadn't stopped it." He paused and then added, "But that is the past, Cilla."

Ancilla listened to him in silence, her eyes never leaving his. She knew in her heart that his feelings were entirely reciprocated. A part of her, the part that was Sir Edmund Crosby's dutiful daughter, Jack Martin's loyal wife, wanted to run, to escape; as much from herself as from him. But the woman that she was beneath this veneer acknowledged that this was where she truly wished to be.

He raised her chin and kissed her lightly, like a butterfly caressing her lips. "I shouldn't have said to you what I did that afternoon," he continued softly. "I shouldn't have tried to force you to admit that you felt as I did. But I believed it when I said it and I still do. Was I wrong, Cilla?"

A full half minute passed before she answered. "No," she said at last and in the barest whisper.

He kissed her again, still gently but this time insistently, and after a moment the two sides of her merged into one and responded to him as completely as he could wish. The voice of her conscience was not completely laid to rest, but it went unheeded. Everywhere he touched her, her skin warmed to the contact and she relaxed completely in his embrace as the one dream she had never quite allowed herself to have became reality.

Ancilla lay quietly wrapped in his arms and listened to the gradual steadying of his heartbeat. She watched the shifting pattern of shadows cause by the flickering candlelight on the low ceiling and thought about the enormity of the commitment she had made. Desire vanquished, her principal emotion now was confusion. Though her education had taken place more in the stables than in the schoolroom after her mother had died, she did not have the moral principles generally attributed to that place. She had never lain with a man before her wedding night and she knew she would have been shocked if Jack had tried to make love to her before that, but she also knew that her feelings for the man now lying beside her in the narrow bed were very different from those she had had for her husband. She moved away from him and raised herself up on one elbow. He opened his eyes halfway and smiled slightly. He took her hand and brought the palm to his lips, then buried it in his. It was meant to be a reassuring gesture but Ancilla did not feel sure of herself or him.

He saw the uncertainty in her eyes and sighed. "What is it, Cilla? Regret? Guilt? I won't have that," he said gently. "There may have been circumstances in the past that made it wrong for us to be together, but this time there is nothing to keep us apart." He drew her closer and kissed her just below her ear.

Ancilla smiled a little at the understatement of the word "circumstances." "I know," she said. "I suppose it is just ... residual. For the past eighteen months I have tried not even to think of you."

"Were you successful?"

She shook her head, laughing. "No."

"Neither was I."

Somehow this admission that she had been in his thoughts—perhaps his fantasies—as he had been in hers, gave her the reassurance she sought. She lay back and buried her head in his shoulder, fully acknowledging the deep contentment that she felt in his arms.

4

Ancilla was standing in the front hall of Littlelands Cottage and someone was banging loudly on the door. Though she opened the door and found no one there, the knocking continued.

"Miss Cilla? Are you awake?" said a voice from a long way off.

The hall and the front garden of Littlelands Cottage receded and Ancilla opened her eyes. Sunlight filled the room, filtered through the thin curtains on the window. She stretched luxuriously and sat up. The knocking sounded again and a decidedly anxious "Miss Cilla?" came from the other side of the door. So that had not been part of the dream.

Before she could reply, the door swung open and Sally hurried into the room. She came to a sudden stop when she saw Ancilla sitting up in bed and said in a relieved yet offended voice, "You *are* awake. I was ever so worried. I thought something had happened to you. Thank heaven the door was only stuck and not locked."

"What could possibly have happened to me?" asked Ancilla, and then, as the last confusions of sleep evaporated and the memory of the previous night came flooding back to her, she quickly grabbed at the sheet to cover her nakedness. But she wasn't naked. She was wearing her demure white cotton nightdress, although she had no memory of putting it on. Her amber silk dress, which she had last seen lying in a rumpled heap on the floor beside the bed, was draped neatly across the chair in the corner. She smiled a small, secret smile to herself, which went unnoticed by her maid, whose eye had been caught by her mistress's trunk, which stood open.

"Whatever have you been doing to your things, Miss Cilla?" Sally said, stooping. "It looks like there's been a madman in here tossin' everything about."

"Oh, dear, I forgot," Ancilla said contritely. "I was looking for something in a hurry last night and I meant to refold everything before I went to bed, but ... well, I forgot. Do you know what time it is?" she added. The sunlight seemed strong for early in the morning, and she was concerned that her long sleep was keeping Devin waiting for her at breakfast.

"After nine by the clock in the hall," Sally said absently, already absorbed in refolding the clothes in the trunk.

It was later than Ancilla had meant to sleep but not so late as she had feared. It was likely, though, that he was already up, since he had planned to be under way as soon as possible. She threw back the sheets and swung her legs out of bed. "I'll wear the blue muslin today, if it isn't too badly creased," she told Sally.

Sally looked up from her work with surprise. "The blue muslin? For traveling?" This dress was Ancilla's best after the amber silk, and not usually worn for every day.

"It is comfortable and light. The day will be warmer now that it is not so damp, and the carriage was stuffy and close even when it was cold and raining. You are sounding very much better, Sally," she added to turn the subject.

"I'm more the thing, Miss Cilla," the maid replied, and then clucked over the state of Ancilla's gray cotton dress, which was all over wrinkles. She finally extricated the blue muslin and handed it to Ancilla.

She went out to the hall to fetch Ancilla's morning can of hot water and took it to the basin. She stooped to pick up a piece of paper, which had fluttered to the floor from the dressing table. It had writing on it, but Sally could not read. Ancilla had offered to teach her several times, but Sally had always said that being able to sign her name was good enough for her.

"There's a paper on the floor with writin' on it," she said. "Is it somethin' you're wantin', Miss Cilla?"

Ancilla was inspecting the dress Sally had given her and didn't bother to look up. "No, it's just a list I made up of some things I wanted to purchase in town, but I don't suppose I shall have the money for them now. Throw it in the grate."

Sally did as she was told, then stoked the last remnants of the night fire and added a few more coals so that Ancilla would have more warmth for dressing.

"There is only a crease or two near the hem, which I am sure will come out with hanging," Ancilla said, sounding very pleased.

Sally put the last neatly folded item, the amber silk gown, into the trunk. If she thought it odd that her mistress had worn such a formal dress for a simple dinner in a country inn, this time she kept her thoughts to herself. "If you're not needin' me just yet, Miss Cilla," she said to Ancilla, who had gone to the washbasin, "I'll be seein' to packin' my own things now. Meg brought me up a bite for breakfast a while ago, but I expect yours will be waitin' for you downstairs."

"No, I don't need you, Sally." She was in fact glad to be left alone. "You do what you have to so that we may leave as soon as I have eaten. I'll dress myself."

After Sally had gone, Ancilla washed and put on her petticoats and stockings. All the while, she mused on the previous night and what she and Devin would say to each other this morning. Last night they had been far too taken up with their need for each other to be concerned with the future, but Ancilla didn't really doubt what the future would be. She consulted her own heart and, in doing so, believed she knew his as well.

She put her cotton nightdress into the trunk and closed it firmly. The faulty latch sprang into place, but she paid it no heed. The idle thought came to her that small annoyances such as that would be a thing of the past when she became Lady Langley.

She returned to the dressing table and sat down to remove the night tangles from her hair before dressing it for the day. She picked up her brush and, looking down as she did so, discovered a folded ten-pound note beneath it. She slowly put down the brush and picked up the money. It was not one ten-pound note, but five of them folded together. She stared at the money uncomprehendingly for a moment, but the truth was obvious. She threw the money down on the table and stood, but quickly sat down again; her legs felt rubbery and the room was suddenly hot.

She wanted to believe what she was thinking could not possibly be true, but the evidence lay on the polished wood in front of her. He had paid her. Was this the usual thing for a man to do when he had spent an agreeable night with his mistress? Was it a token of his appreciation?

Perhaps it was even expected. She had no experience of such things.

One thing she was sure of: it was not the behavior of a man toward a woman with whom he was in love. If that was what the night before had meant to him, he would not have offered her such an insult. Unsophisticated she might be, but she knew this for a certainty.

And she had hardly been able to bear the delay until her return to Littlelands. To be with him, to plan their future together. She had even dared to think of herself as Lady Langley.

She felt more deeply ashamed than she ever had in her life, as much for her own foolish innocence as for any other reason. He had said that he wanted her, that he needed her, but not once had he spoken of love. What had been commitment for her had been only a business transaction for him. She felt almost sick.

She placed her elbows on the dressing table and buried her face in her hands. She sat that way for some time until a brief knock heralded the reappearance of Sally. Ancilla quickly pushed the notes under the runner on the dressing table and picked up her brush.

"Aren't you dressed yet?" Sally asked when she saw her mistress still in her petticoats. "I thought you'd have been down for your breakfast by now."

"I'm having a little trouble waking up this morning," Ancilla replied in a controlled voice. "I'll be dressed in a moment."

With Sally to help her, she dressed quickly. During a moment when Sally was occupied with placing the last of her things in her dressing case, Ancilla transferred the notes to her reticule.

While dressing, Ancilla made up her mind what she would do; it was the only thing she could do. Though she hated the thought of facing him again, the desire to throw his money in his face was stronger. Telling Sally that she meant to have only chocolate and toast for breakfast and that she would inform the coachman that they wished to leave as quickly as possible, she went downstairs.

When she entered the common room, she saw Matchem talking to two unfamiliar, coarsely dresssed men, who she assumed were local farmers or laborers, but with that exception, the room was empty. Matchem looked up from his conversation to wish her good morning, and Ancilla hastily returned the greeting and asked, "Has Lord Langley come down yet?"

"Aye, ma'am," said Matchem with his usual cheerful smile. "These two hours since. The mail goes by—not at its usual crack pace, mind—just as he's sitting down to his breakfast, and I says to his lordship, 'All's clear, then,' and he says, 'Have the ostler ready my carriage,' and within the hour he was off."

"Do you mean he has already left for Fairfeld?" Ancilla asked, trying not very successfully to keep the dismay out of her voice.

"Can't say where he's gone, ma'am," said the landlord kindly, "but he's been gone from here this hour past."

Ancilla thanked him and went to the table set for her breakfast, though she felt too numb to eat.

At last the carriage was in front of the door and their baggage safely stowed. It was not soon enough for Ancilla. The White Hawk had become hateful to her; Matchem's cheerfulness grated on her nerves; Mrs. Matchem's motherly bustle became officiousness to her.

The worst part came when she had to pay the reckoning. The expense had been greater than she had even dared to imagine, and she was left with the bare minimum necessary for them to stay one night in London, and their return the first thing the next morning so that they might not be delayed overnight on the road was now a necessity. Devin's five ten-pound notes lay rolled in the bottom of her reticule, but she had made up her mind that not even the most dire necessity would force her to spend so much as a penny of it.

The prospect of returning to Littlelands at once was now as repugnant to her as just a short time ago it had been her dearest wish. She now wished with all her heart that she could afford a protracted stay in London, or anywhere for that matter, so that the diversion might cast Devin Langley from her mind forever. It would be necessary, of course, to see him one last time to return his money, but after that her most earnest desire was never to see him or hear of him again for the whole of her life.

Though the rain had stopped, and the sun was now brilliant and the water in the shallow places in the road had receded, the conditions of the road were still deplorable. Their progress was as slow as ever and they were as batted about the carriage as before. But this time, lost in introspection, Ancilla barely noticed the discomfort.

Sally made a number of remarks to her that received the barest monosyllables in reply. "What is it, Miss Cilla?" she asked with concern. "Are you feelin' poorly? You haven't taken my cold have you?"

"No," Ancilla said in the same toneless way she had spoken all morning. "I am just rather tired, Sally, and if you don't mind, I think I shall try to sleep for a while." She closed her eyes at once and rested her head against the squabs of the jostling carriage.

This was a patent excuse to be left to her own thoughts, for no one could have slept in such conditions. But Sally merely sighed and fell silent. She drew her own conclusions to account for her mistress's mood and they were not so very far from the truth.

The midafternoon sun beating down on his shoulders felt hot on Devin's skin even through the layers of cloth that covered him. He thought of stopping to remove his driving coat, but he was so near now to his destination that he wished nothing to delay him any further. In a matter of minutes, he told himself, as he steered his horses in a sweeping arc between the wide-open gates of Fairfeld Park, he would be able to change into clothing more suitable to the day and to his activities. But as he neared the fork in the drive, one arm of which led to the house and the other to the stables, stud farm, and racing course, he made up his mind on the moment and took the latter branch. His natural desire to change and wash off the dirt of the road, to make at least a presentable, if belated, appearance before his guests, when weighted against the prospect of missing more, even, in view of the hour, possibly all of the day's racing, sank into unimportance.

Though most of the land on the estate was relatively flat, the house itself and the early portions of the drive were built on a rise, and as he came to the summit before descending, he could see the panorama of buildings and lush green pastures spread before him, liberally dotted now with people and animals.

He drove past another, smaller spur of the drive, which led directly to the course and the racing stables, and continued on to the carriage house, which had its own stables, set apart. He consigned his curricle and horses to the care of a groom and, deciding against walking back to the course by the more roundabout way of the drive, risked adding a bit more dirt to his person by climbing over the fence that separated the carriage stableyard from the pastures and headed across the fields by the most direct route. He was challenged only once by a groom scraping down a sweating horse, and the challenge turned to a greeting as he was recognized. He entered the large, double-winged racing stables by the wide door leading into the pastures and went through to the central part of the building; he was virtually unnoticed in the teeming activity taking place in there.

He tracked down his trainer, John Bosley, just as the latter was about to leave the stables by the main door. After Bosley expressed his surprise and pleasure that his lordship had not, after all, missed the whole of the meeting, he gave Devin the gratifying news that Golddigger had won his match race by two lengths and that the mare they were grooming for the next Oaks had placed second in the third race, which was a sweepstakes race. After parting from Bosley, Devin stopped to have a word with his head groom, who was entrusted with the care of Nimbus; then he left the stable and headed for the course.

The stableyard had a view of the grandstand, which he had had erected shortly after inheriting the estate. It improved the informal course that his father had laid out nearly a decade ago, when the first meeting at Fairfeld was held. As Devin stepped again into the sunshine a roar went up from the grandstand, a clear indication that another race had begun.

He quickened his pace and, rounding the corner of the east wing of the stable, ran squarely into a nattily dressed man whose fair complexion was flushed from his quick pace. The man staggered backward from the impact and Devin grasped his arms to steady him.

Devin smiled in recognition. "Dreaming of future glories for Claret Cup, Cholly?"

Ethelred Cholbeck, known to his friends, for obvious reasons, as Cholly, was a fair young man of medium height with pale blue eyes that always looked on the verge of tearing. He blinked rapidly at Devin and said, "The *devil*," as though he meant it literally, but after a brief moment he returned Devin's smile wholeheartedly.

"Damme, didn't think to see you here today. You were so mysterious about your plans that we just gave you up. Conclude your business, did you?"

"There was no business, after all," Devin replied, "but I'll tell you of that later. Is that the match race between Hammerhead and Peerless that has just begun?"

Cholly nodded. "Hammerhead'll take it, I should think. Put a monkey on him to win."

"I'm glad I haven't missed the cup race. I suppose you're on your way to have a last look at Claret Cup before he's made ready."

"Yes," Cholbeck replied, a frown creasing his brow. "Wish he weren't running, but Carter insisted. Good as done in that case. Wish you hadn't put it in his head that the Blue was getting past his prime and beatable. I don't think Claret Cup has gotten rid of all his winter fat yet, and if he loses, Carter will think of some way to make it my fault."

Devin sighed in resignation. He had been listening to Cholbeck, who was of a pleasant disposition at most times, animadvert on his friend Francis Carter for the past three years. Carter, a Bond Street beau with a fancy but not an ability for things Corinthian, seeking to impress his acquaintances in that illustrious set, had purchased Claret Cup. But, having no knowledge and little entrée into racing circles, he had come to an agreement with Cholbeck, who possessed both, but not the necessary funds to own a competitive runner; the latter would be given a percentage in the ownership of the horse in exchange for his expertise and management of the career of Claret Cup. There were times, though, when Carter, who had retained the controlling interest in the horse, was of a mind to exercise his authority and challenge the decisions of his partner. There were inevitable clashes between the two, which Cholbeck was inclined to bemoan at length to anyone who would listen.

"I am sorry if I have made difficulties for you, Cholly," Devin said to his friend. "Carter merely asked my opinion one afternoon at White's and I gave it to him. I understand that he has also challenged Pomfret to a match race against the Blue at the next Newmarket meeting."

"Getting cocksure," said Cholly with rare gloom. "Did it without so much as a word to me. Wants my advice but don't care to take it. He's beginning to think he don't need me, if you ask me."

'Well, if you are right, and Claret Cup loses, you will be vindicated," Devin said reassuringly. "And your horse should certainly be in top form by the Newmarket meeting."

"Oh, I agree with you about the Blue," Cholly admitted. "But now's now, and then's then," he added cryptically.

Devin murmured sympathetically and changed the subject by asking how the house party had fared in his absence.

"Geoff did the thing as well as you could have yourself, Dev. To the manner born and all that. Everything went so smoothly," he added with a teasing smile, "we almost forgot you weren't here. Course, he had a bit of help."

"If Geoff was able to get your mind off horses and keep you away from the stables long enough for you to be a help to him with our guests, that was an accomplishment, indeed, and more than I've ever managed."

Not blind to his shortcomings, Cholbeck laughed. "Always willing to do my bit, of course, but I didn't mean me." He paused and added abruptly, "Been to the house yet?" Ascertaining that his friend had not, he continued, "Don't know then, do you? Well, mum's the word. Won't be the one to let the cat out and all that."

"What the devil are you talking about, Cholly?" said Devin with genuine puzzlement.

Cholbeck refused to explain himself. "Geoff and the rest of the usual lot are at the course," he said. "Go see for yourself what I mean." And with a quick, enigmatic smile and a brief nod of his head, he continued on to the stables.

Devin took his advice.

The distance from the White Hawk to London was not great, but it took nearly double the time to get there than it would have under more favorable conditions. The two women who debarked from the chaise in the courtyard of the Golden Cross late that afternoon were weary in body and in spirit. The room Ancilla had bespoken by post had long since been given up to someone else, but another was found for them and fortunately it was large enough to accommodate them both.

When they were in their room, Sally began to unpack

some of their things, but Ancilla advised her to let it go until later. "I know how tired you must be, for I am exhausted and I have not been sick. Lie down for a bit, Sally. I wouldn't want you to suffer a relapse and there is nothing here that won't keep."

Sally did so gratefully, but sat up again when she saw her mistress redonning her merino cloak. "Where are you off to, then, Miss Cilla? You should be restin' a bit yourself."

Ancilla shook her head without looking up. "I must see George at once. I only hope that he is at home and that we may be able to settle the matter quickly so that we will be able to see his man of business today. Then no doubt we will have to go to his solicitor as well for the proper papers to be drawn up."

In the common room, Ancilla asked a waiter if he could direct her to Half-Moon Street, where George lived. The waiter offered to have an ostler fetch a hack for her, but, conscious of saving every possible penny, Ancilla declined his offer. Half-Moon Street turned out to be farther from the inn than she had hoped, but to a woman born and bred in the country, used to traversing miles on foot to visit friends, the distance was not all that great.

London, though, proved to be quite different from the country. Ancilla had not gone far before she became aware of the ogling stares of several men she passed. One of them was even bold enough to attempt to approach her, but a single frosty glare was sufficient to put him off, and after this Ancilla walked more quickly despite her tiredness, keeping her head down lest she catch the eye of anyone else.

She reached Half-Moon Street and located George's house, and not a moment too soon for her liking. The door was opened to her by a tall, cadaverously thin man with a hooked nose, who looked her up and down with cold insolence, and then informed her, in a voice directly from the polar caps, that Mr. Martin was not at home.

"Do you expect him soon?" Ancilla asked hopefully. "I am Mrs. Martin, his sister-in-law, and I have come from Littlelands especially to speak with him. I would prefer to wait for him rather than go back to my inn, if you do not think that he will be too long."

The majordomo's manner toward her thawed slightly at the mention of her name, but her unprepossessing appearance prevented him from melting into recognizable human form. "I am afraid that is impossible. Mr. Martin cannot have been expecting you, for he is away from town, visiting friends. I do not expect him to return this evening at all."

This was all but a mortal blow to Ancilla, and one that she had not been expecting. "When do you ... expect him?" she asked, faltering.

"Not before tomorrow midday, and then there is always the possibility that he may change his mind and decide to extend his stay."

After several moments of silence the butler cleared his throat, and Ancilla became aware that she had been staring at him blankly. She thanked him because there was nothing else for her to do, then watched as he accorded her a brief nod and closed the door in her face.

Ancilla retraced her steps to the inn, but this time she would not have noticed if a horde of men had attempted to proposition her. She could hardly believe that this was happening to her. How simple everything had seemed on Monday, when she left Littlelands; how complicated it had all become.

Devin carefully scanned the freckled face of the small
man standing before him. There was concern in the man's
eyes, which was proper to the occasion, but his voice held
no trace of a tremor or hesitation.

"I just don't think it's possible, my lord, or likely," the
man said. "Sammy Duncan had the usual night watch.
He always has it on the night before a meeting because
he's the lightest sleeper in the lot."

"I am not saying it's likely, Smitty, but it isn't
impossible, and in view of the circumstances, it is a
suspicion that must be entertained." Devin's voice held a
trace of dry weariness. He was beginning to think that
there was a malevolent star shining upon him; with two
exceptions, the events of the last few days had provided
him with one annoyance after the other.

The latest of these unfortunate happenings had occurred earlier that day when the Fairfeld Cup race, for
which he had had such hopes, had been run. The racing
of horses had for too long been a part of his life for him to
become upset at a mere loss of a race, but his colt Nimbus,
of which he had spoken in such glowing terms to Ancilla,
had not only not taken the race, he had finished a dismal
last, a full length behind the horse before him. An embarrassing loss for a good or promising horse was always the
subject for a possible inquiry, but Devin, Bosley, and
Lord Brisbane, a steward of the jockey club who was
staying at Fairfeld, with fifty years of experience among
them, had gone over the colt and found no cause to
indicate that the horse had been deliberately nobbled.

Brisbane had decided against making an official report,
agreeing with Nimbus's unhappy trainer that the colt
had simply had an off day. Devin, though, was not
satisfied. It had not been his experience that a truly good
horse was capable of such wide inconsistency as Nimbus

had shown between this race and his training gallops, and he simply did not agree with Bosley's verdict that perhaps they had seen more in the colt than was truly there.

Lord Langley's head groom, Patrick Smith, stood before him now as Devin attempted, despite the fatigue of travel and a very hectic day, to get to the bottom of the matter.

"You are quite certain, Smitty," Devin said after a pause, "that you were with the horse from the time that you aroused Duncan until he was led to the course?"

Color came into the groom's face. "Aye, that I am, my lord," he said, a small note of prideful belligerence coming into his voice. "That's my job, ain't it? To see to my ponies till they're on the track and ready to run."

Devin smiled, amused at his groom's vanity. Smitty might be small in stature, but he was clever and tough and no man's fool. He had been born and bred on the Fairfield estate and had succeeded his father as head groom, not through patronage but by hard work and an ability matched by few.

"Yes, it is your job," Devin said, "and you do it very well. I was only suggesting that as head groom your duties encompass more than just the care of the horses assigned to you. It would be perfectly natural for you to be taken away from your duties toward Nimbus to see to some other matter demanding your attention."

Smitty looked down at the small, peaked cap he was turning in circles between his fingers. Being head groom of the Fairfeld racing stables was not just a job to him, it was a vocation. "Any lad of mine caught givin' short shrift to his charge would be findin' himself at another stable, and there'd be no exceptions even for me," he said, sounding almost fierce.

"I am not questioning your integrity, nor your diligence, Smitty. Raikers said that Nimbus ran sluggishly, as if he had a bellyful of water, and you know as well as I that there are few professional riders with more feel for a horse than Raikers."

If your lordship is thinkin' I'm after givin' my ponies a bucket or two of water afore a race"—Smitty paused and squared his shoulders—"then maybe I know the thing you'll be thinkin' next, and I'll be givin' my notice afore you can get to it."

Devin smiled patiently. "What I *am* thinking, Patrick, is that I wish you would come down off *your* horse." He sat down and motioned for Smitty to do the same. "You know perfectly well that I am not accusing you of doing anything so corkbrained. What happened this afternoon is a puzzle to me and I am simply trying to understand it." His tone became confidential. "Not even Bosley is as close to that horse as you are. What do you make of it, Smitty?"

Though he would have much preferred to stand, Smitty perched on the edge of the brocade chair near his lordship's desk. "Mr. Bosley says every horse is entitled to an off day," he said evasively. "Reckon it's just a shame it had to be today."

"I didn't ask you for Bosley's opinion."

Smitty wiped his hands on his breeches and grasped the arms of the chair to push himself farther into it. "Well," he began hesitantly, "Mr. Bosley is a downy one and that's a fact. It ain't for me to tell him his business."

"But you do not share his opinion?" Reluctance and discomfort were written plainly on the countenance of the groom, and Devin knew he would have to lead him gently. "I know you would never be guilty of disrespect toward Mr. Bosley," he said helpfully, "but you would be doing me a great favor if you told me what you do think. I promise you nothing said here will go beyond these walls."

"Nimbus was as fit as a fiddle this morning." The groom did not look at his employer as he spoke. "But not as perky as you might expect on racin' day. They always know, the ponies do, and they get excited. Since you said Nimbus was to run this meeting, his gallops have been good, but hard. He's been comin' back to the stable a bit frothylike for the time of year." Smitty clamped his mouth shut and set his jaw like a man aware that he has said too much.

"Are you saying that he has been overtrained?" Devin prodded. His head groom's eyes flicked up to his and then rested again on the cap in his lap; he shook his head slowly and said nothing. Knowing the loyalty of the man to his superior, Devin supposed this was the nearest Smitty would come to criticizing him, and let it go. "Thank you, Smitty. You have helped me to put things in a better perspective." He stood to indicate dismissal, and the groom, touching his forelock in the prescribed manner, murmured something unintelligible and left the room.

Outside the study door, Smitty straightened his shoulders and the lines of concern smoothed out of his face. He began walking toward the back of the house, but halfway there, he turned, took a few faltering steps in the direction he had come, and stopped. For perhaps a full minute he stood perfectly still, then, turning once again, he made his way out of the house.

Devin sat at his desk, deep in a brown study. He was not even aware that someone had come into the room until a pair of bejeweled hands were placed on the blotter in front of him. He recognized their elegant shapeliness and looked up with a welcoming smile.

"I was just thinking before," he said to the young woman who stood in front of him, "that only two good things have come my way in the past sennight. You are one of them."

Lucina Wyndham pulled the chair recently vacated by the groom closer to the desk. She was a fine-boned, well-figured young woman with the same dark auburn hair and green eyes as her brother. "What was the other one?" she asked, slouching comfortably in the chair.

Devin did not answer her question but said, "I'm very pleased that Tom was able to spare you to come to me after all, though I am sorry his duties prevented him from joining you. But you alone are a wonderful surprise and a tonic that I need just now."

"Tonic enough to make up for Nimbus's disgrace?" she asked tentatively.

He shrugged slightly. "I've certainly lost races before. Many times."

"Not so many," she disagreed. "But this one mattered to you, didn't it?"

"Yes."

The study door opened and Cholbeck and Geoffrey Drake came into the room. Geoffrey did not wait while his companion carefully closed the door behind them, but crossed the room with his characteristic long, quick strides. His hair was the color of wheat and his eyes were a solemn gray with a serious cast of countenance to match them. He greeted Devin, pecked Lucina on the cheek, then set on the edge of the desk as if impatient of the time it would take to draw a chair of his own over to them.

Have you seen to it that everyone is safely snuggled in his bed, Geoff?" Lucina asked looking up at him.

Geoffrey nodded shortly. While Devin had been away he had willingly taken on many of Devin's duties as host in addition to his own as steward, regarding this as his responsibility; but now that Devin had returned, he could not help bristling a bit at Lucina's words.

Geoffrey was second cousin to Devin and Lucina; his branch of the family, however, had not prospered as theirs had. He and Devin were separated by little more than a year in age and had been at Cambridge together.

When Devin's father had died and Devin had offered him the post of steward to Fairfeld, he had jumped at the opportunity, and though untrained for the position, he had learned by doing. In his way, Geoffrey had proved to be as successful as his cousin. Devin had been a rich man when Geoffrey had begun the task, and it gave Geoffrey great pride to know that at least in part through his efforts, that fortune had almost doubled in the five years he had worked for Devin.

But his pride was not without tarnish. The two men, each recognizing the skills of the other, had become closer during this time, and this caused Geoffrey, at least in his own mind, to hold a very ambiguous position in the household. On the one hand, he was the cousin of the lord of the manor; on the other, he was his servant.

These feelings might easily have come between the cousins, but Geoffrey, in the practical way that was his nature, had worked out the means of giving himself some peace of mind. He was unmarried, and his needs, since he lived almost exclusively on the estate, were small. Most of his large salary each quarter was put aside and safely invested in the five-percents, and he had hopes that he would eventually have the means to purchase an estate of his own. Nothing, of course, on the scale of Fairfeld, but size and scope were not important to Geoffrey; it was the knowledge that he would be meeting his cousin and other of his friends as an equal that mattered to him.

For the time being, to keep his unhappy emotions in check, he had contrived a way of dealing with them. While on the estate, or in his office at the back of the stud farm, or in any other situation where he served as agent for his cousin, he was Mr. Drake, steward of Fairfeld; but once he entered the house, where he had a comfortable suite of rooms, he was simply Geoff, and part of the family.

Devin understood the ambiguity of Geoffrey's feelings, although he did not share them, and was careful to respect the drawn lines at all times. Lucina, too, knew enough of Geoffrey to be considerate of his feelings and had in fact not meant to imply that it was a part of his duties to see to the settling in of the houseguests for the night.

In his way Geoffrey understood that she had not, but simply could not help being on his dignity. A little ashamed of his curt response, he looked at Cholly, who was now pulling up a chair beside Lucina's, and attempted to make light of the matter. "Except for Cholly. No amount of fresh air and sunshine is enough to put him in his bed before the small hours. This is caused, no doubt, by his inbred dislike of rising before noon."

Cholly paused in the act of moving the chair to cast his friend an injured look. "Not fair. I was up bright and early this morning, wasn't I Lucy?" he said, appealing to her.

Lucina reached over and patted his hand with affection. "You made an appearance at the course by eleven. A noble feat for a man I heard was playing cards till nearly dawn."

"Gaming again, Cholly?" Devin asked. "I thought you'd given it up since that time you thought you'd been fleeced at Mrs. Merribeck's hell."

"Chicken stakes," Cholly said disdainfully. "Just to keep my hand in. Won, too."

"He played whist with Kilbain, Colliard, and Dunning," Geoffrey said with a dry smile, "who have to be among the worst cardplayers ever to sit at a table. Their sort is always grateful to find any decent player who'll cut a deck with them, and they don't mind if they're on the fleeced end. You should have upped the stakes, Cholly."

Ignoring this bait, Cholly turned his attention to Devin. "Saw Smitty coming in here a while back. Nothing the matter, is there? Claret Cup hasn't gone lame, has he? With the Blue coming through to win the Fairfeld Cup, Carter would be wild if we had to scratch him from the match at Newmarket."

Devin and Geoffrey exchanged amused glances at their friend's monomania, and the latter said, "Surely he would have come straight to you with that earth-shattering news."

Devin cast his cousin a quelling look and said to Cholly, "I wanted to talk to him about Nimbus's condition before the race and to get his opinion of the matter."

Lucina, who had been idly listening to their conversation while waiting for the chance to talk to her brother alone again, now looked up. "You aren't going to go on teasing yourself about this, are you, Dev?" she asked with concern. "I know how you feel about that horse, but, well . . . you can't always be right, you know."

"Of course I'm not," Devin agreed, smiling. "But I just find it impossible to believe I could have been *that* wrong. I have to begin to wonder what sort of judge I am of a good runner if I was that far off."

"What did Smitty say?" Cholly asked.

Devin shrugged. "Nothing, really. Said the horse wasn't as bright as might have been expected on a race day, but other than that, he saw nothing to cause concern."

"And Dr. Tentrees is certain that he is sickening for nothing?" queried Lucina.

"As far as he could tell," Devin replied. "We'll know the truth of that in a day or two."

Cholbeck yawned and stretched. "Think I will go up to bed," he said. "All that gadding about at the crack of dawn seems to be taking its toll on me. Perhaps I can persuade Chalmers to join me in a hand of piquet before bed to relax a bit."

"And if you win," Geoffrey taunted, but not unkindly, "you can cut expenses on his wages."

Cholbeck, who had indeed had a tiring day, was much shorter of temper than usual. He looked up sharply, but as he started to retort Lucina cut in.

"You mustn't be so hard on poor Cholly, Geoff. This hasn't been the best of days for him. Claret Cup came in second in the cup race and you know that he and Mr. Carter had hopes that he would win it."

"Well, Carter did," Cholly corrected her. "Never did think it myself."

"Oh, I don't know," said Devin, musing. "The Blue won over Claret Cup by only half a length. Last year it would have been his race by three times that, at the least. I'm sure we are right about the Blue, Cholly, and the match at Newmarket could well belong to you."

"I expect Claret Cup will be fit enough by then," Cholly agreed. He then rose and, wishing them a good night, went up to bed.

When he had gone, Geoffrey stood also and said he supposed he had best seek his bed as well.

"Before you go, Geoff, I want to ask you something," Devin said. Geoffrey raised questioning eyebrows and Devin went on. "Have you seen any of Nimbus's recent gallops? I was wondering if anything about them particularly struck you."

Geoffrey was surprised by the question. "You've seen them for yourself. It was because of his superb form that you decided to run him in the cup race. If you mean during the time you were in town, I didn't notice anything in particular. I was too busy to watch the gallops every day, but Bosley never mentioned any concern about him, and he certainly would have come to me if there had been any cause for it."

Devin agreed that this was true. "But what I primarily meant," he added, "is whether or not you noticed what sort of condition the horse was in after the gallops. Did he seem to be blowing hard, or extraordinarily tired, or even just frothy?"

"I can't say that I noticed any such thing," Geoffrey said, looking puzzled. "Are you wondering if Bosley worked him too hard? One of the things that make him such a good trainer is that he knows just how to push a horse to his maximum without taking him beyond what he can reasonably do."

Devin regarded his cousin thoughtfully for a moment. "Did you know that he disagreed with me about entering Nimbus in the cup race? He thought we ought to give him lighter competition for the beginning."

"So you think he might have overtrained the horse to bring him up to scratch?" Geoffrey suggested. "It isn't impossible, but I don't believe it. You ought to let this thing go, Dev. You're getting addlepated over it. You know John Bosley wouldn't do such a thing. The horse had a bad day or for some unobvious reason was unfit. The race is run, and groping about for some sort of answer won't change the outcome."

"Geoff is right, Devin," Lucina put in. "Please stop teasing yourself about it."

Devin agreed, out loud, at least, that he would try not to concern himself over it any longer. Geoffrey then made his departure, and brother and sister were alone again.

"Do you know," said Lucina, "it does amaze me that a person who is as sensitive in his own feelings as Geoff is can be so insensitive to another's. It really was very cruel of him to quiz Cholly that way about his gaming. It is not as if Cholly has ever been a hardened gamester, but he does love to play and I think he feels badly that it must always be for penny points because of his income. Geoff should certainly understand that as well."

"I'm glad you didn't say so to Geoff," Devin said with a tired smile. "You ruffled his plumage enough for one evening, and Cholly certainly doesn't need your defense. He'll get his own back, if not tonight, then tomorrow. Those two are always quizzing each other, but it's as friends. Neither means anything by it."

"I think Cholly was genuinely upset by Geoff's remark about fleecing his valet," Lucina insisted.

"Cholly was just tired," he said, "and I must confess, so am I."

"I don't wonder at it," Lucy said with sisterly sympathy. "Traveling half the day over rain-rutted roads and then having to play host to a lot of people you probably wish at the devil, not to mention all the things you had to see to when you got here. No doubt you haven't even had good sleep for the last two nights. The beds in inns are never what they are at home."

"I was comfortable enough."

"Maybe," Lucina conceded, "but it must have been so tedious stranded at an inn by yourself with only strangers for company and nothing to do but fret over the delay."

His sister and friends had assumed that he had put up at the inn at Chelmsford, as was his usual custom when delayed from reaching Fairfeld in a day from town, and he had not bothered to correct their error. "There was someone there that I knew," he said now.

"Somebody traveling here for the meeting?"

"No, traveling in the opposite direction, to London, but equally stranded. It was Ancilla Martin."

"Ancilla going to London?" said Lucina, surprised, for she knew that Ancilla's income was not large. "Does she have friends there? I know she has no family but Sir Waldo and Lady Crosby, and even if they did take a house for the season in town, I cannot imagine them being generous enough to have Cilla stay with them."

"No, it is not the Crosbys she is going to see, but she does have family of a sort there," he said. He went on to explain Ancilla's predicament and added, "I *am* worried for her. I don't believe for a moment that it was an oversight. It is just like George to cheat her of the property if he can."

"It is shocking if he means to do that," said Lucina indignantly. "Isn't there anything you can do for her?"

"I shall if she'll let me. She is very independent, you know."

"Perhaps it would help if I talked to her," said Lucy, accepting the glass of wine that Devin had poured for her. "I didn't come to know her as well as you did, but we rather liked each other, and if she should need help, I think an offer of it from me would be easier for her than if it came from a man."

Devin poured out wine for himself as well, then paused to sip at it before speaking again. "You shall probably see Ancilla if you stay with me until the end of June, as you've promised. I don't believe she means to remain long in town."

"But *we* shall be going to town for a while," Lucina reminded him. "You aren't going back on your promise to open the London house for me so that I may see all my friends and do some shopping before I go back to Tom, are you?"

"No," he said, smiling at the apprehension that had crept into her voice. "But it will be at least a month before I can get away from here, and I cannot remain in town above a month, for I must attend the meeting at Newmarket. Then, of course, it will be only a fortnight until the second meeting here, and I can't neglect my responsibilities toward that a second time."

"*Horses*. Always horses," Lucina exclaimed with mock exasperation. "I think that while I am in town I shall have another chore. I have been so wrapped up in my own life that I have sadly neglected you, Devin. But I think the time has come that I find you a wife. It would be just the thing, I think, to help you put your life in proper perspective. The world, in case you are unaware of it, does not revolve around the Stud Book or the Racing Calendar."

"Since you think I am so besotted by my horses," Devin said, laughing, "I am surprised that you would wish me on some poor woman whom I would probably neglect."

"If she were the proper woman for you, you would not do so."

"Perhaps not," said her brother, "but I wish you would save your pains. I haven't any interest in being leg-shackled just yet."

"That is what every man says," Lucina assured him.

"Well, if you can find me a suitable bride who will not be jealous of my horses, and who will have a greater liking for my person than for my purse, I promise I will at least study her points and give it consideration."

"You are becoming a cynic, Devin," said Lucina censoriously. "I cannot like that. And you value yourself too cheaply. I am sure there are any number of women who would have you even if you were not Lord Langley of Fairfeld Park. The thing is, you have never taken the trouble to find one of them."

"Perhaps it is just that I have had the experience of the other sort finding me once or twice too often," he said dryly.

"Nonsense," she said, airily dismissing his remark. "If you will look only in the highest circles, where most of the females are more concerned with matters of position than of the heart, you must expect that. You should follow my example. Stop being so high in the instep and look for a woman who is worthy of you not because of beauty or position but because she values the things that matter in life. And it must be a love match, Devin," she added positively. "After a year of experiencing the rigors, intimacies, and adjustments of married life, I am tolerably certain that without love it would have been unbearable."

Amused, Devin laughed at her new matronliness, then suggested that as it was becoming quite late, they too should retire for the night.

6

Ancilla had told herself that not even the direst emergency would cause her to spend a penny of the fifty pounds that Devin had left for her. Now that the emergency was at hand, she found that words were one thing, reality another. At the very least one more night at the Golden Cross would be necessary, and there were meals for her and for Sally to pay for as well, she had no choice at all, for to have returned home at once without seeing George would have been foolish beyond permission.

George's servant had told her that the soonest he would be expected would be midday the next day, and Ancilla had meant to wait until later in the afternoon to return to his house, to give him ample time to arrive, but when the time came, she found herself restless and impatient to see him, and it was just shortly after one when she started out, again on foot, to his house.

The door was opened to her by the same servant, who gave her the same insolent stare. He admitted grudgingly that Mr. Martin was returned, and then rudely left her standing in the hall while he went to ascertain if his master was receiving.

When he returned to say that George would see her, Ancilla followed him down a dark, narrow hallway to the back of the house. She entered, at his indication, a room that would have been the better for a broom and a dustbin. It was obviously intended as a study; there were several scattered comfortable-looking chairs, low bookcases with what appeared to be account books, several display cases holding a variety of snuffboxes, and, as the centerpiece, a large, dark wood desk. The effect of the room was ruined, though, by numerous articles of discarded clothing scattered over the chairs, and by the untidy bookcases, which had some of their contents spilling over onto the floor. The top of the desk was littered with papers, and wine from a decanter, which stood on top of the papers, had spilled, making a sodden mess.

As Ancilla came into the room her brother-in-law, a tall, dark-haired man with brown eyes, stepped over a pile of newspapers to reach her and held out his hand. "*Cilla.* I had no idea you were in town. Doing a bit of shopping, are you? Nothing like it for you females, eh? Soothes the spirits, I've heard."

"Actually, George, I have come to see you."

"See *me?* Have you? Well, and so you are. But allow me to introduce you to Sir Robert Purcell first," he said, indicating a man to Ancilla's left, whom she had not noticed until now. "Robert, this is Ancilla, m'brother Jack's wife."

Sir Robert, who had graying brown hair, a long, thin face, and light brown eyes that were almost amber, came over to her and bowed elaborately over her hand. "It is always an exquisite pleasure to meet so lovely a woman," he said silkily.

Ancilla allowed him to take her hand but not to keep it for a moment beyond what was necessary. She did not care for the familiarity in his tone, and, on her mettle after her unhappy encounter with Devin, she was not now inclined to offer her trust or friendship unconditionally.

George hurriedly cast a crumpled cravat and a copy of *The Sporting News* off one of the chairs, and invited her to be seated.

"Well, now," he began, a little too buoyantly, "what is it you wanted to see me about, Cilla?"

Ancilla looked at Sir Robert, who had seated himself on the edge of the desk and now regarded her with interest. "It is a private matter, George," she said with a meaningful glance in Sir Robert's direction.

"What? Oh. Never fear, Robert is a good friend and most discreet. Say what you like in front of him."

Ancilla did not like it at all, but she did not care to argue about it. "It is about the deed to Littlelands Cottage."

"Deed?"

"Yes. When I last saw you," Ancilla reminded him, "you promised that you would see to it at once, and instead I received this letter just a short while ago from Mr. Grogan, who wrote to me as your man of business." She removed the letter from her reticule and held it out to him. George looked discomfited and reluctant to take it, but finally he did, and Ancilla watched as he read. "You can see that it makes no mention of my right to the property and implies that I am simply a charge on the estate," she said after a few minutes. "You know that Jack purchased the cottage and the land it is on from you when we were first married, but no doubt you neglected to mention this to Mr. Grogan when you made your decision to sell Littlelands."

He handed her back the letter. "Yes. Well." George looked in Sir Robert's direction as if to find guidance there, but Sir Robert appeared absorbed in the study of a brown stain on the faded Turkey carpet, and did not look up at him. "I've had some reverses of late," George said awkwardly. "You know, a little speculation here and there that didn't quite pay off. Nothing to do but sell the place up. Never had any use for it anyway."

"I see," Ancilla said unemotionally. This conversation was not going as she had imagined it would. A tiny knot of apprehension began to form in her stomach. She took a deep breath before she spoke again. "I am very sorry that you are forced to sell up, but the cottage is not yours to sell, George."

George had been sitting on a chair opposite her, but now he went over to the desk and appeared to be looking for something. "The thing must be sold as a whole. I can't go carving pieces out of it," he said defensively. He found what he had been looking for, a small, figured snuffbox. He took a little of the mixture and placed it on the side of his hand. "It wasn't really a settled thing between Jack and me. More of an option to buy, really."

The knot in her stomach grew and made her feel a little sick, but she kept her voice steady. "You know that isn't so, George."

"Well, it *is*, damm it," George said loudly, and then softened his voice. "Jack always thought he'd make his fortune in the army, and he meant for the two of you to have a proper place of your own one day. He didn't intend to saddle himself with a little cottage on the edge of an estate."

"Jack never said any such thing to me," Ancilla said quietly. "I think you know my circumstances, George. I am not asking you for charity. I have come here simply to receive from you what is my own. You know it is the only home that I have and that I haven't the means of purchasing another. In fact, this journey here to see you on the matter has cost me far more than I can afford."

Distracted by their conversation, George inhaled the snuff too deeply, and there was a pause while he succumbed to a mild sneezing fit. The time it took him to recover also helped him to recover some of his composure. "You mustn't think I haven't thought of you in this, Cilla," he said, putting an avuncular note into his voice. "I've been thinking for some time that it isn't at all the thing for you to go on living alone with just a servant for company. In the first place, you are young and attractive, and in our class it just isn't proper for you, and in the second, the cottage is quite isolated. If some wandering vagrant, or worse, should come along . . . well, you would be quite on your own. I don't like the idea of that and I am sure Jack would not have wanted it," he said heartily, warming to his theme. "No, not at all. I know that Waldo offered to take you in again after Jack died, and I think that would be the very thing for you. You would have a comfortable home, be in the bosom of your family. Much the best thing."

Ancilla regarded him dispassionately for a moment and then spoke, keeping her voice even. "If that is what you have convinced yourself of, George, you are very much mistaken. I would not be at all comfortable at Crosby Hall. Perhaps you are unaware of the reason for Waldo's generous offer? It was not because he wished me to come to him or even because he felt that it was his duty to offer me a home—though, heaven knows, he is careful enough of what he perceives as his duty.

"A friend of his, a Mr. Beecham from Colechester, was widowed about the same time I was. He is at least twenty years my senior, and the father of nine children, the oldest of whom is two years older than I am. He and Waldo decided between them that I would make an excellent wife for him and a mother for his children. That is the reason Waldo asked me to come to Crosby Hall, so that I might observe the time of my mourning by preparing myself for Mr. Beecham and his ready-made family. I sympathize with Mr. Beecham's misfortune, but I have no desire or intention of becoming his wife."

"I don't see why not, Cilla," said George. "It sounds to me like an excellent scheme. And you said yourself that

your circumstances aren't exactly plush. Seems to me
you would be bettering yourself."

It was obvious to Ancilla that no progress was being
made, and that the only way to deal with this was directly.
"It is beside the point. I am not going to marry Mr.
Beecham, nor do I intend to take up residence again with
my cousins. The matter at hand is my right to Littlelands
Cottage. You know that I have the right to it, George—
you admitted it yourself when you came to the service for
Jack."

"Well, I meant to do something of the sort at the time,"
he admitted, "but as I've said, I don't think it's in your
best—"

"In *my* best interests?" she interrupted. An angry flush
had come into Ancilla's cheeks. It was seldom that she
raised her voice above its normal, well-modulated tone,
but anger and fear for her future had combined to make
her do so. "You mean in your *own* best interests, do you
not? What you said in the beginning is the truth, George.
When the estate meant nothing to you, it didn't matter if
you carved a piece out of it to help your brother, but now
it is inconvenient and your brother's widow can go to the
devil for all that you care. If I mean nothing to you, and I
suppose there is no reason that I should, you at least
should think of Jack. He loved and respected you, though
why is a mystery to me. You are worse than the bully
you used to be when we were children—you are a selfish
cheat. You and I both know the truth of the matter and I
shan't let you deprive me of what is rightfully mine. I
don't know what means I shall have of stopping you, but
you may depend upon it, I shall find them." After this
last brave but, she feared, empty threat, she rose, intending to sweep out of the room, but Sir Robert Purcell, who
had been all but forgotten by her and George, stood at
the same time, and spoke into the brief silence that
followed her outburst.

"I can see," he admitted belatedly, "that this is a very
private matter between the two of you and that you are
both probably wishing me at Jericho. I know it is
unsolicited, but may I offer you both a bit of advice?
There is no need for you to come to verbal blows in this
matter. George is a reasonable man, are you not, George?"
George stared sullenly ahead of him and said nothing,
and Sir Robert went on. "I am sure that if you are both

willing to listen to each other's side, you can come to terms and reach an amicable solution."

"I don't see that there can be but one amicable solution," Ancilla said coldly, turning her wrath on him.

"But you have not yet tried to see it," he said smoothly. "George, you are a dreadful host. Pour out a glass of wine for Mrs. Martin. All business is best discussed at one's ease."

George poured the wine and ungraciously pushed it into Ancilla's unwilling hand. "I don't wish for any wine," she said. "I think it would be best for me to leave."

"To please me, Mrs. Martin," said Sir Robert with an ingratiating smile. "It will soothe your nerves, I promise you." He possessed himself of her empty hand and brought it to his lips in a courtly fashion. "It has been a very great pleasure to meet you, Mrs. Martin, even though the circumstances have been less than propitious. I hope that the next time they will be equally agreeable to us both, and I hope that that time will be very soon."

He then turned his attention to George, who had still not spoken since Ancilla's verbal attack on him, and requested that George walk with him to the door, as he had some business to discuss with him.

Ancilla had wanted to retort to Sir Robert that the only thing that would soothe her nerves was the deed to the cottage in her hands, but the heat of her anger was seeping away, and she knew that there was at least truth to his words that nothing would come of argument. She remained behind as the men left the room. She was tempted to follow them out and leave of her own accord, but after several minutes she sat down again.

The truth, she realized, was that she had little choice. She had known that the things Sally had said of George in the carriage had not been entirely false, but she had truly not believed that he would deny her right to the ownership of the cottage when faced by her. However distasteful, she had to talk to him, to reason with him, to persuade him, for there wasn't much else she could do. She still had in her reticule the name and direction of the solicitor that Devin had written on his card, but what was that without the funds to pay for any litigation that might be necessary?

She sat and sipped the wine until her glass was empty. It occurred to her that a considerable time had elapsed since George had left her, and she began to wonder if he had any intention of returning. She began to think that perhaps he meant to leave her sitting there until she took the hint and left, and she was about to do just that when he came back into the room.

He did not look sullen now; in fact, he was smiling, if uncertainly. "Finished your wine, have you?" he said as he advanced into the room. "Let me get you more."

Ancilla stood and placed her glass on the clutter of the desk. "Thank you, George, but I do not wish for any more. Unless you have changed your mind about the subject at hand, I do not think it would be proper for me to remain any longer."

George gave her another brief smile, licked at his lips as if he found them dry, and went to pour himself some of the wine, which he drank off in a single swallow. "Well, the thing is, Cilla, you took me by surprise. I wasn't expecting you, you know, and you come here telling me what I must do, and it put up my back a bit. Robert and I had a little talk just now, and he made me see that I'm being pigheaded and a bit unfair."

"Did he?" Ancilla said noncommittally. Perhaps she was wrong to have taken Sir Robert in dislike, but she intended to withhold judgment until she heard just what it was that George had to say.

"Why don't you sit down, Cilla, and we'll work this thing out," he said as he went to the chair behind his desk.

Ancilla did not wish to sit, but she did so.

"It isn't so much your having the cottage that I care about," he went on, "it's the land. Littlelands isn't a big estate, nothing like Fairfeld or even Crosby, and to take a big slice out of it would make it much less salable."

"A big slice?" said Ancilla, not comprehending. "The cottage stands on less than an acre. I cannot think that what amounts to no more than space for a kitchen garden should make a difference to the salability of the estate."

George opened his eyes with staged surprise. "You mean Jack never told you that our agreement was for the twenty acres that march alongside Fairfeld?"

It was her turn to be surprised. "No, never. Surely he would have."

"Perhaps he didn't think it important for you to know,"

George said, shrugging. "But the point is, that's a third of the entire estate. I didn't think much of it at the time. Maybe I thought he'd buy up the whole place one day. He knew I had no use for it, and he was fond enough of it in his way. But as I've said, now it's best for me to sell up and, well . . ."

Ancilla considered what he had told her. She could not understand why Jack had never told her that so much of the property was theirs, but she could think of no reason for George to lie about it. On the one hand, if Jack had purchased the twenty acres from George, then she was entitled to it; on the other, if this was the sticking point, to demand it as well as the cottage might be foolish and leave her with nothing. After all, she would not miss what she had never known was hers, and it was unlikely that she could ever put it to use.

"If that is the only difficulty, George, then perhaps we can come to an agreement," she said. "It is the cottage itself that is important to me. If you will agree to acknowledge my right to that and have the proper papers drawn up to make it legally mine, I will relinquish my claim to the additional acreage."

"*Splendid,*" said George, breaking into a relieved grin. "I'll get the legal thing under way at once. You must have more wine now, Cilla. Bit of a celebration, don't you know."

But Ancilla declined his offer again. "I think it would be best if we were to go to your solicitor at once, if you don't mind. I really must leave first thing in the morning and I would like to take the papers with me."

"I'm afraid that isn't possible, Cilla. These things take time. You know what lawyers are. Then there will have to be a land survey, that sort of thing."

"Something will have to be managed today," she told him firmly, her suspicions toward him reawakening. Was this compromise just a means of getting her out of his way? Would she return to Littlelands to wait once again for the papers that would never come? "I have already explained to you that this journey has been very expensive and I haven't the means to make an extended stay in town. Perhaps your solicitor could make out a letter of intent or something of that nature. That surely could be accomplished today."

"It's possible, but I've had a thought," he said. "It

wouldn't be expensive for you to stay in town if you came here to live until the thing was done."

"Thank you, George, that is most generous, but we are not blood relatives and you know it would not be proper for me to live here alone with you."

He appeared to think on this for a moment. "Of course," he said suddenly and brightly. "I should have thought of it at once. It's the perfect solution. I'll have Vera come to stay. She's given up her house in town and gone to live in Kensington, but she likes to come up when she can during the season to see her old friends. You've never had a proper season in town, have you, Cilla? This is just the thing. She'll introduce you to *ton* circles and take you about to parties, and at the end of it, you'll have your deed to the cottage and have had a bit of a treat besides."

"That would be very nice, but I would still need money while I was here, and, to be frank, the funds that I have brought with me are all but depleted." They were in fact entirely depleted, and she was living now on the money that Devin had left her. She was determined to spend as little as possible so that she would be able to replace what she had used.

"Well, as to that," said George, ready with an answer. "It's only right that I should give you some sort of compensation for giving up the extra acreage. I'll tell you what—when Vera comes she'll take you out and help you choose some new dresses to wear to the parties you'll be going to. I'll wager it's been a while since you've had a new gown, and you're a pretty woman, Cilla. You ought to show yourself to advantage. She'll have the bills sent to me and, well, this thing shouldn't take more than a month or two—do you think thirty pounds in pin money would do for you?"

George's proposition was so unexpected and had come so quickly after her fears that she faced ruin that Ancilla had difficulty thinking the offer through. Thirty pounds just to spend was a fortune to her. If she had perceived it simply as charity, her answer to him would have been quick and negative, but this was compensation for land she had given up, and that was different. It was on the tip of her tongue to tell him that she could better use the money and what he would spend for the clothes as a single sum to take home with her, but this was the chance she had longed for to get away from the neighborhood of Fairfeld for a time.

For the first time in her life, she decided on an utterly selfish course of action. She told him she would be happy to accept his offer, and they then agreed that it would be best for her to return to the inn for the night. He would send a message at once to his sister so that she would arrive in town as soon as possible.

When Ancilla returned to the Golden Cross and told Sally of her decision, the maid was frankly skeptical. "All I ask," she said, "is what's in it for Mr. George?"

Having made her decision, Ancilla was not prepared to be anything but happy in it. "He is getting the land that he wants. That is what is in it for him," she told her maid quellingly.

Sally's prejudice toward George Martin was of long standing, and she simply could not believe that there had been no motive other than kindness behind his act. It seemed to her from what Ancilla had told her that George could have gotten what he wanted in an even exchange. But it was obvious that for reasons of her own, her mistress was prepared to take his generosity at face value, so, after a few obligatory animadversions on George's character, Sally subsided and continued with their packing.

Just before noon on the following day, a message arrived from George to tell Ancilla that Vera had arrived from Kensington, and that Ancilla might come as soon as she pleased. Because of their baggage, a hack was necessary, but this time Ancilla had no thought for the expense.

"Since he's been overcome lately with kindness, you'd have thought he'd send a carriage for you," Sally could not resist saying as they got into the hack.

"Perhaps he does not keep one," Ancilla said reasonably, settling herself against the squabs. In a moment they were on their way to the beginning of a sampling of town life.

When they arrived in Half-Moon Street, Ancilla was greeted by George and his sister. Vera hugged her warmly, as if this were a common thing between them, though in fact their acquaintance was slight. Ancilla had been little more than a schoolgirl the last time she met Vera, but she had always considered her haughty and stand-offish, and had never been able to like her over much. And now she could not help noticing that beneath her surface warmth, Vera regarded her with cool appraisal. They went into luncheon almost immediately, and afterward Vera offered to go to Ancilla's room with her to see her made comfortable in her room.

The room she had been allotted was not large, but it was very comfortably appointed. Ancilla expressed her delight in it, and then began to thank Vera for dropping everything in Kensington to come at once so that she might be spared the expense of remaining at the Golden Cross.

Vera extended her thin lips in what passed for a smile, and cut her off. "There is no need to thank me. I am sure I am pleased to be able to help you if I can, but it would be best, I think, if we understood each other from the beginning. I am here as much for my own sake as yours. Cummings," she added, speaking of her late husband, "was a wealthy man, but he had a penchant for dabbling on the 'Change, and unfortunately he passed away during a time of reverse. Staying in town, as you've mentioned, is ruinously expensive. I come up whenever I can, but that isn't often, and I'm not likely to refuse a direct invitation. George is a dear man, of course, but not always as thoughtful of others as one could like. I understand there is some business between you. You would be wise, my dear, to see to it that whatever it is, is not permitted to slip his mind."

She then went to the wardrobe, where Sally had already placed Ancilla's clothes, and, uninvited, began to go through them. "You must have let yourself become buried at Littlelands. There isn't a thing here that is less than five years out of date, and that is being generous. A friend of mine, Lady White, the wife of Sir Edward, a man of considerable standing in Parliament, is having a little card party tomorrow night and I'd hoped we might attend, but that is impossible. We will have to begin shopping at once, for you won't be able to go anywhere until we do."

Ancilla suggested that her amber silk was not inappropriate, but Vera Cummings vetoed it firmly, and because Ancilla was utterly ignorant of the fashionable world of the *ton*, she subsided meekly and allowed herself to be guided by the older woman.

Ancilla's assumption that George did not keep a carriage was correct. He hired a vehicle whenever he had need of one from the local livery, and at Vera's insistence, one of these hired carriages was put aside for their use for as long as they were to be in town. It called for them that afternoon, and she and Ancilla set out for the shops at once.

Ancilla felt as if she were caught in a whirlwind, and this was just the beginning. For the next few days all of her time was filled poring over pattern cards of the latest fashions and examining bolts of material. Dresses held together only with basting were eased over her petticoats and pinned to fit her, to be made up at once; and designs and fabrics were chosen to be done a bit more leisurely. At the milliner's she selected several bonnets that Vera assured her were all the crack, and at other stores, lacy petticoats and underpinnings, stockings and shoes, and every possible accessory that a lady of fashion could wish for were purchased.

On Saturday, the third day of their breathless activity, Ancilla became concerned enough to suggest to Vera that their purchases must be costing a great deal. She had no idea what the modistes and drapers of London charged for their wares and dared not ask, for Vera had informed her at the outset that to do so was considered very déclassé, but she knew that the volume of things they had bought would have cost quite a bit at even provincial prices, and she mentioned that perhaps George had not intended her to be so extravagant.

But Vera merely laughed at her, and said that the things that they had acquired were the meerest necessities for a woman going about in society, and that George perfectly understood these things, if she did not. Ancilla, for the first time in her life the possessor of fashionable garments, was not inclined to press the argument, and she allowed her concern to subside.

She had seen very little of her brother-in-law during this time, as he was from home a great deal, and most of her time not spent shopping was taken up with Vera's instruction as to how Ancilla would be expected to go on in the *ton*. Vera also told her all of the latest on dits (for though out of town, she was never out of touch), and she nearly made Ancilla's head spin with the variety of names and characters that she was expected to remember.

On Monday a coiffeur came to cut and dress Ancilla's hair à la Méduse, which Vera assured her was in the first mode, and although unsure of it at first, Ancilla was forced to admit that it was most becoming. The bell of the service door rang incessantly that morning as the parcels of those things that had been made up quickly began to arrive. An exquisite cream satin evening gown embroidered with seed pearls was one of the first items to arrive, and Vera insisted that she try it on at once. Her hair newly styled, she faced her reflection in the tall mirrors of her wardrobe with something like awe. She had not the vanity to call herself beautiful, but she knew that she had never looked better in her life, and she had a wish, quickly banished, that Devin might see her looking so.

Dressed once again in her blue muslin, which Vera had insisted be given to one of the housemaids the moment her wardrobe was complete enough to allow of its loss, she was trying on a newly arrived bonnet when a brief knock heralded the arrival of George.

When she saw him, she cast off her bonnet and impulsively ran to hug him. He accepted her embrace and kissed her chastely on the cheek. He then held her at arm's length to better view her. He critically examined her hair and the effect of it, and said admiringly, "Well, well. Always did think you'd be worth lookin' at got up properly."

Ancilla accepted this odd compliment with a smile and thanked him for his generosity.

He looked embarrassed and brushed her thanks aside. "Before I forget," he said, drawing a packet out of his coat. "Now don't go gushing all over me, it's just the pin money I said you were to have and a little something extra. I thought about what you'd said the other day about the cost of your journey, and I'd like to make it up to you."

"Thank you, George," she said sincerely, "but it is unnecessary. You have already been most generous to me."

"Nonsense," he said. "Here, take it. You can have a flutter with the horses when we go to Newmarket for the next meeting."

"Will we be going to Newmarket?" she asked with surprise. "I had no idea you were interested in race meetings. When you lived at Littlelands you seldom bothered to attend the meeting at Fairfeld."

"Oh, I've come to enjoy it. Belatedly, you might say," he replied. "Actually it's Robert who has the interest in it. He has a house near Newmarket, where we'll be staying, and runs a horse from time to time."

Ancilla did not welcome this news. In the first place, though she had seen little of him since their first meeting, she did not feel that Sir Robert improved upon acquaintance, and though she did try for George's sake to like him, she simply could not. In the second place, Devin had told her that he meant to attend that particular meeting personally, and she was almost certain to see him. This she did not wish to do until it could be upon her terms.

"Perhaps by that time the papers will be drawn up," she suggested, "and I shall be back at the cottage."

"I shouldn't think so. These things take time. I know you want everything done proper and legal, and it won't do to rush it."

"I suppose," Ancilla admitted. She told herself she was being foolish to wish to deny herself what would undoubtedly be a special treat just because she did not like the attitude of one man toward her and because she wished to avoid another.

After George had left her, Ancilla was able to enjoy a few hours of unaccustomed rest before Vera came to supervise her dressing for the very first *ton* party she was to attend, a musicale at the home of one of Vera's friends.

When they first arrived there, Ancilla felt awkward and feared that she would forget all of Vera's instructions, but the people proved to be very nice—the men especially were attentive—and she was soon at her ease. It was her first experience at being so admired, and she enjoyed it tremendously.

Her pleasure was destined to continue, for Vera's circle of acquaintances was large, and every night and even some afternoons were thereafter filled with a variety of entertainments.

Though many of the people that Ancilla met were titled, and Vera's conversation was still liberally peppered with famous names, none of the lions of the *ton* ever made an appearance at any event they attended, and Ancilla came to the conclusion that, though fashionable, these were not the highest circles of society, as Vera had claimed they were. She suspected that many of the people that the older woman spoke of with such familiarity were probably little more known to Vera than to herself.

Several older men and one or two nearer her own age began to appear constantly at her side, and though flattered at first, Ancilla soon learned enough of the polite world to be cynical of its ways. She was a penniless widow, and however attractive most men might find her, marriage was not likely to be what they would offer. She began to realize just how naive and how much of a fool she had been about Devin. This was the world to which he belonged, and compared to the men who now dangled after her, he was an infinitely greater catch. To have supposed that his lovemaking that night had been a prelude to marriage had shown an innocence akin to simplemindedness.

Still, Ancilla had no intention of giving up her newfound popularity. After a lifetime of being taken for granted by the people who had known her all her life, the experience of having attractive men argue over their position on her dance card, and vying for the opportunity to fetch her champagne whenever she gave the smallest hint that she had a thirst, was heady. She delighted in the company of all equally, and simply took care that no one of them ever had the opportunity to place her in an awkward or compromising situation.

There was one man, though, whom she would very much have liked to discourage, and that was Sir Robert Purcell. His manner toward her as time passed became increasingly familiar and at times even possessive. She was forced to remind herself on several occasions that he was George's friend, and for that reason she owed him at the least her civility. But more than once she spoke to him more sharply than she intended and yet, instead of taking offense, the provoking man became more attentive than ever. She tried to hint to George that the attentions of Sir Robert were unwelcome, but George either couldn't or wouldn't understand her and, in fact, it seemed to her, encouraged situations that brought them together.

One day, about a month after she had come to town, Sir Robert called late in the afternoon, and though George was from home, he remained with the ladies for luncheon. Ancilla successfully fended off an invitation from him to drive her out in his phaeton by the lie that the prospect of driving in one of those high, unbalanced-looking vehicles would be too nervous-making for her. He countered by suggesting that they use instead his barouche, and Ancilla found herself trapped into accepting, but managed to do so in such a way that Vera was included in the invitation as well.

To Ancilla's surprise, for Vera was not one likely to miss the opportunity to drive out in the park at the time that all the fashionables would be there, Vera tried to cry off, but when Ancilla then said that if she did not go, she too would remain at home, the older woman changed her mind and was ready when Sir Robert arrived.

As they were about to leave the house, Vera realized that she had forgotten her gloves and returned upstairs for them, leaving Ancilla alone with Sir Robert. Ancilla suggested that they wait for Vera in the hall, but he prevented her from making the move to do so by standing in front of her and taking one of her hands in his.

"You must permit me to tell you how lovely you look today," he said earnestly. "That particular shade of green is most becoming. I knew the moment I saw you that you were a diamond of the first water, still uncut, perhaps, but unquestionably a diamond, Ancilla." He raised her hand to his lips and planted a lingering kiss on it.

The moment she could, Ancilla withdrew her hand and, under the cover of putting on her gloves, lowered her head and turned one shoulder to him.

Mistaking the principal cause of his offense, he apologized. "I beg your pardon, Mrs. Martin. I know you have not made me free of your given name, but George and Vera have been so kind as to make me feel a part of this family, and that is how I find myself thinking of you."

"I am flattered, Sir Robert," she said with the bite of sarcasm, careful to stress the formal address.

Vera returned then and they went out to the carriage. Vera was handed in first and she took the seat facing the horses, planting herself squarely in the middle of it. Ancilla was then assisted into the carriage and attempted to sit next to her, but Vera would not have it. "You must take the other, dear," she said sweetly. "I know Sir Robert would not have it any other way."

Stifling a sigh, Ancilla sat in the farthest corner of the opposite seat, unable to take pleasure in the drive because she so heartily wished herself elsewhere. Acquaintances were met and spoken to, but most of the conversation within the carriage was carried on by Vera and Sir Robert, with Ancilla decidedly not keeping up her end of it. Even this languished after a time and a not very comfortable silence fell that was finally broken by Sir Robert, who, turning to Ancilla, said, "You do not care for driving, Mrs. Martin? Forgive me, but you seem bored. I wish you had not allowed your politeness to keep you from telling me so, for it is my most earnest desire to please you."

"I am not bored, *precisely*, Sir Robert," Ancilla could not resist saying. "I enjoy driving well enough, but if I had my choice between riding and driving, I would far prefer to be mounted as that gentleman is over there," she said, nodding in the direction of a lone rider on a high-stepping black gelding. "That horse is Spanish bred, if I am not mistaken."

"Do you ride, Mrs. Martin?" he asked, and then added, "But of course you do. You are country bred and I believe George mentioned that your father was a great man for hunting."

"He bred hunters, Sir Robert."

"And do you follow in his footsteps? You must be a famous rider," he said. "I only wish you had told me sooner, for then I should have had the sure means of gaining your regard at once."

Ancilla was not really paying him mind. Her attention was taken by a small group of riders coming toward them. They were still too far ahead and the crowd of carriages and riders between them in the lane too great for her to make them out clearly, but it seemed to her that there was something familiar about one of the men. As they came nearer she caught her breath, recognizing Devin Langley astride a bay hack, speaking to a woman riding beside him who was unfamiliar to her. Behind them were Lucina and Geoffrey Drake. Their carriage was momentarily stopped in the press of traffic, but the riders coming from the other direction still approached and, as they drew abreast, Ancilla knew a meeting was inevitable and braced herself for it.

Lucina was the first to see her, and, kicking her horse to go around the others, she came up to the side of the carriage. "Ancilla?" she said uncertainly. "I nearly did not know you, but then it has been a time and you are become so fashionable. You look magnificent."

Ancilla greeted her former friend in a like manner and then made Sir Robert and Vera Cummings known to her. The others had stopped next to the carriage by then, and Lucina in turn introduced the unknown woman as Mrs. Loretta Folliet. The woman, an attractive brunette with high cheekbones and perfectly sculpted features, inclined her head politely and then turned to Devin and said something that made him smile. The look that they exchanged was intimate, and for no discernible reason, Ancilla found this upsetting. She quickly turned to Geoffrey Drake, who was waiting to greet her.

"I saw Sir Waldo in the village the day before we left for town, which was Monday," he said. "He told me that he'd had a letter from you that you were going to be in town for a part of the season and staying with George Martin. I promised him I'd call upon you at Martin's to see how you were getting on, so we are well met."

"Unless you can inform Waldo that you found me completely given over to dissipation, you won't please him, I am afraid," said Ancilla, laughing. "I had a letter from him in reply to mine which was strongly disapproving. He believes that the very best I can expect from my stay in town is that my health and complexion will be destroyed and my taste for the simple life of the country utterly vanquished. I would blush to tell you what he viewed as the worst possibilities."

"And did you answer him?" asked Geoffrey, amused.

"I probably shouldn't have, but I was not in the best of humors the day his letter arrived, and I am afraid I told him that what I did with my life was no concern of his and that I would appreciate it if in future he kept his opinions to himself."

"He wouldn't like that. Concerning himself with things that are none of his business is a principal pastime for Waldo." After the briefest of pauses, Geoffrey added, "He is certainly very wrong about the effect of town life on your health and complexion. You look positively glowing, Ancilla. I have never seen you look lovelier."

The earnestness of his compliment disconcerted Ancilla a little, and she chose to treat it lightly. "I don't know if it is town life that makes it so," she said, smiling, "but I am sure that most of the credit must go to its silken trappings. At a fashionable modiste's even a sow's ear would have a chance at becoming a silk purse."

"I won't have you say so," he said sincerely. "I agree that, properly outfitted, even the unattractive can be made to appear presentable, but genuine beauty such as yours must be there from the start."

Used to the fulsome compliments of her admirers, Ancilla regarded them as so much dalliance, but she knew Geoffrey Drake well enough to know that he would not say such a thing lightly and she flushed with pleasure. Sir Robert then queried Drake on his opinion of how things would fall out at the meeting in Newmarket next month, which turned Geoffrey's attention. Vera was conversing with Lucina and Mrs. Folliet in an animated way that was too familiar for an acquaintance that had begun only minutes earlier.

Ancilla turned slightly and looked up and found Devin directly beside her. The flush brought on by Geoffrey's compliment had faded, but it now returned, and, determined that he would not know how shamed she felt in his presence, she refused to let herself avoid his gaze. For want of something to say to him, she asked in a voice as casual as she could make it if he had discovered the perpetrator of the hoax that had been played upon him.

"No," he replied, his voice equally casual. "If it was someone at Fairfeld for the meeting, there was no one who would admit to it. But, then, I did make it plain that I was not very amused by it, so perhaps that is not surprising."

Horses were a safe, noncommittal topic, and Ancilla pursued this. "I'd heard that the Blue won the cup race. You must have been disappointed. I know you had great hopes for your horse."

"Yes, but it developed into more of a mystery than a disappointment. Nimbus put in a dreadful showing, though in his training gallops before the race and since then, he has shown all of the form and performance that we expected of him on that day." There was a dry inflection in his voice, as if there were more to his words than was on the surface.

Ancilla wondered what this could mean, but before she could ask him, he leaned over his horse's neck, coming quite close to her, and said quietly, "Is everything all right with George? Did your business with him go well?"

Ancilla nodded. This was as close to a private word as she would have with him, and, coming to a quick decision, she took advantage of it. "I must see you alone," she said in an urgent undertone. "It is most important that I speak with you and it must be in private."

He looked taken aback and there was a hesitation before he spoke. "Is it to do with us?" he asked, keeping his tone *sotto voce* as well.

Ancilla merely nodded and then looked to Lucina, who was speaking her name. "I have just been telling Mrs. Cummings that I am the worst sort of friend to have," Lucina said. "More than once I have thought of writing to see how you were going on, but my excuse, poor as it is, must be that I have been so busy being a new bride and a diplomat's wife that this is really the first time I have had to myself since I married. But now that we are both in town at the same time, I hope we'll see a great deal of each other, Cilla. Mrs. Cummings has very kindly invited me to call upon you in Half-Moon Street. May I?"

Ancilla said that she would be very happy to see her, which was not entirely true, for though she wished for Lucina's company, she could only hope that it would not bring her brother's as well.

Sir Robert, who never took very kindly to the attentions of other men toward Ancilla, had heard the exchange between her and Drake and had noted the whispered conversation with Devin. Deciding to put an end to it all, he told his driver to move on, pleading as his excuse that they were holding up traffic.

"As I was saying, Mrs. Martin," he said when they were moving again, "I wish you had told me before how much you enjoy riding. I keep several hacks in town and I would be more than happy to mount you whenever you should wish it."

Upset from her encounter with Devin, or, more accurately, upset that he still had the power to disquiet her, she used no circumspection in answering him. "Thank you, Sir Robert, but accepting such a favor from one who is neither a very close friend nor a member of my family would be improper. It bespeaks a familiarity that does not exist."

"Now, *that* is a masterful setdown. You wound me grievously, fair maid," he said with mock sorrow, but with an underlying edge to his voice. "I have been bold enough, as I've told you, to feel quite a part of your family."

A fierce glare from Vera made Ancilla modulate her response to him, but she remained firm and Sir Robert was unable to persuade her to accept the use of his horses.

When they arrived at the house, Vera asked him to take dinner with them that evening, but he declined, casting a sidelong glance at Ancilla and saying, "I fear Mrs. Martin is out of sorts today and would be better left to rest than forced to entertain guests. In any case, I have business in the city."

The ladies took their leave of him on the doorstep, and Ancilla went directly to her room without a backward look, so it was with surprise that she turned after throwing her bonnet on the bed to find Vera standing near the open door, hands on her hips, her features grim.

"I knew that I could not expect to find in you that degree of refinement that someone more sophisticated would have," Vera said angrily, "but I did not suppose you to be ill bred. Sir Robert is a busy man but he takes the time to drive you in the park—do you show appreciation? He pays you the compliment of putting his excellent stable at your disposal—are you grateful? You threw his attentions and his efforts to please you back in his face and sneered at him in the bargain. I was never so ashamed."

Ancilla was too astonished by the attack to take immediate offense. "I am sorry that I made you feel that way, but I spoke only the truth to Sir Robert. He wishes for a degree of familiarity between us that I cannot think proper to permit."

"You don't like him very much, do you?"

"No, I don't," Ancilla said baldly.

"May I ask why?"

Ancilla carefully considered this. "I think," she said after a moment, "it is because he is so clinging. Whenever we are together he is always there beside me. He hovers over me like a bird of prey and I feel as the fieldmouse must when she sees a hawk circling overhead."

Vera came farther into the room and closed the door. "That is an absurd analogy," she said, sitting down on the stool with her back to Ancilla's dressing table. "Sir Robert is an attractive, personable man."

"Perhaps some find him so. I merely expressed my own feeling toward him." Ancilla drew off her gloves and began to undo the back of her dress, hoping that Vera would take the hint that she wished to undress, and leave.

But Vera remained where she was. "Sir Robert is a wealthy man, Ancilla, and a very influential man in some circles. It is not every provincial nobody who can come to town and attract the interest of such a one."

"I did not willfully attract his interest," Ancilla told her. "And, frankly, I wish he would take it elsewhere."

"Then you are a fool." Vera rose and went to Ancilla, taking her arm and turning her to face the mirror. "Who are you, Ancilla Martin? The derelict of my poor foolish brother who grew up playing soldiers, dreamed of becoming a general, and wound up only dead. What do you have now? A small cottage on an insignificant patch of land. A widow's pension from the horseguards that barely pays the wages of your servant and puts food in your mouths. You came here dressed in rags I would not permit my housemaid to wear.

"Look at you now, Ancilla," she continued, speaking to their reflections. "I heard what that young man said to you today. You were pretty when you came here, but now you are a beauty. And don't pretend that means nothing to you. You enjoy the admiring stares and the flattering words of the men who dangle about you—I have been with you in company and I know."

Ancilla pulled away and turned to face her, angry spots of color in her cheeks. "What I have is my integrity. I may be provincial, but I know what it is that Sir Robert wants of me. Do you think it a fair trade? Honor and independence for superficial beauty? I do *not*."

"You could do worse," Vera said flatly. "Dreams of a grand match are just wasted. Men of our class take their pleasures where they may, but when it comes to contracts, they think with their heads, not their hearts."

Ancilla did not really wish to argue with Vera. If she

were to go on living here until the papers for the cottage were ready, it would be very uncomfortable if there were bad blood between them. And though it was of Sir Robert they were speaking, it was Devin of whom she was thinking, and Vera's words were painful to hear. "I do not wish for a husband or a lover," she snapped.

"When George told me about your arrangement with him for the cottage," Vera said with a smile that was more of a sneer, "I thought you very clever to have jumped at this chance. It is not likely that you will have another. A woman alone in the world and without funds must learn to do what she can to get on. I know. A cold bed and an empty stomach are just different sorts of evil."

"That may be *your* notion of getting on in the world, but it is not *mine*."

Vera, still sneering, calmly looked her up and down, turned to leave, then said, "You're still little more than a girl, Ancilla. I am ten years your senior and I know what I am speaking of. Your miss-ish ideas will not strike you as so very noble when you return to the cottage and find yourself on your knees pulling potatoes out of the dirt for your dinner. Think over what I have said to you—now, while opportunities are still open to you."

Thankful to be alone, Ancilla did not change but lay down on the bed still in her forest-green carriage dress. Her temples were beginning to throb. The memory of something she had once read came to her. A wife, some cynic had written, is nothing but a legal whore. A man promises to protect her and provide for her, and, in turn, she lets him into her bed and lays down her body for him. At the time she had read these words, she had been scandalized by such thinking; now, having been exposed to Vera Cummings's brand of cynicism and that of the fashionable world at large, the sentiment did not seem so outrageous to her.

Hadn't she dreamed of becoming Devin's wife and the mistress of Fairfeld? If that was not wishing to "get on in the world," she did not know what was. There had been no calculation to her behavior with Devin at the White Hawk, but the result was the same. She had given herself to him and in return she had had expectations. Value for value. She had been more seduced by her dreams than she had by him.

7

When Sally came to dress her for dinner that night, her
head ached in earnest, and Ancilla took only a light meal
on a tray in her room and cried off for the evening's
entertainments.

The following morning, her headache had vanished,
but her spirits had not benefited from the rest. Before
going down to breakfast she sat at the dressing table and
removed the roll of ten-pound notes, once again complete,
from her reticule, and sat staring at it for some time. She
thought of the lovely Mrs. Folliet and the handsome
chestnut she had been riding; she remembered, too, that
on the woman's right hand had sat a diamond so large as
to be almost vulgar. She saw again the smile that had
passed between Mrs. Folliet and Devin, and wondered if
those things had been "gifts" from him. She realized that
the fifty pounds might be thought of as an insult in quite
a different way.

George was a late riser and she found Vera alone in
the breakfast room. After the words that had passed
between them yesterday, Ancilla expected Vera to treat
her with coolness, but Vera behaved as if nothing at all
had occurred, and Ancilla was glad enough to take her
lead. When Vera asked her to accompany her on a round
of visits to some of her friends, Ancilla declined, pleading
letters to write, but in fact she wished to be about when
George got up, for she intended to talk to him about
speeding up the legal processes of guaranteeing her right
to the cottage. Though what Vera had said about her
enjoyment of town and the attentions she had received
was true, Ancilla had come to the conclusion last night
that this sort of life was not for her. How long would
it be, she had asked herself, before she slipped into
their world, before their values became hers? It was obvi-

ous that cynicism had already permeated her, and this had never been a part of her nature.

She remained in the breakfast room after Vera left to change, slowly sipping a cup of morning chocolate and waiting for George to come down. She heard the peal of the doorbell and cringed inwardly. Sir Robert frequently called early in the day, and Ancilla wished she had told Slocombe, the cadaverous butler, to deny her to all callers. Sir Robert observed the outward proprieties, though, and always asked for Vera or George first. Ancilla thought that while the butler was upstairs fetching one or the other, she would slip up the service stairs to her own room and think of some excuse for not coming down should she be requested to do so. But the butler did not go upstairs; he came directly to the breakfast room before Ancilla could escape.

"Lord Langley and Mrs. Wyndham to see you, ma'am," Slocombe said with that touch of insolence toward her that had been there from the beginning. "I have placed them in the green saloon."

Ancilla inclined her head coolly. "I'll join them in a moment. Inform Mrs. Cummings that we have visitors," she added, for she feared that she might find the meeting awkward, and even Vera would offer her some support.

She remained in the breakfast room a while longer, to give Slocombe time to go to Vera and thus reduce the time she would be alone with brother and sister.

At the doorway of the saloon, Ancilla took a deep breath and entered with all the composure she could muster. Devin stood at once and looked at her with an intimate smile. Lucina stood as well and met Ancilla halfway into the room with a quick, affectionate hug.

"I cannot get over how beautiful you are become," Lucina said, holding her friend a little away from her. "You look so different that I truly didn't know you for a moment yesterday. Which I know is a strange sort of compliment, but I mean it as one. Isn't she looking delightful, Dev?" she added, turning toward her brother.

"Exquisitely so," Devin agreed, "but I think you are embarrassing Cilla with your effusiveness. Come and sit down like a proper guest on a morning call, and allow Ancilla to do the same."

Ancilla could not help casting Devin a brief, grateful glance. It was the first time she had really looked at him since entering the room and it was enough to increase her heartbeat. She might have been able to convince herself intellectually that she despised him for his treatment of her, that he meant nothing to her, but physically, her response to him was what it had always been, and beyond her ability to control.

"Oh, Cilla knows me," Lucina said, laughing. "I am forever saying just what comes into my head. A very poor thing for a diplomat's wife, I fear."

Ancilla sat down, and in response to her question, both assured her that they required no refreshment. This commonplace helped to put Ancilla more at her ease. "I'm happy to see you again, Lucy," she began, to open the conversation. "Are you and Tom in England for an extended stay?"

"No, I am here quite on my own," said Lucina. "We were supposed to come together two months ago, but poor Tom was laid low with a dreadful cold and we could not. But he is such a dear. He has a great deal of business to attend to just now, and cannot get away, but he insisted that I come to England myself, to see our families, and to do a bit of shopping.

"He will regret the latter," she went on in her cheerful way, "for we have not been in town a sennight and I have already made enough purchases to require a second carriage for my journey home, and I still have much to do. Will you join me for some of it, Cilla? Shopping is always so much more fun when you have a friend with you to confirm your good taste."

"I'd be very happy to come with you," Ancilla said formally; she did not know what else to say. The friendship between her and Lucina spanned several years, but contact had been sporadic. Ancilla didn't doubt that Lucina had other, closer friends to share her time, and she wondered if Devin had put her up to this. She was then ashamed of herself for doubting Lucina's sincerity, for there had always been an empathy between the two women that had nothing to do with Devin.

Vera made her appearance at last and after an excessive expression of delight that they had called, the conversation became general. Though Devin and Ancilla joined in occasionally, most of the talk was between Vera and Lucina, and the latter would have found something to say to the scullery maid had she been required to converse with her.

When the proper period of a morning call had been completed, Lucina gathered up her gloves and reticule, and began the usual words of leavetaking. Then she said, as if a sudden thought had come to her, "On the way here Devin told me that George collects snuffboxes. My husband does too. Do you think George would mind if I viewed his collection before we leave? I know Tom would be very interested in hearing about it when I return to Dublin."

Vera knew nothing and cared less about her brother's collection, but she had no intention of declining the wish of a young matron with entrée into circles that were top of the trees. "Oh, I'm sure George would be delighted to know that you take an interest in his collection," she said. "If you could stay a bit longer, I'll have Slocombe see if he is up and dressed yet and he can show it to you himself."

"Oh, no," said Lucina quickly. "I don't wish to inconvenience him. If you could show it to me yourself, Mrs. Cummings, that would be quite enough."

"Do you mind, Lucy, if I don't join you?" Devin said. "I have a few matters of neighborhood business to discuss with Ancilla, which I know would bore you and Mrs. Cummings. This is the perfect opportunity for me to do so." He turned his head and looked at Ancilla, and their eyes met in understanding. This, at least, he had put Lucina up to, to give them the opportunity for the private conversation she had requested. Ancilla felt herself growing warm wondering just what he had said to his sister to account for his wishes.

Lucina readily agreed, then literally talked Vera Cummings out of the room so that she would have no chance to object to Devin and Ancilla being left alone. But this, of course, was wasted effort. Vera's notions of morality were not so nicely refined, and, always quick-witted, she had come to the rapid conclusion that their leaving the room had been prearranged. If there was something between this man of stature and fashion and her temporary charge, or likely to be in the future, she would cast no rub in their way. Who was to say that it might not play to her benefit eventually?

The two women left, and Devin sat down again, closer

to where Ancilla was sitting. He thought he knew what was troubling her and his primary wish was to reassure her. She did not speak at once as she gathered her thoughts on how best to begin, and he misunderstood her hesitation.

"You may speak frankly to me, Cilla," he said gently. "And you may rely on me as well. My only wish is to help you in any way that I can."

Ancilla lowered her head and opened her reticule. He supposed it was to search for a handkerchief for the tears that he believed would soon follow. He reached out a comforting hand toward her and was astounded when she placed a tightly rolled wad of money in it. He looked at her, at the money in his hand, and back at her again.

"What is *this?*" he asked, his voice expressing his astonishment.

"It is your money," Ancilla said levelly.

"My money?" he parroted.

"You may count it, if you wish. It is all there."

The great Cribb himself could not have dealt Devin a better leveler. "But what is this to the purpose?"

Ancilla had anticipated this reaction. She had no doubt that having his largess returned to him was a unique experience. "It is to every purpose," she said with cool command of her voice. "I can see that I have surprised you, but your amazement is nothing to what mine was when I discovered the money under my hairbrush. How *dare* you do such a thing."

He watched her face as she spoke and gradually the pieces fell into place for him. A slow smile lifted the corners of his mouth and broadened into a grin that stopped short of an outright laugh.

"Don't you *dare* laugh at me," Ancilla said fiercely.

He gained control of his features, but his eyes still spoke generously of his inner amusement. "I'm sorry, Cilla," he said a little haltingly. "It is at myself that I am laughing. We are entirely at cross purposes. I thought"—he paused to gain control of his voice, which was slipping away from him—"I thought you were going to tell me that you were breeding."

"Breeding."

"I know it is rather soon, but the seriousness and urgency of your manner made me think it must be something of great importance, certainly not this," he said, indicating the money he still held.

"Money is of no importance at all to you, is it?" she asked scathingly. "If I were breeding, it would be nothing to you but a minor inconvenience. You would just throw more of your filthy ten-pound notes at me. A fine, honorable man who lives up to his responsibilities. There is nothing too expensive for purchasing power of your wealth, including the pride of those less fortunate."

His mirth vanished completely. He had realized at the time that her pride might be offended by the money, which was why he had left it for her so surreptitiously, but her virulence went beyond mere injured pride. "Dear Lord," he said slowly, as serious as she could wish. She started to stand but he caught her hand and held her still. "I knew, of course, that you might not like it," he admitted, "but I never guessed you would feel so strongly."

"Didn't you?" she said, her voice trembling with anger. "No doubt you expected me to express my gratitude for your generosity like a proper lightskirt. I may be a fool . . . I was certainly a fool to be taken in by you, but I am not for purchase, whatever you may think."

"Purchase? But . . ." He stopped and unwisely grinned again. He saw the sparks in her eyes and said quickly, "Didn't you read my note, Cilla? This money was a loan, not payment. You can't have thought I meant to offer you such an insult."

"You know there was no note."

"There was," he said calmly, in marked contrast to her heat. "I left it on the dressing table."

"Do you suppose to mollify me with a lie? There wasn't any note." But this last word was said very slowly and in an entirely different voice. A vision came to her of Sally holding up a piece of paper and asking her if it was anything that she wanted. She had assumed it was the list she had made earlier and had told her to throw it in the grate. "I never read any note," she said, but there was no anger in her voice now; it was simple statement of fact.

"I don't know why you never saw it," Devin said, "but I did write it. In it I explained to you that I realized that you might be having financial difficulties and that I wished you to use all or as much of it as you might need. I also apologized for doing it so underhandedly, but, you see, I knew that you would never have taken it from me if I had offered it to you openly."

Ancilla regarded him for a long, silent moment. "If we hadn't . . . been intimate that night, would you still have left me that money?"

"You *will* think badly of me, won't you?" he said unhappily. "The two things have no relation to each other."

"No?" Ancilla said with a touch of sarcasm. "If indeed your intentions were good, then I must thank you for your concern for me, but it wasn't necessary."

"I'm sorry, Cilla," he said with sincerity. "I see now that the thing was stupidly done. But for what it's worth, I did mean well. We're friends, and I had to do what I could for you even though I knew you might not like it."

Friends. No more, simply friends. "But we have been more than friends to each other," she said, meeting his eyes squarely, "and I think that was a grave mistake. I don't know why it happened, or rather I can think of a hundred reasons, but none of them satisfy. But I think it would be best if we were to understand each other for the future. It was an . . . an episode. It will not be repeated." She stressed this last firmly.

He stared at her for several moments, his eyes searching hers. "You can't be serious, Cilla," he said at last. "You don't feel as I do? That night had no significance for you?"

It had significance. Far too much. "I have not been long in town," she said, looking down at her hands, which were now folded in her lap, "but I have heard all the latest on dits, the crim. con. stories. I know that most people need nothing more than the sort of attraction we have had for each other to become lovers. But it isn't enough for me. I was raised to believe . . ." That love was for marriage, she finished in her thoughts, but could not bring herself to say the words aloud.

"Are you afraid of what I may think of you?" he asked, misconstruing her words. "Is it because of the money? I wish you would please never think of that again." She was sitting on a small sofa next to his chair, and he left it to sit beside her. "Half the women in this town may be round-heeled, but I have never thought of you as among them. I know that if you had not felt as strongly as I did, it would never have happened."

Pitted against Ancilla's values was a longing stronger than she had ever felt in her life. It would be easy to succumb, so very easy. Was it impossible that his need for her might not deepen into more, as hers for him had done? But then he spoke again, and his words dealt the final blow to the last vestiges of her dreams.

"Are you afraid of your reputation?" he asked softly. "You should know that I would never do anything to bring you to harm. We shall be as discreet as you wish."

Discreet. Not proclaiming their love to the world, but keeping it hidden like the dishonorable thing it was. She did raise her head, but she didn't look at him. "For how long, Devin?" she asked very quietly. "Until you tire of me or we tire of each other? Or perhaps it would only last until I came to hate you as much as I would hate myself."

"I don't understand you, Cilla," he said, genuinely puzzled.

She shook her head slowly and stood up. "I am not sure that I understand myself," she confessed. "But I do understand that I can't be your mistress." She met his eyes so that he would see that she meant what she said. "Not ever, Devin, so please don't tease me over it." Tears made up of anger, disappointment, and regret threatened, and she would not cry before him. "Please," she added, her voice tremulous, "make what excuses you will to Lucy." And she went quickly out of the room. She left behind her a very confused young man.

He honestly did not know what to make of her. He knew her well enough to know that her nature was not capricious; he would have understood her better had he thought it so.

He was not an excessively vain man, nor an especially immoral one, but he had honestly thought that she cared about him, that she understood his position and family obligations, and that she looked forward to a future in which they could be lovers, and friends. Even now it was difficult for him to put aside the vision he had had, of being able to make her life comfortable, of being able to share it in part. There would have been afternoons of riding—he could have added a horse for her to his stables—long evenings of conversation, longer nights of love. And when the day came that he had to make a socially advantageous marriage . . . well, she was aware of the necessities of his station, and he would make certain that she did not suffer, financially or emotionally.

In fact, he had been certain that she shared his dream. Why else would she have spoken so warmly and asked to meet with him? After all, she could have returned the money without seeing him. If her rejection of him had been consistent, he would have come to the conclusion that he had mistaken her feelings or that her values would not permit of their being together. But what was he to think now?

He got up and went over to the window overlooking the street, where his groom was walking the four dappled duns attached to his phaeton. Another man might have given the thing up, but he admitted that he was not yet ready to do that. He might not understand her, or even his feelings for her, but he knew that he did not want her to go out of his life again, and whatever the cause of her skittishness, he was willing to take the time to overcome it. He was too good a horseman, though, not to realize that a light hand was always preferred to a heavy one, and for now, at least, he would play the game according to her rules.

Lucina called again the very next afternoon to keep Ancilla to her promise to go shopping with her. The day before, Ancilla had all but decided that should Lucina do so, she would think of some excuse to fob her off, but further reflection had changed her mind. After the incident at Fairfeld, she had gone out of her way to avoid Devin as much as possible, to the point of refusing most invitations when he was in residence for fear of meeting him even on neutral ground. The result was that she had had far too much time to herself to brood, to dream of the impossible. And what had that brought her? It would have been far better, she now convinced herself, if she had continued to see him until doing so became commonplace again. Then it might all have been forgotten, never have resurfaced. If she were destined to meet Devin here in London through Lucina, then so be it. Perhaps by the time she returned to the cottage she would be able to view Devin Langley and the portion of her life that he had touched as just misadventure.

Accordingly, she put on her pelisse and bonnet and went downstairs to find Lucina engaged in conversation with Vera. She discovered that Lucina had another purpose to her visit. She wished to invite her and Vera, as the latter was acting as duenna, to a party her aunt was giving for her in two days' time. Ancilla accepted at once, and thought it was as well that she had, for she had not a doubt that Vera would have made her life very uncomfortable if she had declined for them an invitation to such a *ton* social event.

So, in two days' time, Ancilla once again found herself in the same room as Devin. He was not in the receiving line at the top of the stair on the first floor of Lady Culbreath's elegant town mansion, and it was several minutes after they had entered the main room before she saw him. Once again she felt the familiar rush of warmth and the quickening of her pulse when their eyes met; and the softness that came into his eyes at that moment did nothing to help her composure.

For the first few minutes of conversation she felt uneasy. Vera monopolized most of the talk, though, and Ancilla was pleased to discover that she was soon feeling more composed. When Vera discovered, across the room, an old friend from the days of her come-out and left them alone, Ancilla was able to remain at his side discussing commonplaces as if it were the most natural thing in the world. They were not left alone for very long. Geoffrey Drake soon came over to them, accompanied by a young woman about Ancilla's age and by another, considerably older. He introduced them to her as his sister and mother, who lived near Hampstead but who had come to town to see Lucina. After several minutes of conversation, the two women drew off Devin's attention and Geoffrey turned to Ancilla with an admiring smile.

"Lucy didn't tell me that you would be here tonight," he said. "Most of the other women probably wish that you weren't. You take the shine out of them all."

Ancilla returned his smile. She knew she was looking well in a celestial-blue silk gown that only a few short weeks ago she would have considered cut indecorously low and far too clinging for modesty. "I think you would get an argument from many people on that, but I thank you for a prettily turned compliment."

He moved closer and leaned toward her to say confidentially, "Don't you see all the envious stares I am receiving from the other men in the room? I shall probably be bombarded with requests to be presented to you the moment I leave your side."

Ancilla laughed at his nonsense. "Isn't that Lady Granville and the duchess of Devonshire talking to Lady Culbreath?" she asked. "I know that everyone says that the duchess hasn't the beauty or style of the duke's first wife, but I think she has a very pleasing countenance and carriage."

"Well, you see," said Geoffrey, "it is just that the great Georgiana was so beloved that her successor was bound to suffer by the comparison. Then there are other reasons that she is not taken to as the first was," he added, but without explanation.

"Oh, you need not fear wounding my sensibilities, Geoff," said Ancilla, laughing. "Even at Littlelands I have heard on dits of that magnitude. They say she gave the duke a second family before she had the right to do so, do they not?"

In another gently bred young woman, Drake might have found the admission of a knowledge of such scandalous gossip a bit offputting, but in Ancilla he was prepared to think it refreshing. "Yes. And while posing as the first duchess's bosom crony as well. The whole of that family keeps us busy gossiping as though it were their purpose in life. You may see Caroline Lamb here tonight. Her grandmother, Lady Spencer, has been a good friend to Devin's aunt since their salad days."

Ancilla did not need to be told why she might be interested in meeting Lady Caroline. That ethereal and troubled young woman had caused a stir with her behavior, and her name was just becoming seriously linked with that of the lionized young poet, Lord Byron. Ancilla voiced a hope that that young man might be present as well, for she had heard it said that he was the handsomest man in England, and she very much wished to see for herself if this was so.

"He looks well enough," said a voice behind her. "Too pale, though, and they say he does up his hair in curl papers at night."

Ancilla and Geoffrey turned, and Cholly Cholbeck grinned at them. "Looking lovely, Cilla," he said, bowing over her hand. "Mightn't have known you if Dev hadn't warned me you might be here. Haven't seen you for a bit. How have you been keeping?"

"Very well, thank you, Cholly," she replied, smiling. She was becoming used to the odd compliments the change in her appearance was eliciting from her old friends. "It has been a while, nearly two years. That was Claret Cup's maiden season, wasn't it? I haven't been following such things as closely as I once did, but I understand he has been doing very well."

"Takes his share," Cholly allowed. "Carter had a thing or two to say to me over the Fairfield Cup loss, but couldn't go his limit because he knew I had told him so before the thing was run."

The three remained to talk awhile of horses, a peculiar subject on such an occasion but one of interest to all three. Lucina, freed from her duties in the receiving line, soon came over to them and took Ancilla by the hand to lead her around the room and introduce her to the other guests. Here at last were the people whose names came so easily to Vera Cummings. Ancilla found herself being presented to Lord Alvanley and Lord Palmerston; Lady Cowper had a polite nod for her; and the famous—some said infamous—Lady Jersey quizzed her almost rudely for several minutes on her antecedents and background, and was apparently satisfied, for as she and Lucina turned away, Ancilla heard her ladyship refer to her to a companion as a charming girl. Geoffrey's prediction proved true. A gratifying number of men asked to be presented to her, and soon her circle of acquaintance among these people was as great as it was among Vera's friends.

There was music for those who wished it, but the principal entertainment for the evening was cards and conversation, with a supper to follow at midnight. Ancilla passed a good portion of the evening playing whist with three of her new acquaintances, who were all excellent players and kept her on her mettle lest she disgrace herself. Afterward she simply drifted about the rooms, conversing with old and new friends. Vera was making the most of her good fortune at having found her old friend, Lady Tallboys, and left Ancilla to her own devices, which Ancilla did not mind in the least.

She had seen Devin only in passing for most of the evening, and it was not until it was nearly time for supper that he deliberately came over to her.

"I'm pleased you were able to come, Cilla," he began, "and so, I know, is Lucy."

"Well, Lucy particularly wished me to do so and I have done so for her sake," she replied pointedly.

He laughed briefly and self-mockingly. "Having been properly put in my place, I don't doubt we shall now go on very well together."

"Why should we not?" she asked with seeming innocence.

This question drew from him an appreciative smile. "You have made rather a point of avoiding me in the past. You must have known I would be here tonight. I feared it would keep you away."

"Oh, have you not guessed?" she said, choosing to treat the situation lightly. "I have determined to become most fashionable and you and your friends are certainly that. You couldn't have kept me away."

"I don't think you need me to succeed at that. Lucy was right when she said that you have never looked lovelier. Or, for that matter, more ..." He broke off abruptly.

"More what?"

"Desirable," he finished with an apologetic smile. She turned her head away from him and he added quickly, "You needn't think I mean to importune you, Cilla. You have made your feelings clear, and though I own I don't understand them, I shall respect them. I would be lying if I said that my feelings have changed, but if friendship is all that you will have of me, then I accept it, and gladly."

She looked up at him. "I won't change my mind, Devin," she said with quiet seriousness.

"I know. Friends?" he extended his hand toward her.

After a moment's hesitation she placed her own in his. "Friends," she agreed with a light smile, but in her heart she prayed that time would work its magic quickly, for the cost to her of speaking that one word was greater than she would have imagined possible.

It was after two in the morning when Ancilla and Vera finally returned to Half-Moon Street. Ancilla changed quickly and fell into bed, exhausted physically but mentally very alert. She was happier than ever that she had made up her mind to make seeing Devin ordinary to her, for if she had not, she would have missed one of the most enjoyable evenings of her life. Whether or not the scheme would be successful was, of course, for the future to say, but in the meantime she had furthered her friendship with Lucina and renewed her acquaintance with Geoffrey Drake and Cholly Cholbeck. Best of all, Cholly, when he heard that she had never learned to drive a sporting vehicle, had quickly offered his services in teaching her. This was a thing that she had always wished to do, but had supposed she would never have the opportunity to learn.

She let her thoughts slip away into an imaginary future: she saw herself driving about in the park in an ultrafashionable high perch phaeton, the dashing cynosure of all eyes. She laughed aloud at her self-indulgence, but shortly afterward the physical overcame the mental and she was soon asleep.

8

Ancilla and Vera very naturally slept beyond their usual hour, and for once they came down to breakfast even later than George. Vera chatted endlessly during the meal on the subject of Lady Culbreath's gathering, the people who had been there, and the latest tidbits of gossip that she had heard. Ancilla was still feeling the effects of being out so late and was quiet, and George, who always stayed out late and usually drank too much, was seldom a conversationalist before midafternoon, so Vera had the floor to herself, which was in fact the way that she preferred it. She was especially pleased that she had renewed her acquaintance with her friend Lady Tallboys, who had married very advantageously, and hinted that in a day or two they might expect an invitation to an entertainment that lady was holding at the end of the week.

The very next morning the invitation did come, but it was by no means the only one that did. In addition to the usual two or three that arrived daily from Vera's circle of friends, there was a small stack of those from people she and Ancilla had been introduced to at Lady Culbreath's. Ancilla suspected that Lucina or Devin had had a hand in this, and from the way that Vera looked at the invitations and then at her when they arrived, she knew that Vera was thinking the same.

But Vera did not concern herself with their source. All that mattered to her was that for the next month until they went to Rockhill, Sir Robert's estate near Newmarket, they would be dining and dancing every night of the week with the most *ton* people in town. Many of the events to which they were now invited conflicted with those from her old friends, and though Ancilla suggested that they accept some of those or at least put in an appearance, Vera sent their regrets to all but the most fashionable entertainments. The friends who had remembered her even during her exile in Kensington were firmly put aside for Vera's new acquaintances, most of whom would probably have been hard pressed to remember her face when they saw her again.

Ancilla's old habit of early to bed and early to rise fell by the wayside. It seemed to her that every waking moment was filled with an activity, and as more and more of these hours were demanded of her, the time for sleep became less and less. She supposed that such unaccustomed dissipations would catch up with her eventually, but after a few days of getting used to it, she found she had never felt better.

Her friends from Fairfeld were constantly in evidence. Geoffrey called on her nearly every day, and he willingly escorted her to all the landmarks and sights of London whenever her busy schedule would allow. He even gallantly went with her and Lucina to the Pantheon Bazaar one afternoon and suffered the ride home in Lucina's carriage completely penned in by their packages.

Ancilla saw a great deal of Lucina, who seemed to be present at every event that Ancilla attended, and their friendship blossomed with close companionship. After the first few days of sounding each other out, they began to exchange confidences, and Ancilla's biggest regret was that she could not tell her friend of the one thing she most wished she could discuss with someone she could trust. But Lucina was Devin's sister before she was Ancilla's friend, so it was impossible.

During this time Ancilla spent almost as much time in Devin's company as she did in his sister's, and for much the same reason; wherever she went, he was there, too. At first, though consistently friendly, she was very guarded with him, but as time passed and his behavior toward her was never less than that of a gentleman, she soon began to relax with him again, and in a very short time their relationship took on the easy quality it had had during the time before he had first attempted to make love to her at Fairfeld.

Cholly Cholbeck, too, became her frequent companion. He had kept his word about teaching her to drive, and Ancilla discovered that this was a considerable compliment to her. Cholly, a member of the very exclusive Four-in-Hand Club, was considered one of the finest whips in the kingdom. He was also, as he himself readily admitted, not much in the petticoat line, and it was rare that a young woman found herself seated beside him in his phaeton, so Ancilla considered that the compliment was doubled. Every fine afternoon, precisely at three, he called for her to take her for her lesson, and in less than a fortnight he declared that she was becoming so proficient that she would soon be driving him about.

Ancilla laughed and thanked him for the compliment, but added, "Though what I am to drive you about in, heaven only knows. I have always wanted to learn to drive such a carriage, but it isn't likely that I shall ever have one to drive in the future unless you bring yours with you to Fairfeld sometime and take pity on me."

"Be happy to," said Cholly agreeably. "Always thought, though, that it isn't so much what you later do with a thing that you learn, but knowing that you know how to do it. Self-satisfaction."

"That's an interesting philosophy," Ancilla said, handing him the reins as they headed back toward the city.

"That's another thing I've learned. Being philosophical, that is," he said as he turned the horses onto the road that would take them through the park on their way home. "Lot of things I could do if I had the blunt to show off, but I expect we can't all be born rich and there's not much sense crying over it. Best just to do what you can to get on and be philosophical about what you can't help."

Ancilla concurred in this sentiment and then asked, "What would you do if you did have money, Cholly?"

"Horses," said Cholbeck promptly. "Been about them all my life. I know how to breed them, and train them and run them, but I've never had a runner of my own."

"What about Claret Cup?"

Cholly took his eyes off the road and turned to her with a brief smile. "Still in an advisory capacity, aren't I? Everyone considers him my horse, but he's Carter's, and that's a fact. Overrules me when it suits him, and the Fairfeld Cup is a case in point. Told him it wouldn't do, but he wouldn't listen."

Ancilla watched with admiration as he expertly flicked the ear of his leader with the point of his whip as they came to a straight stretch in the road. "I hope I shall be able to do that one day," she said with proper reverence.

"Might."

"Now that Claret Cup has lost against the Blue, will you still keep him in the match race at Newmarket that you told me about?" she asked.

Cholly nodded. "He'll take it. Almost sure of it. The Blue didn't win by much—in fact, he had me worried for a moment. Not that I wanted Claret Cup to lose, precisely," he added, "but it would have made me look every kind of fool with Carter. The purse for the cup was handsome, but I think I'd rather have Carter at heel than the money," he said with a grin. "Makes things easier all around."

Understanding him, Ancilla returned his smile and remarked that she hoped she would see him at Newmarket. Cholly and the others from Fairfeld were to stay with Lord Pomfret, she knew, and she wished that she were staying there as well; not just to be with her friends but because of the one thing that dulled her expectations of pleasure at attending the meeting: she and George and Vera would be staying with Sir Robert at Rockhill. She hoped that his house would be so full of guests that he would have little time for her.

There was an additional advantage to her new social life, that she had seen almost nothing of Sir Robert for more than a fortnight. After her coolness to him when he had taken her and Vera driving, he had not called at the house for a day or two, and then, when he had begun to do so again, she had usually been from home. Nor did she come across him at the parties and balls she attended, for in spite of his good birth, it was apparent that Sir Robert did not have the entrée to the highest circles.

As if conjured by her thoughts, Ancilla spied him astride a showy bay just ahead of them as they came into the park. Happening to glance her way, Cholly saw the direction in which she was looking, and immediately maneuvered his horses to the farthest side of the road so that a heavy stream of traffic in both directions separated them. This strategy prevented Sir Robert from stopping to speak to them, but it did not prevent him from seeing them, and after a moment of staring at them that plainly showed his surprise, he nodded in their direction and continued on his way.

Aware that Cholbeck's action had been deliberate, and assuming that Lucina, to whom she had confided her dislike of Sir Robert, had told him that she disliked meeting him, she thanked Cholly for his effort. "It might have been especially uncomfortable meeting him today, for I recently refused to go driving with him in his phaeton, and after seeing me with you, I'm afraid my excuse is blown to pieces," she added. "I wonder what he must think. Not that I care, but I am glad that you knew I wished to avoid him."

"Didn't know it," said Cholly. "Wished to avoid him myself."

Ancilla was mildly surprised. "Are you acquainted with Sir Robert?"

"Might say that. He's my uncle. My mother's eldest brother."

Ancilla was astonished. It was reasonable to assume that Cholly and most of the people she knew had friends and connections beyond the set of people they generally associated with, but not even in her fertile imagination would she have put together a connection between the pleasant, open Mr. Cholbeck and the cool, oblique Sir Robert Purcell. She had never met Cholly's parents, who were both deceased, but she didn't doubt that if his mother had been anything like Sir Robert, Cholly took after his father's side of the family.

Her amazement was written plain in her expression, and Cholly favored her with one of his quick smiles. "Surprise you, does it?" he asked. "Don't let it be known much, especially wouldn't care to have Carter hear of it. The thing is, he may be my uncle and all that, but he's bad *ton* and there's no denying it. Been involved in a few things that have left a bad taste in people's mouths, and he ain't received. Not where it counts, that is."

"You don't acknowledge him, then?" Ancilla inquired, a bit shocked by Cholly's blunt condemnation of so close a relative. Sir Waldo certainly left a bad taste in her mouth, but she would not have dreamed of shying away from an admission of the relationship.

"Oh, I tip my hat to him when we meet," Cholly owned, "but I don't look for his company and, if it comes to that, he don't look for mine. Might be better for me if he did, or if I did. Plenty of blunt there, and no issue to pass it on to. Could be me if I played my cards right, but I don't care for the way he's gotten his money."

"How has he gotten it?" Ancilla asked, fascinated by this new insight into the character of Sir Robert.

"Point is, nobody's sure," Cholly replied. "Didn't inherit it, that's for certain. My grandfather was a shocking gamester and Mother was lucky that she married when she did or she'd have had no dowry at all. Purcell got himself involved in a scandal not long after my grandfather died, while I was still in leading strings. Don't know much but family gossip, but it was something to do with a young sprig from a ducal family, who got into play with my uncle at a hell that was the rage at the time and found himself parted from twenty-five thousand of the best. Some talk that Purcell fudged the cards, but nothing proven, and there was a similar incident sometime later. Not saying he *is* a Captain Sharp, mind, but there are those who believe it."

"Including you," Ancilla suggested.

Cholly shrugged and was silent for a few minutes as they pulled into Half-Moon Street. "Live and let live, I always say," he said matter-of-factly. "He doesn't go about poking his nose into my business, and I steer clear of his. Best all around. We don't get on together. Never have."

Cholly seemed to be disclaiming that he shunned his uncle because of his reputation, but Ancilla thought that was his primary reason. Good *ton* was as important to Cholly as was the career of Claret Cup.

When they reached George's house, Cholly declined her offer of refreshment, and she went into the house alone. She was halfway up the stairs when she heard a door slam loudly and, turning, she saw George coming quickly toward her.

"Where have you been?" he demanded.

Ancilla blinked at the note of command in his voice. "Out with a friend," she replied coolly, and continued up the stairs.

George followed her up the stairs and deftly caught the door that she attempted to slam behind her. He entered her bedchamber without invitation. "What friend?" he asked imperiously.

"Is that a concern of yours?" Ancilla inquired sweetly. "I certainly do not ask after all of your friends."

"Was it Cholbeck?" persisted George, unperturbed.

As Ancilla studied him she realized that he was genuinely agitated. Curiosity as to the cause effectively cooled her anger. "Yes, it was. Is there an objection to this? I have known him for a number of years, you know."

George waved an impatient hand. "The point is," he said, "you were out driving with him in the park but you tell Robert that phaetons make you vaporish and refuse to drive with him in his."

"But how . . ." Ancilla began, stunned by both his attack and his knowledge of her recent whereabouts. But the solution to the latter, at least, was obvious. She did not know how Sir Robert had managed to reach Half-Moon Street before them, but he had wasted no time in doing so. Her anger returned on the instant. "I refused Sir Robert's invitation to drive out with him because I frankly cannot abide him," she said curtly. "I have tolerated him for your sake, George, but that is the truth. He makes my flesh crawl, if you want it as bluntly as I can put it."

George was the one who now looked stunned. "How can you *say* such a thing?" he said, almost spluttering with anger. "Maybe Alanetta Crosby was right about you. She told me that you were a selfish ingrate. You ought to be on your knees in gratitude that a man like Robert has condescended to show the least interest in you."

"From what I have heard of Sir Robert, he should be grateful that I have deigned to know him," Ancilla responded tartly.

"Who's been talking to you? Cholbeck, I'll wager."

"Do you know the relationship? Then you must know the reputation of Sir Robert as well. I wonder that you would allow yourself to become so closely allied with such a man."

"*I* don't listen to scurrilous rumor and take it as gospel," George retorted.

Ancilla flushed. It was true that she was ready and willing to believe anything bad she might hear of Sir Robert. "Whether the things said of him are true or not," she said more reasonably, "is beside the point. I do not like the man and his insinuating ways."

"You'd better start liking them if you know what is good for you," said George intently. "In less than a fortnight we'll be staying with him at Rockhill, and heaven help you if you behave toward him the way you have been doing of late."

"And if I do, George, what then?" she said hotly, too angry to think that it might be unwise to argue with George until she had the deed to the cottage safely in her hands.

"There is a little matter of something you wish from me," he said unpleasantly, not hesitating to use this weapon.

"Are you saying that if I do not accept the attentions—I should say, *pretensions*—of Sir Robert, you will stop the proceedings for my title to the cottage?"

"I'm saying that it takes a great deal of bottom to displease me when you are seeking a favor, and have already received many more than you'd hoped for or deserved," George said bitingly.

Ancilla gasped. "If you mean letting me stay here and the things that you have purchased for me, you know perfectly that I did not especially want them but that you insisted. And in any case, you yourself said that it was no more than payment for what I was giving up to you."

"You had nothing to give. Where is your proof of ownership, Cilla? You came begging to me for that."

That, of course, was the final straw. Though it was certainly not in her best interests to lose her temper completely or act hastily, she was about to do just that. She would throw his baubles in his face and leave this hateful house and his hateful friends. That in doing so she would be sealing her future, and would be no better off than she had been when she had first come here, was a thought for cool moments, and this was not one of them.

Before she could speak, the door flew open, and Vera came hurrying into the room. "What on earth are you two about?" she demanded. "George, I could hear you shouting all the way down the hall. Is that any way for brother and sister to behave?"

"George Martin is no blood of mine," Ancilla said furiously.

"I should have known better than to acknowledge any connection at all," snapped George, not to be outdone.

"Listen to yourselves, *both* of you," Vera said scoldingly. "You sound like two infants. What has happened to put you in such a pelter?"

They both began to speak at once, but Vera shushed

her brother and heard Ancilla out, then asked her brother if he had anything to add. George reluctantly admitted that the essential facts were correct.

"Then, if you ask me, I think you are both behaving stupidly," was Vera's comment. "Ancilla, as a woman of breeding you should be more circumspect or more clever with your excuses so that you do not offer a direct insult to a man who, whether you like him or not, has never been anything but polite and kind to you. And, George," she continued, turning to her brother, "you certainly do no favor to your friend by trying to thrust him down Ancilla's throat. I do not know all the details of the business that is between you and Ancilla, or who is in the right of it, and frankly I don't care. But it seems to me that *neither* of you is being served by picking at each other in this stupid way."

Ancilla had never thought of Vera in the role of mediator, and was startled enough by this departure from her picture of the older woman's character to give her words more credence than her headstrong anger might have otherwise allowed.

She swallowed her bile and took the first step; she apologized to George for having insulted his friend and said that she truly had not meant to do so, and George, with equal reluctance, took her lead and begged her pardon for having attempted to hold the deed to the cottage over her head.

But he could not refrain from adding, "You've an unreasonable prejudice against Robert, Cilla. He's really a very decent sort of man if you give him the chance to show it to you."

"I shall always be civil to him, George, for your sake, and as long as he does not go beyond the line of what is pleasing, I will not be rude to him." That was the only promise she would make and George had to be satisfied with it.

But Ancilla might not have been so polite had she heard the continuation of the conversation after Vera hustled George from the room. "You're a fool, George," she hissed at him in the hall.

"I want a word with you, Madam Justice," he said waspishly. "Bring along your scales, if you please."

"You ought to be thanking me instead of sneering at me," Vera said as she followed him. "You should cer-

tainly know by now that Ancilla is no biddable young
innocent. From the expression on her face, and the bit
that I heard of the argument out in the hall, I'll wager
she was within an inch of consigning you and Robert to
the devil, whatever the cost to herself. Whom would that
have served?"

"Don't talk to me about serving," her brother said
angrily. "You know why you were brought here. What
the devil are you about letting her run with that Fairfeld
set? Robert has had about all he intends to take of it, and
seeing her out driving today with that nephew of his
nearly sent him into an apoplexy."

Vera favored him with one of her cold smiles. "Is Robert in a pet because his protégée is doing so well without
him, or because he himself cannot attain to such heights?
If he had social ambitions, he should have behaved himself in the past."

"He don't give a damn for such things and you know it.
You know what he wants and he's been paying handsomely for it. He's beginning to wonder if it's just wasted
money, and he blames us for it."

"If he wanted her instant regard he should have abandoned the subterfuge and simply told her from the start
that it is he who is paying the bills," Vera suggested.
"Then, if she turned her back on him, he would have had
no one to blame but himself."

"You've just said that you understand Ancilla," George
said. "You know she has too much pride to have taken a
penny from a stranger, even if it would have meant
saving her from the workhouse. Robert saw her spirit the
moment they met and knew that directness wouldn't
answer. I had to talk her into taking it from me, and
then I had to make it sound like it was no more than her
due. Thank heaven she knows nothing of legal matters
and believed me when I said that such things take time.
Only because of that was I able to keep her here. The
pretense of the extra acreage was Robert's idea and that
made it easier."

"Well, she might have had some gratitude toward him
for saving her home for her. As it stands, she can't take
him at any price."

"We'd damn well better see to it that she starts."

"How do you propose to do that?" Vera jeered.

"I don't know, but you'd better begin applying yourself

to the answer, too. That dress you're wearing wasn't brought to you by kindly elves."

Vera brushed this remark aside and sat down in a chair near the window, advising her brother to do the same if they were to put their heads together to come up with a solution. "Frankly, I think the things that Robert has allowed me to purchase for myself are trifling payment for casting me as an abbess," she said with brutal plainness. "Even *I* don't care for that. Are you liking your role as procurer, George? I can't believe you were stupid enough to sit down at play with a known leg."

"It isn't just the gaming debts, and you know it," he said, sitting down across from her. "He's bought up most of my other debts as well, and he can call them in when he pleases."

"You never should have taken a fancy for the 'Change, George. You've never had any more business sense than Mr. Cummings did. You've escaped debtor's prison so far, but what manner of prison are you in now?"

"Why the devil do you think I'm selling Littlelands?" he retorted. "There'll be enough from that to pay him off and a bit left over to recoup my losses."

"Have you had any offers for it?" his sister asked.

"A nibble or two," George said, "but only one that is really serious, and if *he* wants it he'll damn well pay for it. He already owns half the world, and if he wants my bit of it, it'll be at my price."

Vera advised him not to be a gudgeon and to take what he could get for what was little more than a crumbling ruin of an estate. Then she turned her attention to the problem at hand.

9

Blithely unaware of the true source of her recent largess, and with no knowledge of any nefarious plans for her future, Ancilla, with no more than minor misgivings, journeyed to Newmarket a fortnight later with Vera, George, and Sir Robert in the latter's traveling carriage. She was a bit dismayed when they arrived at Rockhill, after two days on the road, to discover that they were to be the only guests.

Sir Robert's recent demeanor toward her had been characterized by a certain distance. She thought that perhaps some good had come from the exposure of her lie to him, and hoped that he would cease his attentions to her. But by the evening before the first day of the meeting, he had thawed toward her considerably, and after dinner that night she had found herself in the uncomfortable position of being completely alone with him. He began to pay her extravagant compliments again and went so far as to take both her hands in his, an unpleasant situation saved only by the arrival, before he had gone too far, of Vera, searching for her needlework.

The next morning at breakfast, Sir Robert was again rather cool, not toward her this time but toward Vera and George. But Vera seemed unconcerned and George only mildly discomfited, and Ancilla decided it was some private dealing of their own and no concern of hers.

As she entered the large, airy breakfast room Ancilla admitted that Sir Robert had a lovely home. It was only a conventional manor house, with none of the grandeur of Fairfeld, but in its way it was as elegant and pleasing to the eye. The house itself was graciously proportioned and a fitting home for a gentleman of birth and breeding. The interior was furnished with consistent good taste. Most of these things were relatively modern, and, remembering what Cholly had told her, Ancilla wondered if any of the possibly bilked ducal money had gone into their purchase.

After breakfast it was still a bit early in the morning to go to the meeting, but Sir Robert preferred to leave at once. The men were already in the hall when Vera and Ancilla came down from their rooms and the carriage was at the door ready to take them to the course. Sir Robert stood aside to allow his guests to precede him out of the house, detaining Ancilla for a moment to comment in his usual way about her loveliness. As Ancilla stepped out of the house, a man who had just dismounted from a horse behind their carriage nearly walked into her as he headed purposefully toward Sir Robert.

"I need a word with you, Purcell, before you leave," he said insistently.

"Not now, Henry. I'm on my way to the course. It will keep until tonight," said Sir Robert behind her.

"It *won't* keep," the man said so forcefully that Ancilla stopped and turned briefly to look at him. It surprised her that he would speak in such a tone to Sir Robert, and surprised her even more that Sir Robert would heed such a command. But it was apparent that he meant to do so, for Sir Robert called to George to go on without him to the course, and then went into the house with the stranger.

"Come along, Cilla," George advised her crossly. "Stop gawking at what don't concern you. If we had to get up at this ungodly hour to watch a lot of blasted horses trying to run each other down, we might as well get on with it."

But Ancilla was still curious, and as George got into the carriage after her she asked, "Is that a friend of Sir Robert?"

"Fellow he has business with from time to time, that's all."

"Who is he?"

"What the devil does that matter?" snapped George. "He's just a tout or some such thing."

Ancilla did not press him, for her true interest was in the day that lay ahead of them. Her father had frequently attended important meetings but she had never been permitted to accompany him. He had always returned with tales of the color and panoply of these events that had kept her wide-eyed interest throughout.

As their carriage approached the course now, she saw

that her father had not exaggerated. If anything, his descriptions had not been vivid enough. The day itself was sparkling clear, and the first thing to strike her was the brilliance of the green that everywhere served as a backdrop to the myriad of other colors. There were vendors of every sort offering for sale almost anything one could wish to purchase, and the variety of foods offered— sausages and meat pies for the common people, delicacies set out in striped tents for the upper classes—made the smell of the place vie with sight of it for precedence. There were prizefighters and fanciers of the Fancy, young women whose style of dressing proclaimed their trade, rough-looking men and foppish gentlemen amongst the crowd of race goers; a cock fight was in progress. And everywhere there were horses. Ancilla had never seen such an array of exquisite horseflesh in one place before, not even at Fairfeld.

Sir Robert's coachman let them down beside the principal grandstand, where George suggested they wait for Sir Robert. Ancilla searched for a familiar face amongst the press of people. After a few minutes she saw a brightly shaded pink parasol being waved in her direction, and as the owner came into view she recognized Lucina.

Vera saw her too. "No doubt you will wish to spend some time with your friends before the racing begins, Cilla," she said. "I told Lady Tallboys, who is here with her husband for the meeting, that I would look for her when we arrived, so you needn't concern yourself about me."

George glared at his sister. "Robert will be expecting us to wait for him."

"You may wait for him here if you please," Vera said, ignoring the warning in his voice, "but I think it is foolish to just stand about on such a lovely day. We'll meet up again after he arrives." She turned and moved off into the crowd. Ancilla also moved quickly away before George could again protest, and soon came up to Lucina.

"It's a good thing we were able to meet up with each other so early in the day," said that young matron, smiling. "In a very short while there will be such a sad crush of people about here that we might spend half the day just searching for each other. Must you rejoin your own party, or will you be able to watch the racing with us? Devin has two likely winners racing today and I promise you we intend to be very merry."

"I wish I might spend the day with you," Ancilla said with sincere regret, "but it would be very rude for me to abandon my friends for the entire time."

"Then we'll just let them come looking for you later, shall we?" asked Lucina, linking her arm through Ancilla's and leading her toward the grandstand. "Devin and Cholly are at the paddocks with Mr. Bosley. Devin's newest acquisition, Royal Commoner, an incredible bargain he picked up at an auction at Tatt's a few months ago, is running in the first sweepstakes race, and Claret Cup's match against the Blue is directly after that. Have you seen Devin's new horse yet?"

"No."

"Then we must proceed to the paddocks at once," said Lucina, laughing. "Once you have seen this horse, and if he does win, you will realize the depth of my brother's insight into what makes a good racer, for I promise you, there is nothing in this beast to catch the eye."

This turned out to be an understatement. When they met up with Devin and Cholly, they were standing beside the most unprepossessing horse Ancilla had ever seen. The horse was not only an undistinguished brown in color, his head and ears seemed too large for his body, which was excessively bony.

As they approached the men Lucina called out a greeting and said, "Look who I have found, Dev."

The men returned the greeting, and as Ancilla came up to him Devin said apologetically, "He's not much to look at, I know, but his form is better than his conformation."

Ancilla smiled at him. "If he is good, I'll believe with Lucy that you have a faultless eye."

"Oh, that he does," said Cholly cheerfully. "For horses and for women."

Devin could not forebear casting Ancilla a brief, wicked smile at this remark, and so easy were relations between them now that she was in no way flustered; she merely smiled in return.

The exchange was noted by two other people: Lucina, who was standing beside Ancilla, and Geoffrey Drake, who had just joined them. The latter seemed preoccupied and nodded briefly, and even curtly, to Ancilla when she greeted him.

A number of people began to gather a little to the left of them and voices were raised in alarm. Geoffrey started to go to see what was happening but got only a few paces away when Mr. Bosley emerged from the circle of people and came up to them. After a few moments of consultation Geoffrey hurried off toward the stabling, and Bosley continued toward them.

"Trouble, John?" Devin asked him.

"Aye," said the trainer, puffing a bit from his haste. "The Blue was just being led into the paddock when he suddenly went to his knees."

There was a collective gasp from the small circle around Royal Commoner. "Opium," Devin said succinctly and with flat disgust.

The trainer nodded and looked grim. "Most Like. I've seen it happen before. He was given too strong a dose, and instead of just slowing him, it brought him down.

"Damn," said Cholly, furious.

"We all hate to see something like that happen to a good horse, sir," agreed Bosley. "God be hoped the dose wasn't too much, like it was for those that got poisoned last year. Hanging's too good for one who'd do a thing like that."

"I wouldn't have had this happen for the world," Cholly said with feeling. "I suppose the match is Claret Cup's now by forfeit, but I don't want the damn purse. The Jockey Club can have it for the pension fund that Bunbury's been talking about setting up. Claret Cup would have taken the Blue today, and proving that he could was what mattered."

"Well, the touts certainly agreed with you," Devin said soothingly. "Claret Cup was the odds-on favorite." Turning again to his trainer, he said, "Is Geoff gone to see to our horses? If this sort of thing is going about, I want one of our grooms to be on guard with them at every moment."

"He's seeing to it, my lord," said Bosley, "and as soon as this race is run, I'll have a word with the lads who'll be watching them."

It was nearly time for Royal Commoner to be gotten ready for his race. Lucina, Ancilla, and Cholly, who was still quite upset, went to take their places in the Langley private box in the stands, with Devin promising to join them just before the race began.

"Damn shame for Pomfret," said Cholly as they walked. "I know how I'd be feeling if it were Claret Cup. Damn shame for me, too, if it comes to that. Carter will be fit to be tied."

"Really, Cholly," said Lucina with exasperation. "Claret Cup is an excellent horse and I am sure that Mr. Carter is a sore trial to you, but there are times when I wonder if you have any other conversation."

Cholly looked hurt at this, and Ancilla, knowing him to be unsettled by what had happened, quickly engaged him in conversation on other topics to help soothe his feelings.

They did not have long to wait before the race began. Devin soon joined them, and Ancilla watched for the black, white, and red colors of the Fairfeld stables. Royal Commoner took his place in the ranks with the other horses. The sun gleamed on the coats of the horses as they waited, many prancing in anticipation, for the starter to give them the signal to leave the post.

Finally they were off, and Ancilla entered into the spirit of the event as the straining pack thundered past them. Royal Commoner started out at the middle of the field, but Devin's judgment proved sound. With only a few furlongs to the end of the course, he gained fast on the leaders and took the race in a close heat with the favorite.

"Oh, well done," exclaimed Cholly, recovering his spirits in the excitement of the event. "I had a monkey on him to win at eight to one."

In the excitement of the moment, Ancilla permitted Devin to put his arms around her and hug her. "Do you know which horse he beat?" he asked, his eyes shining with pleasure. "Breakaway, the Derby winner."

Ancilla's eyes, too, danced with delight; she could not have been happier if Royal Commoner had been her own. "You are vindicated," she said, laughing.

"Yes, and not a moment too soon. If this had turned out to be a disaster, as Nimbus's performance in the cup race was, I fear my reputation would have been in shreds."

Ancilla would not hear of this. "Your credit is too good for you to fall so easily. But the importance of the outcome surely makes its success all the more exciting and enjoyable."

"More exciting, certainly," he agreed, "but the thing that makes any triumph enjoyable is sharing it with someone who thinks and feels as you do," he added meaningfully.

"That always makes the difference," Ancilla said, and their eyes met in silent understanding.

"I have been thinking about us a great deal of late," he said without preamble. "I have something I wish to say to you, but it isn't for here. Will you be coming to Pomfret's ball the night after tomorrow? I know you have been invited."

"Yes," Ancilla replied, a little breathlessly.

Lucina came over to them and tugged at Devin's sleeve. "Are you so blasé to success, dear brother, that you don't wish to be presented with the purse? Everyone is waiting for you."

Ancilla remained where she was, listening to the flutter of her heartbeat. She could only guess at the meaning of his words, but the tone of voice he had used, the way he had looked at her as he spoke, had sent hope surging through her.

Afraid to refine too much on his words, yet lighter of heart than she had been in many weeks, she decided that to think on them too much would only result in giving her an unnatural optimism or pessimism, depending on which way she allowed her thoughts to turn. It would be best if she could put his remarks out of her mind as much as possible and wait to see just what he did say to her at the Pomfrets' ball.

She left the grandstand to go after the others. There was now a very large group standing about Royal Commoner, and she approached them slowly, standing a little apart.

She felt a touch at her elbow and looked up into the thin, smiling face of Sir Robert. "I am glad you are not like so many of the ladies who attend race meetings, Mrs. Martin," he said. The sun was on his face and his amber eyes shone like gold but were in fact as cold as any metal. "They come here merely because it is fashionable to do so, but you, it seems, enjoy taking an active part in the events."

Though there was nothing much in his words, they had an accusatory sound, and Ancilla, always quick to bridle in his presence, replied coolly, "You know my history, Sir Robert. I am used to being around horses, and I enjoy it very much."

"I wish you had allowed me to present you with my mare for your use in town," he said reproachfully. "George has told me that it is a rare treat to behold you in a saddle, and I feel we have both been denied a pleasure."

Ancilla inclined her head in cool acknowledgment of his compliment, but otherwise did not reply.

"If I had not seen my carriage when I first arrived," Sir Robert went on, "I would have feared it had taken a wrong turning on the road. There was no one of you to be found. Perhaps my business took longer than I'd supposed, but I must not be selfish and blame you for wishing to get on with your pleasures for the day."

"Wasn't George waiting for you at the grandstand?" Ancilla asked. "I thought he meant to do so."

"No. I looked about in the crowd for one or the other of you for a time, but then I applied my wits instead of my feet to the problem, and made certain that this, at least, is where I would find you."

Again there was that note in his voice that she could not like, but she bit back the retort that sprang to her lips. "My friends were kind enough to invite me to join them," she said, letting the ice in her voice be setdown enough.

At that moment Devin chanced to look her way and saw the plea in her eyes. He ended his conversation with Geoffrey and came over to them. "Good morning, Purcell," he said, stopping close at Ancilla's side. She instinctively moved a step closer to him, effectively setting them apart from Sir Robert.

This alignment was not lost on the man. His welcoming smile was almost a grimace. "How are you, Langley? It's been a time since we've met. I was most distressed to hear about the disastrous performance of your colt in the cup race at Fairfeld. I'd heard that you had hopes of him for the Derby. You'll enter this horse now, I suppose. Breakaway gave it everything he had but he couldn't nose him out."

"The Derby is a different course," Devin replied repressively, "but if I think his performance warrants it, I suppose I shall."

"I wish you well of him," said Sir Robert. "It would make up for the disappointment of the other, no doubt. It is always the greatest pity when one discovers one's judgment has been at fault and the one we'd had such hopes for turns out to be fit for little more than the knacker's cart."

Ancilla was not looking at Devin, but she sensed the tightening of his muscles as he spoke in a perfectly ordinary, if slightly dry, voice. "I am not yet ready to consign him to horsemeat."

"Ah, yes, but inconsistency is the very devil in a racer. It is generally wiser to admit one's mistake and take the loss. It is less expensive in the end."

"That doesn't overly concern me."

"Some things turn out to be expensive in ways that have nothing to do with money," said Purcell with his superficial smile.

"Occasionally," Devin concurred tonelessly.

"Morning, Uncle," said Cholbeck with a cool nod toward Purcell as he approached them.

"Ah, Ethelred," said Sir Robert deliberately. "I didn't need my wits to tell me you'd be here. Running Carter's horse today, are you?"

"Intended to," replied Cholly curtly, "but some damn fool decided to shorten the odds on his own." He briefly told his uncle what had occurred, adding, "The crime of it was bad enough, but the fellow who did it was a bumbling idiot to risk going after a champion like Bolting Blue. I don't suppose we'll ever know who did the thing, but if we did, I'd want him dealt with, and severely."

Cholly spoke with more emotion than Ancilla had ever heard him put in his voice, and it was obvious that he was still disturbed. It was also obvious that the meeting with Sir Robert gave him no pleasure, but Sir Robert certainly did nothing to make himself likable to his nephew. If that was an example of a common exchange between the two, it did not surprise Ancilla that Cholly had avoided his uncle that day in the park.

Sir Robert returned his attention to Ancilla, saying, "We had best search for Vera and George, who must be wondering what has become of both of us."

"George knows where I am," Ancilla said promptly. "But I am sure he is anxious about you. No doubt he was searching for you and that is why you missed him. Please go on without me, Sir Robert, for I wish to remain a while to speak with Mrs. Wyndham."

Sir Robert was anything but pleased with her defiance of his wishes, but Ancilla didn't care. She had no intention of going off alone with him to be subjected to his ponderous gallantry. Short of creating a scene by insisting that she leave with him, Sir Robert had no choice but to retire gracefully.

But the end of the next race also signaled the end of Ancilla's reprieve. It was George who came to fetch her this time. He had only the minimum of words that politeness demanded before he insisted that she leave with him at once.

As they walked toward Vera and Sir Robert, George made several pithy comments on Ancilla's growing habit of spending more time with her friends from Fairfeld than with the people she was supposed to be attending, and because this *was* a cool moment, Ancilla held her tongue against the day when it would no longer be necessary for her to do so.

Though the racing and flurry of Newmarket continued, the rest of the day was rather a letdown for Ancilla. They left the course early to return to Rockhill, and the evening brought her no greater enjoyment. Immediately after dinner Sir Robert excused himself to return to his study, claiming business that needed tending to, and George, after poking about the drawing room for an hour or so, said in a bored voice that he supposed he might as well go to bed.

Ancilla and Vera remained, plying their needles in silence until the tea arrived, but they, too, for the first time in a month, were in their beds before midnight.

10

The next morning saw them early at the course again, for Sir Robert had one of his horses, Ebb Tide, running in a plate race scheduled for before noon, and he wished to have the time to confer with his training groom beforehand.

Their arrival coincided with that of several people from the Pomfret house party, but the only one known well to Ancilla was Lucina. As soon as she saw Ancilla she left the others and came over to her, obviously big with news.

"The most dreadful thing has occurred," she said in a hushed voice, "though you may not hear it spoken of generally just yet. A man was found killed late last night in an unused box at Lord Pomfret's stables."

"Killed? Do you mean murdered?" Vera asked, her eyes shining with morbid interest. "Who was it?"

"Henry Lippcott, a bloodstock agent," Lucina replied, then added, addressing Ancilla, "He is the one who took part in that dreadful hoax that was played upon Devin." She then told them all the story as she knew it. "After the incident with the Blue yesterday Lord Pomfret placed a guard on his horses, as had Devin and most of the other owners. But just after midnight last night there was a fire in a haystack—mercifully not near enough to the stable to endanger the horses—and everyone, including the grooms who were guarding the horses, went out to see what was happening and to help put it out. It was set deliberately, of course.

"About an hour later, after the men had returned to their duties, one of the grooms stumbled over Lippcott's body." She lowered her voice for dramatic effect. "He was found to have opium balls in his pocket, and that, you know, is what they suspect was given to the Blue to nobble him earlier in the day." She had the satisfaction of seeing four pairs of eyes riveted to hers.

"Lippcott? *Murdered?*" George said, looking dumbstruck.

"Did you know him, George?" Ancilla asked.

"No," he said quickly. "That is, knew him to see, of course—I've seen him about at meetings—but he wasn't a friend or even an acquaintance."

"I can't say I am very surprised," said Sir Robert. "His was far from an unblemished character and I can well imagine him taking to nobbling. Caught at it and shot, was he?"

"No," Lucina replied, "for that must have made a noise and that would have caused him to be found at once. I believe my brother mentioned that he was struck down with a shovel. Lord Brisbane and Sir Compton Cross, who, you know, are both stewards of the Jockey Club, are staying with Lord Pomfret, and they believe that Lippcott set the fire to get to the horses and that he was discovered, as you have suggested, Sir Robert, when he was about to feed one of the balls to the horses. They think that whoever it was simply struck out at him without thinking, but, of course, when he realized he had done murder, he took fright and ran off and is now too frightened to admit to it."

"Nor is that surprising," Sir Robert commented. "It would be his word alone that it was not deliberate, and he would hang for certain. In any case, if that was the sort of thing that Lippcott was about, he got no less than he deserved."

"What he was doing was certainly wicked, but he shouldn't have had to die for it," Ancilla said, shocked by Sir Robert's harshness.

"The laws of our land do not agree with you, Mrs. Martin," he replied condescendingly. "A man was caught in a similar act last year and there is little doubt that he will hang for it before this year is out."

"In that case the law is as unjust as the crime it seeks to punish," Ancilla insisted.

"Well, that it was done accidentally is only one theory," Lucina said. "But I know that this time the Jockey Club plans to investigate it seriously, though with the fear of scandal, they mean to do it as much on their own and as privately as possible. At Fairfeld Lord Brisbane, because he did not wish to go looking for trouble, brushed aside Devin's belief that Nimbus had been nobbled, but now even that will be looked into again, for they suspect there may be a connection between these occurrences. Devin and Brisbane are at this moment closeted with Lord Pomfret, deciding the best way to go."

The four continued to discuss this interesting, if unpleasant, matter for several more minutes, then Sir Robert left to see to his training groom, and Lucina, saying that the others must be wondering where she had gotten to, left them as well after inviting Ancilla to join their party later in the day if she could manage it. Ancilla fully intended to do so, for she had hopes of spending some portion of the day with Devin, but events did not fall out that way.

The first two races, viewed from an undistinguished section of the grandstand, were uneventful and won by horses unfamiliar to Ancilla, so that her interest was no more than that of an observer. When the horses began to line up for the third race, an important guinea stake, the first to come onto the course, a compact chestnut with a small star on his forehead and one white stocking, was very well known to her. It was Golddigger, the champion of the Fairfeld stables. Sir Robert joined them at this point and, sitting next to Ancilla, pointed out his own horse.

Ancilla knew that out of politeness to her host she should cheer for his horse to win, but in her heart it was Devin's Golddigger that she wished to see take the race. The field of horses was large, but at last they were all at the post and the race began.

Both Golddigger and Ebb Tide started out among the leaders, but by the end of the race Ebb Tide had flagged and the chestnut was out in front, the winner by more than a length. As he crossed the finish, Ancilla could not help herself from exclaiming with delight.

"You must have mistaken the horse that I showed you, Mrs. Martin," Sir Robert said dryly. "I'm afraid we lost."

Ancilla had the grace to blush and murmured something about having known Golddigger since he was foaled. Sir Robert let the matter drop. The conversation lagged, as it had all morning. Sir Robert was not as talkative as usual, even forgoing his usual unwelcome compliments to Ancilla, and George was become so quiet as to appear sullen. Vera, whose scannings of the crowd had produced no acquaintances to whom she might escape, was bored and did not hesitate to show it.

Ancilla hoped they would soon leave their places to go to the refreshment tents or to wander about the crowd, so that she would be able to slip away and be with her friends from Fairfield, but only a short while after the guinea race was run, Sir Robert suggested that as there was little else to interest them that day, they might as well return to the house. Neither Vera nor George objected; in fact, the latter seemed relieved to be leaving, and though Ancilla would have objected, she could hardly say that it was because she hoped to be in company other than theirs.

She consoled herself with the thought that even if she did not see Devin today, what mattered was that they would be together tomorrow night at Lord Pomfret's ball. But in the carriage on the way to Rockhill, Sir Robert stated his intention of returning to town on the following morning and, of course, that meant they would all be leaving Newmarket.

This news came as a dreadful blow to Ancilla, and as soon as they got to the house she tackled Vera on the subject. "I thought we were to be staying here for the entire meeting," she said. "We have even accepted the invitation to the Pomfrets' for tomorrow night."

Vera shrugged as she removed her shawl and threw it over a chair. "You heard what he said as well as I did. He has business to attend to in town. We are his guests and came in his carriage, so we will just have to adjust ourselves to his wishes."

"Surely this change of plans was very sudden?" Ancilla persisted. "We had no plans to be in town again before next week and he knows that we meant to go to the ball—he even quizzed us about purchasing new gowns just for the event. I wish we might stay another day for that, at least. Perhaps he has forgotten about it and if you were to mention it to him, he might put off his plans to leave for another day."

"Is this ball important to you?" asked Vera curiously. "Yes, I can see that it is." She paused for a moment and then said speculatively, "I doubt he has forgotten—his memory is superb—but if you were to ask him if we might remain, I am sure it would carry more weight with him than anything I could say."

Ancilla did not care for the implication and said so, but Vera merely shrugged again, saying, "It was only a suggestion. You must decide how much you wish to be at that ball tomorrow night."

Attending that ball, seeing Devin and hearing what he wished to say to her, were the most important things in the world to Ancilla at that moment. Though she had told herself that she would not think about it, that, of course, had been impossible. Her hopes were so high for this meeting with Devin that to be told it must be put off was like having cold water dashed in her face.

She wondered what he would think when their excuses were sent to Lady Pomfret. She teased herself at first that he would assume that she wished to avoid the meeting and did not want to hear what he would say, but her common sense reasserted itself and she knew that he would realize that she was at the command of others and her absence not of her choosing.

Still, it would be a full fortnight before they would be together again. She knew that he meant to return directly to Fairfeld from Newmarket to see to the preparations for the second meeting at Fairfeld, and he would not again be in London until the day of the ball, which he himself was giving in his sister's honor.

The temptation to go to Sir Robert and to coax him into remaining was powerful, but in the end she knew she could not. It would require feminine wiles to do so, perhaps even half promises that she would not intend to keep, and this sort of behavior was abhorrent to her.

Her spirits were low for the rest of the day, and she did not look forward to dining with the others, but the meal was pleasant enough after all. George was still quiet, as he had been all day; he ate little and contributed nothing to the conversation, spending most of his time rolling tiny pieces of bread into balls. But beyond wondering if he were sickening for something, Ancilla gave him little thought. Sir Robert and Vera were both in excellent spirits, and after a time her own rose as well.

No one seemed inclined to retire early that evening, not even George. After a very brief time with their port, the men joined the women in the drawing room, and Sir Robert suggested that a bit of music might be amusing. Vera obligingly went to the pianoforte in a corner of the room, then played and sang, quite proficiently, several songs that were popular. She then turned to Ancilla and informed her that it was her turn to provide the entertainment. Ancilla demurred, aware that her own performance—owing to the fact that she had spent more time with her father and his horses than she had with her studies—left much to be desired; but, overruled by Sir Robert and Vera, she reluctantly got up to go to the instrument. The sound of the front bell echoed through the house, and Ancilla paused, hoping for a reprieve.

"Who the devil can that be?" said Sir Robert, sounding displeased.

In a few minutes the butler appeared and said that Lord Brisbane and Sir Compton Cross wished to have a few words with them all. The two men were shown into the drawing room, and after the usual greetings and apologies for their intrusion, Lord Brisbane came immediately to business.

"No doubt you have heard," he said, addressing himself to Sir Robert, "of the unfortunate business at Pomfret's stables very early this morning."

"Yes," said Sir Robert. "Most unpleasant. Not only for Lord Pomfret but for the good name of racing as well."

Lord Brisbane agreed to this heartily. "It is for that reason we are here, Sir Robert. I know that you and your friends will want to do all you can to assist us so that our investigation will be successful while remaining private. If the authorities were to become too involved, I am afraid a full-blown scandal would be impossible to avoid."

"And, of course, that *must* be avoided," agreed Sir Robert. "I am sure we will be most happy to do whatever we can, but I fail to see how any of us can be of assistance. I myself was only vaguely acquainted with Lippcott, and I think I can safely say that none of my guests knew him at all."

"I am sure that is the case, Sir Robert," said Brisbane carefully, "but if you don't mind, I still would like to be certain of it." He then turned to George, who had risen at their arrival and was now standing next to the mantel.

To the question of whether or not he was acquainted with the murdered man, George answered in the negative, and so sharply that Ancilla stared at him, noticing for the first time that his complexion had become ashen and that the hand grasping the mantelpiece was showing white at the knuckles. But Lord Brisbane apparently noticed nothing out of the ordinary, and merely turned to Vera to ask her the same question, and then to Ancilla, with a special smile for her because he knew her from the days when he had hunted with her father.

Both women disclaimed any knowledge of the man, and Brisbane then said to Sir Robert, "You did know him, though. Can you say when was the last time you spoke with him, Sir Robert?"

"About two months ago in town," said Sir Robert without hesitation. "He approached me to tell me that a certain horse I had expressed an interest in was soon to be put up for auction at Tattersall's and that if I wished it, he could arrange a private sale beforehand. I only dabble in racing, my lord, as you know, and at the time I was not prepared to expand my stable, so I told him that I wasn't interested."

"And you have not spoken to him or seen him since that time?" Brisbane probed. "You did not, for instance, meet up with him at any time yesterday?"

"Perhaps if you would tell me what you are getting at, I would better understand you," Sir Robert said with a caustic edge to his voice.

Lord Brisbane shifted a little uncomfortably in his chair. He exchanged glances with the silent Sir Compton before speaking. "Early yesterday morning," he said presently, "before the meeting got under way, someone passing on the road near here saw Henry Lippcott passing through your gates. There was no mistaking him, for Lippcott was well known to this person."

Sir Robert's eyebrows rose, but Ancilla had the impression that it was deliberate, that he was not really surprised. "*Indeed*," he said. "This is the first I have heard he had come here. Perhaps it was after we had left for the course. My servants gave me no message that he had called, but you might question them to see if they recall it."

"Thank you, Sir Robert, we'll do that," said Brisbane promptly. "But this man who saw Lippcott was certain that it was quite early when he saw him. I also understand that you and your friends arrived at the course separately. Is it possible that either of your carriages passed him on the way there?"

"I would certainly have known if I'd seen him," said Sir Robert, sounding impatient, "and my guests, with the exception of Mr. Martin, who at least knew him by sight, did not know him at all and wouldn't be able to tell you even if they had."

Brisbane nodded at the sense of this, but for the first time Sir Compton spoke. "Perhaps," he said, "Mr. Martin could say if he saw him, and the ladies might remember if they had seen any man at all on the drive or entering the estate?"

George and Vera again affirmed that they had seen no one, but Ancilla hesitated. She remembered the man who had come to see Sir Robert just before they had left for the course. Until this moment she had made no connection between him and Lippcott, but now she recalled Sir Robert addressing the man as Henry. It seemed incredible to her that the others had forgotten, as it had, after all, been the reason Sir Robert had gone to the course apart from them. She was about to speak, to remind them of the event; she looked into the faces of the others and what she saw chilled her. The stares of Vera and Sir Robert were cool and watchful, and George looked frankly afraid. She understood at once. Their denial of this information had been deliberate, they were waiting for her to give them the lie. Not entirely sure why she did so, she heard herself tell Lord Brisbane that she had seen no one at all out of the ordinary at Rockhill on the previous day.

The two men did not stay very long after this; Brisbane asked Sir Robert a few more questions, primarily to discover if he knew of any other of Lippcott's associates. He then told them they had come to the conclusion that Lippcott had been responsible for several known cases in which horses had been nobbled before a race, and they had reason to believe that others had been involved with him, though he did not elaborate on this point.

When the stewards had gone, the light spirit of the evening did not return. Ancilla longed to know the reason that the others had denied that Lippcott had come to Rockhill, but George stared at her with such a steady, warning glare, echoed in Vera's eyes, that she held her peace.

Their party soon broke up, with Sir Robert once again retiring to his study and George going up to his room. Vera and Ancilla soon made to follow them, but before they left the room, Ancilla could not help mentioning her thoughts to the older woman. "Surely you remember the man," she said after she had described what she had heard of his words to Sir Robert, "and I can't believe that Sir Robert has forgotten."

Vera pursed her lips and looked her up and down before answering. "Of course he remembers. I've told you his memory is excellent. And so do I remember, but it is not very sensible for us admit to it. This is not a mere asking after acquaintances, but a very serious matter and one in which it would be foolish for any of us to become embroiled."

This sort of thinking was alien to Ancilla. "But isn't the seriousness of the situation all the more reason to have told Lord Brisbane what he wanted to know?" she asked. "Perhaps something Mr. Lippcott may have said to Sir Robert would have given him some hint of Lippcott's later activities."

"Are you suggesting that Sir Robert had any part in Lippcott's deeds?" Vera said coldly. "You would be very wise not to encourage such ideas. You heard yourself that Sir Robert's dealings with him were legitimate and only slight, and that is exactly the reason we cannot allow ourselves to become involved. Mud sticks, you know, and we could all find ourselves caught in the middle of a very pretty mess."

With this, she considered the discussion at an end and left the room, but Ancilla remained there for a few minutes. Ancilla was far from satisfied with Vera's explanation. It didn't really surprise her that people such as her brother-in-law, Vera, and Sir Robert would selfishly regard their own interests above the wish to help others, and she might have let it go at that but for two things.

In the first place, if George and Vera believed Sir Robert's dealings with Lippcott to be so trivial, she did not see why they had been so quick to corroborate his denials and so clearly expected her to do the same. In the second place and, to her mind, more importantly, there was George's strange behavior to be accounted for.

Her brother-in-law was a moody man. That he had been quiet today and sharp when he had spoken at all was nothing out of the ordinary, but early in the morning, before they had met up with Lucina and heard the story of Lippcott's death, his mood had been quite normal and even rather pleasant. Far more to the point, though, was the unmistakable fear he had evinced when questioned by Lord Brisbane.

Ancilla did not know what to think, but she did not wish to jump to conclusions. She determined that she would not seek her bed that night until she had answers to the questions that were knocking about in her head.

She went upstairs, heading not for her own room but for George's sitting room, the door of which was slightly ajar, the light from inside streaming out into the dimly lit hall.

She was reaching for the handle when George's voice came to her so close and clear that she nearly jumped. "Don't tell me that you had no hand in this, or didn't know what was happening, because I won't believe it," he said.

Ancilla instinctively moved back a pace, and there was the sound of another voice, more distant but equally recognizable. "You are, of course, free to believe what you wish," said Sir Robert with a sneering inflection in his tone.

"Listening to you has brought me to the brink of ruin, and I'm telling you I'm done with it."

Ancilla could not see either man, but she could imagine Sir Robert's cold smile as he spoke. "You were not so particular when listening to me was lining your pockets. You needn't bother to pretend innocence, George. You understood perfectly why I had information on what manner of wager to lay on which particular horse."

"Picking up the odd guinea by cozening those that have more than is decent to begin with is one thing. This is different, Robert, and this is the end of it for me."

"I think not, George."

"For now perhaps you may call the tune of my dance," George said angrily, "but when Littlelands is sold, we shall see."

"I would be careful of displaying such defiance, George. Money is not the only consideration."

"Don't waste your breath for hollow threats, Purcell. I never thought it would come to this and I won't be a party to it, not for you or for anyone, and you may tell that to whom you please," George said emphatically.

"There are times when extreme measures are necessary, and you would be wise not to assume any threats are hollow," Sir Robert added in a low, ominous tone. "We are friends, George, but there are those who might not look upon your defection so kindly."

"You expect that to scare me?" George gave a short laugh. "Compared with the shadow of Tyburn Tree? You may fancy ending your days there, but I don't intend to." He was so upset that there was a tremor in his voice. The door swung in a fraction, and Ancilla, who had been rooted to the floor during this exchange, quickly and silently scurried the length of the hall to her room, entering it and shutting the door again as quietly as possible.

She had not brought a bed candle with her and the room was in darkness. She groped her way to the bed and sat down. Her questions had been answered and her doubts vanquished. Sir Robert and George, and perhaps even Vera, were in some way involved in this terrible thing.

She supposed she ought to go to Lord Brisbane with what she had learned, but she had no idea how she might practically contact him before they left for London in the morning. And, considering that she would first have to admit that she had lied to him and that the information she had for him was only her own conclusions based on a fragment of an overheard conversation, she wondered just how good her credit would be.

More than ever she wished she were attending the Pomfrets' ball. Perhaps, after things had been settled between them, she might have asked Devin for his advice in the matter. But further reflection made her realize this would not be the wisest course in any case. In most matters she knew she could trust Devin to advise her fairly, but now, with his own horses probably involved, she questioned his ability to be objective.

Her next thought was to confide in either Geoffrey or Cholly, but she quickly dismissed Cholly as a choice, for she knew that beneath his pleasant exterior, Cholly was a rather selfish man who put his own interests first. She thought it as likely as not that he would try to hush the thing up or convince her that she was mistaken, lest any scandal arise and thereby endanger his position with his friend Mr. Carter. That left Geoffrey, but she supposed she would not see him again before she saw anyone else from Fairfield.

She stood and began to undress in the dark without ringing for her maid. She almost wished that she had gone upstairs with Vera and had never overheard that conversation. She was now involved whether she liked it or not, and she could only hope that her unwelcome knowledge might not not draw her into the mess. Mud sticks, Vera had said, and whatever else was true of her, Ancilla reflected as she got into bed, you could trust Vera to know the world at its least generous.

11

By rising early, using four horses, and having the good fortune of a full moon to guide them when the sun had gone down, London was achieved on the return journey in a single day. By the time Sir Robert's carriage arrived in Half-Moon Street, the occupants of George's house were so exhausted that they sought their beds at once.

Remaining with George and Vera was now repugnant to her and having to be civil to Sir Robert when he called was a severe trial. She and Vera and George had been invited to Fairfeld for the second race meeting, to be held there the week following the ball at Langley House, and she had made up her mind that she would not return to London with George afterward.

She had all but convinced herself of what Devin would say to her when they next met, and as she believed she would soon be his betrothed, and not long afterward his wife, she no longer cared a rush whether George gave her the deed to the cottage or not. It would not be proper for her to remain at Fairfeld after the meeting, of course, but she would return to the cottage until she and Devin were wed. She doubted George's ability to evict her before then even if he wished to, and she doubted it would matter to him in any case.

For the time being she kept her own counsel, behaving, as best she could, as if nothing had occurred to alter her opinion of any of them. Until she had settled her affairs with Devin and relieved herself of the burden of what she had inadvertently learned at Rockhill, she thought this was the prudent course to take.

They had expected to be away at least until the middle of the following week, and consequently had refused all invitations in town until that time. But Vera, without a blush, sought out the old friends whom she had abandoned, and was successful in gaining from them a number of invitations. Ultimately Ancilla was glad, for it made the time pass more quickly.

It was harder for her to behave naturally with Sir Robert than with George or Vera, but if he noticed that she had become more aloof with him, he gave no sign of it. Without so much as mentioning that he had ever seen her and Cholly driving in the park that day, he had renewed his offer to take her driving, and to avoid an unpleasant scene, Ancilla had accepted.

Two days before the ball at Langley House, she allowed him to take her out, and his attentions were even more overbearing than usual. At the end of her tether, as far as he was concerned, Ancilla had not been able to keep herself from snapping at him. Their return from the park was accomplished in an angry silence on both sides, and he was not even gentleman enough to assist her from the carriage when he brought her home.

Ancilla's mood, when she entered the house, was quite black, and when she heard the distinctive creak of the door to George's study, she turned, expecting to find her brother-in-law and intending to tell him once and for all that she would not again suffer the attentions of his friend.

"George," she began, but stopped when she saw that it was Geoffrey Drake. He looked equally surprised to see her.

"I know that Lucy has been in town this week to make things ready," she said, smiling and holding out her hand to him, "but I had no idea you were here. I didn't expect to see you until the day after tomorrow at Langley House. Did you ask for me and get fobbed off with George?"

Geoffrey looked decidedly discomfited. "Actually I had a bit of business with George."

Ancilla opened her eyes at this, for she knew that Geoffrey had no more liking for George than did Devin, but she gave it no time for thought, for the opportunity she had wished for was at hand. She asked him if he could spare her a few minutes, as she had something she wished to discuss with him.

"Of course," he said with flattering quickness, and Ancilla led him into the nearest open door, that of a small saloon.

Ancilla plunged into her story at once. She had rehearsed

it so many times since that last day at Newmarket that she had no need to stop and think what she would say next. It was told fairly quickly, for Geoffrey did not once interrupt her, but when she was done, he asked her a number of searching questions, and, satisfied by these and apparently aware that she was concerned, he smiled reassuringly.

"Poor Cilla," he said indulgently. "You have teased yourself into a pelter, haven't you?" He held up a hand to hold back the retort he saw forming on her lips. "No, I'm not quizzing you. But I do think you have been refining too much on this. The part of the conversation that you overheard between Sir Robert and George *is* especially interesting. I think it is likely that they were up to no good, but more in the sense of lining their pockets than anything else.

"From what he said, I think the likeliest thing is that Sir Robert was getting tips from Lippcott on which horses were to be nobbled and then paying Lippcott a commission on his winnings. That's reprehensible enough, I agree, but it is unfortunately not uncommon. There are those who would not dream of nobbling a horse themselves, but they don't object to profiting from someone else doing it."

Ancilla looked at him dubiously. His explanation sounded reasonable but she was not yet convinced. "Do you really think it was that way, Geoff? I have been agonizing over what I should do. Shouldn't Lord Brisbane be told of this?"

"Yes, but you've done the right thing in coming to me, Cilla. In fact," he added, "I am very flattered that you have trusted me enough to choose me to help you. You may safely leave it to me from here. I'll drop a hint in the proper ears and your name need never come into it."

Ancilla was enormously relieved. She was sitting beside him on a small, spindle-legged sofa and she impulsively reached over and embraced him.

Geoffrey became instantly flustered. He stood up at once and said that he must leave, and then sat down again and took one of her hands in his.

Ancilla stared at him, surprised by this uncharacteristic behavior. Geoffrey, no matter what his surface humor, always had about him a certain dignity, was always self-possessed.

"I . . . I didn't intend this to happen," he said haltingly. "That is, I never meant to tell you . . . but if I do not . . . if there is any chance . . . I would not be able to forgive myself for not putting it to the test."

"What is it, Geoff?" Ancilla asked with sincere concern. "Is something troubling *you?*"

"You might say that," he owned with a self-deprecating smile. "We have known each other for a number of years, Cilla. Since you were first married to Jack and I came to help Devin manage Fairfeld. I thought then that you were one of the loveliest females of my acquaintance, not just physically but inside as well. I truly never thought more than that. Then, when Jack died and you stopped coming to Fairfeld, I supposed you were taking his loss rather badly and I did not wish to intrude. But I have come to realize that during those years when I simply thought I was admiring you, I had really harbored other feelings."

There was no doubt in Ancilla's mind what he was about to say. "Geoff, please," she said, trying to forestall him.

"No, please let me finish," he said quickly. "I may not get up my courage a second time. I don't pretend to think that you feel as I do, but if you will give me the chance, I promise I shall do everything in my power to teach you to love me. Please, Cilla, will you do me the honor of becoming my wife? I know I haven't a lot to offer you at the moment, but I have hopes of being able to set up on my own in the near future and then I promise I shall keep you as a woman of your quality deserves."

Ancilla could have cried for vexation. The last thing in the world she wished to do was to hurt this kind, good-hearted man who was pouring out his deepest feelings to her. She knew only too well what it was to hurt, to love someone who did not have the same depth of feeling. "Oh, Geoff, I wish I could," she said, her voice catching. "I do like you so very much, but I can't pretend that I feel as you do or promise that one day I shall. I think of you as a dear, dear friend."

"It's more than that, isn't it?" he asked quietly. "It's Devin." This was a flat statement. Ancilla did not reply, but he found his answer in her eyes. "I feared as much. That was why I nearly didn't declare myself. But when you came to me with your problem instead of going to him, well, I allowed myself to hope again."

"Devin and I have no understanding," Ancilla said honestly. "I don't know for certain that we ever shall, but I won't lie to you. I do care for him. Very much."

"I'd guessed as much but I didn't wish to believe it." He stood. "Well, I won't lie to *you* and say that I'll gladly dance at your wedding, Cilla, but I do wish you well."

Ancilla rose, too. She felt wretched at having had to so disappoint a man she both admired and respected. If it had not been for Devin, she might easily have found in herself an ability to return his regard.

"Please don't count my chickens for me, Geoff," she said in an attempt at lightness. "Devin has not yet asked me to be his wife."

"He will," Geoffrey said with grim conviction. "If an honorable man could wager upon such things, I'd make the rest of my fortune in a single stroke."

"I hope you will soon make your fortune in any case, Geoff," she said, and again embraced him briefly and kissed his cheek. "I shall always be grateful for the great honor you have done me by thinking me worthy to be your wife," she said with a sad smile. "If things had been different—"

"But they aren't," he interrupted. "And I don't know how much of an honor it is. I don't know why I even thought I could compete with a man like Devin. I'm just a workingman, a glorified bailiff."

Ancilla might have taken offense at the implication, but she knew that it was his hurt speaking. "That isn't true and you know it," she said with gentle sternness. "If Devin has become a great success, he owes no small part of it to you, and I promise you, he knows it. Please don't feel badly toward either of us, Geoff. I know how much Devin values your friendship, and so do I." She realized that she was speaking of Devin and herself as if their future were a settled thing, and knew, too, that Geoffrey's conviction that Devin would offer for her had strengthened her own belief of it.

Geoffrey, in his turn, kissed her chastely on the cheek, wished her very happy in the future, and finally left her.

Sitting as still as she could while Sally dressed her hair on the night of the ball at Langley House, Ancilla moved only her eyes to the small ormolu clock on the mantel. She had never known such a long, dragging day in her life. She had come to her room to begin dressing a full hour before it was necessary, just to fill the time. The clock told her that it still wanted a full half hour before the carriage was ordered to take them to Langley House, and now, with her hair done, she was ready to leave. With a resigned sigh, she thanked Sally, told her not to wait up for her, and dismissed her.

She picked up a novel she had borrowed from the lending library, hoping that reading would quicken the minutes, but she found that she could not keep her attention from wandering from the page. There was a brief knock at her door and Vera came into the room. Ancilla looked up from her book eagerly; any diversion was welcome.

"Aren't you glad now that we did not go to the Pomfrets' ball?" Vera asked. "Now you have a new gown to wear for this one, and very well you look in it, I must say."

Ancilla looked down at the soft folds of sea-green crepe that surrounded her. "Do you really think it becomes me?" she asked anxiously. "I think perhaps the skirt wants a little fullness."

"It is perfect as it is," Vera assured her. "It's important to you to look well tonight, isn't it, Cilla?" she added with curiosity.

"All of my friends will be there tonight," Ancilla said repressively.

Vera was not deceived. "Are you sure there isn't someone in particular that you wish to be lovely for" she asked archly. Ancilla did not answer, but her color deepened slightly and that was answer enough for Vera. "Never mind, I won't tease you. Come to my room and tell me if you prefer the amethysts or the pearls with this gown."

But all waiting must eventually end, and Ancilla and Vera did finally arrive at Langley House in Grosvenor Square. Devin was with Lucina in the receiving line, and as soon as he saw Ancilla he gave her a special smile that lit up his eyes and was for her and her alone. When he spoke to her, his words, though commonplace, were a caress. "You were very much missed by your friends at Lord Pomfret's. Especially by this one."

"Sir Robert had business in town. I very much missed being there," she replied. This unexceptional exchange was only the surface of a very different exchange that went on between their eyes. Ancilla felt a thrill of happiness; if there had lingered in her a soupçon of doubt about his intentions, it was banished.

Devin was forced to turn to the next arriving guests, and Ancilla went on to the ballroom in Vera's wake. She knew that his duties as host would occupy him for a time, but she didn't doubt that he would find time for them to be together as soon as he could accomplish it. Geoffrey and Cholly were there, of course, and most of the people present were known to her, so in conversing with some and dancing with others, her next hour was well filled and passed quickly. She finally saw Devin coming over to her and she smiled in welcome. She had half promised the next set of dances to a foppish gentleman, but now his claims were forgotten.

"At last," Devin said, laughing and taking her hands in his. "We can dance if you wish, but I would rather find a quiet place to talk." Ancilla agreed and he led her into a short hall that branched off the ballroom and into an anteroom at the end. As soon as the door was closed, he gathered her in his arms and held her closely to him. "I know this is presumptuous of me," he said softly into her ear, "but I could not help it. Lord, this has been the longest fortnight I can remember. What a poor sort of lover you must think me."

Ancilla, her breath taken away by both his embrace and his words, did not answer at once, and he added with a touch of anxiety, "*Am* I presuming too much? I know that we have come to be friends—have I been flattering myself that there is more?"

The joy that was in her heart was to be read in her eyes, but the usual misgivings that attend the hope of attaining one's most heartfelt desire made him apprehensive. Still holding her, he stepped back, better to view her.

Ancilla, very light of heart and suddenly mischievous, could not resist quizzing him. "I think of you as a *very* dear friend."

"And that is all?"

She appeared to consider this. "Well," she said in a measured voice, "I have a great respect for you and certainly I must be grateful to you and to Lucy for all the kindness you have shown me."

"*Kindness.* Dear God, I am well served for my arrogance," he said with bitter self-mockery.

Knowing she had carried the thing far enough, Ancilla placed her hand on his shoulder and lifted her face to kiss him lightly and most unexpectedly on the lips. He frowned in puzzlement for a moment as he studied her face. His own then broke into a grin of genuine delight. "*Witch,*" he exclaimed, and then drew her close again and kissed her properly.

As soon as Ancilla had the freedom and air to speak, she said, "Why did you say I must think you a poor sort of lover?"

He smiled. "If we were living between the covers of a book by Mrs. Radcliffe, when you did not come to the Pomfrets' I must have taken a horse from the stables at once and rode neck or nothing until I had found you. Instead I calmly remained at Newmarket for the rest of the meeting and then went directly to Fairfeld to see to the arrangements for the meeting there."

"Idiot," she said, but the word was a declaration of love. "Papa always said that I had too much imagination, but even I know that in real life lovers do not ride *ventre à terre* to be together when there is no cause for it. You knew we should soon be together again and you had responsibilities to attend to. No sensible woman would ever find an adherence to responsibility an undesirable quality in a man."

"It is certainly not a romantic quality," he said dryly. "But I shall make it up to you. I'll sit in your pocket at every opportunity and when we are apart, I shall watch the door expectantly at all times. If you venture to speak to any other man, I shall stand in a corner and stare at you broodingly."

"Oh, most romantic," she said with a gurgle of laughter, "but a bit tiresome, don't you think?"

"Lovers are *supposed* to make cakes of themselves," he said, sounding wounded, and then laughed. "What have I done to deserve such good fortune? Beautiful and sensible. God, but I love you." He kissed her again, but after a few moments they were interrupted by a discreet knocking on the door. "*Damn,*" he said with feeling, and, releasing her, he went to the open the door.

It was Lucina, looking both sheepish and regretful. "I *am* sorry to disturb you, Devin, but . . . is Ancilla with you?"

He sighed. "Yes, and this had better be good, Lucy," he warned.

"Well, it wasn't my wish to disturb you," she said defensively. "Mrs. Cummings said that she thought she saw the two of you come in here, and she felt it would be best if I came to fetch Ancilla personally lest your being alone together be misunderstood." This last was said with a hopeful question in her eyes. She had some notion of her brother's regard for her friend, and she would have been very happy to have had her suspicions in that direction confirmed.

But Devin did not give her this satisfaction. "What the devil concern is it of hers?" he asked, annoyed.

"Why, none, I suppose," said Lucina. "But, you see, she has taken the migraine and must leave, and she wishes Ancilla with her. For support, I suppose."

Devin cursed under his breath. Ancilla had come up behind him and heard what Lucina had said. She moved around him into the doorway. "Tell Vera that I shall be with her in a moment, Lucy," she said.

Lucina nodded, gave them both a brief, apologetic smile, and left.

"Do you wish to leave?" he asked Ancilla. "Migraine or no, Vera Cummings is quite capable of getting to Half-Moon Street on her own."

"How hard-hearted you are," Ancilla admonished. "Now, that is a quality I do not admire." Her face softened into a smile. "It is best if I do go. She may make a fuss if I do not, and if she is genuinely ill, I may be able to make her more comfortable. I own I am surprised at this, though. I have never known her to take the migraine before."

"Perhaps when she saw us come in here she invented it to protect your virtue," Devin suggested half seriously, and when Ancilla favored him with a sardonic smile, he laughed. "Yes, I agree. If ever I have clapped my eyes on a born abbess, it is that woman. And that shows a want of charity, does it not? Surely another undesirable quality. But since you clearly think the same, you cannot condemn me for it."

"I shall, though. My sex is known for its capriciousness. But I shan't let her or anyone interfere with us at Fairfeld,

I promise," she added more seriously. "You're leaving tomorrow, I suppose."

"Yes, and, damnably, I have a great deal of business to attend to beforehand, so it will be Monday before I see you again," he said. "My new romanticism will have to begin at Fairfeld, I'm afraid. If you have not arrived by dinner, I promise that this time I *shall* ride to get you, *ventre à terre* and neck or nothing."

"All of your friends will quiz you for being sent on another wild-goose chase." She laughed. "But I shall be there. Even if I have to come to Fairfeld in a wagoner's cart."

He kissed her lightly and finally let her go, smiling as she turned for one last look at him before she left the room.

Ancilla might have wondered at Vera's headache, but she did not really question it. The older woman, when Ancilla reached her side, did indeed look quite ill. The carriage soon arrived for them, and all the way home, Vera sat in a corner, moaning piteously. She went to her bed, leaning heavily on the arm of her dresser, the moment they reached the house.

Several hours later, not long after the clock in the hall had struck the hour of three, a miraculous cure appeared to have taken place. Vera, dressed in an embroidered dressing gown, was sitting in a wing chair in her room, reading a book, sipping wine, and nibbling on biscuits. She was wide awake and alert, pausing in her reading every so often to lift her head and listen intently. There was no sign now of the drooping, tearful woman that Ancilla had seen being led by her maid to her bed.

Some noise at last caught her attention. She put down her book, drank off the last of the wine, snuffed her candles, and padded quietly to her door. She stood there for several moments, listening, then cautiously opened the door and peered into the hall."

"George?" she called in a low voice. "Is that you?"

George, carrying a bed candle, came up the last of the stairs and went over to her. "Just get in yourself?" he asked. "How was the Langley ball?"

"We came home hours ago," Vera told him, and added accusingly, "I was hoping that you would be early tonight. I want a word with you."

"Let it keep until morning." He yawned in her face. "Damn tired. I've been playing cards since dinner."

"And losing, I suppose," she said tartly.

"Came out about even," George said defensively. "Don't worry, it wasn't with Robert."

"It is still money you cannot afford to lose," she said crossly. "We'll talk now—in your room. Ancilla's bed is just the other side of the wall and I don't want to take the chance of our voices waking her." She closed the door and led the way down the hall to George's room before he could protest.

George followed her resignedly and lit several candles in a branch in his room before sitting down to let his sister have her say.

"It is time that we talked about Ancilla, and Robert's plans for her," Vera said at once.

"As far as I know, he hasn't changed his mind about her," George said wearily. "He means to have her and if she don't soon start softening toward him, it'll be bellows to mend with us. We'll get the blame for it, you can be sure of that."

"Let him blame us," Vera said crisply. "I don't see how it is our fault if the chit doesn't fancy him. For my part, I put more than a word in her ear in his favor, but she has made it clear from the outset that she has no wish to encourage him in the smallest way."

"He claims that he has not had the chance to tender his addresses properly," George told her. "He says it is our fault that he seldom has the opportunity to even see Cilla, let alone fix her interest."

"She wouldn't have any use for his address in any case," said Vera plainly.

"That is beside the point," said George severely as he sank into a chair and began to pull off his shoes. "If he got to do the thing and she sent him about with a flea in his ear, that would be *her* doing. I don't expect you give a damn whether or not I end up in the Fleet, but you may find yourself back in your depressing little hole in Kensington sooner than you bargained for."

Vera shrugged. "I shall find myself there again in any case." She tapped the nail of her forefinger thoughtfully against her front teeth. "Has Robert mentioned Langley in his complaints to you?"

"Langley? No. Why should he?"

"I fancy that is the real cause of his rancor. Oh, don't be so dense, George," she said at his patently puzzled expression. "It's as plain as a pikestaff that he's cut Robert out. Ancilla's a clever puss, after all. She's been playing up to Langley, and my guess is that he means to have her whatever the cost. *There's* one whose addresses she won't spurn, you mark me. When the time is right, our proper little country mouse will prove as lightskirted as any of her city sisters."

George threw up his hands. "That's just damn fine. I might as well go out and be measured for my cell in the Fleet and be done with it."

"I believe it is the best thing that could have happened."

"For Ancilla, perhaps. I suppose one can't blame the girl for preferring a young lover who's as rich as Croesus over Purcell," he said in a dejected way.

"For us, George, for us." She emphasized her point by leaning across the space between their chairs and prodding his knee with her finger. "What do we get out of this by doing it Robert's way? I get a few new gowns, a bit of time in town for the season, and a pat on the head for being a proper abbess—and Robert doesn't call in your debts before you can realize the money to pay them from the sale of Littlelands. But if we are clever, we can beat him at his own game. You'll be able to pay him off and snap your fingers at him, and I'll have a bit of money to put aside for a few luxuries when I wish them."

"How?" asked George, skepticism written all over his face.

"You *are* such a fool, George," she said without rancor. "You really don't deserve to be let in on this, but I shall help you out of family feeling."

"I wish to the devil that you'd get on with it," he said impatiently.

Vera smiled slowly and archly. "Langely wants Ancilla and she wants him. I think it was nearly an accomplished thing tonight, but luckily I saw them going off together and managed to stop it. I fancy it will be an accomplished thing when we go to Fairfeld, so we must act quickly.

"Tomorrow you will go to Langley House," she continued, "and tell his fine lordship that the prize is his for a small consideration. Ten thousand, do you think? It wouldn't pay to be too greedy. He may be a bit taken

aback, of course. He no doubt thinks she is his for the
asking. But he'll get over it soon enough if he wants her
the way that I think he does. It isn't an unusual
arrangement, after all."

"So Ancilla gets a settlement and what do we get?
Commission?" he said without enthusiasm. "She'd have
to be damn generous for me to be able to pay off Robert,
and believe me, he wouldn't waste a minute before seeing
me dragged off to the Fleet after that."

Vera gave an exasperated sigh. "No, George, Ancilla
doesn't get the money. You get five thousand and I get
five thousand. Cilla will do well enough for herself under
his protection and shouldn't begrudge us our little fee.
She won't like it if she finds out, I suppose, but hopefully
by then it won't matter."

"Unless he keeps that sort of money about the house,
which is bloody unlikely, I don't see how we are going to
get it before she finds out," he retorted.

"When you talk to Langley you will be the soul of
discretion, George," said Vera in an instructing voice.
"You will make it clear that it is due to Ancilla's fine
sensibilities that you are handling the negotiations, and
that she does not wish to sully their relationship by
doing the thing herself."

"Hah," exclaimed George with a sneer. "Fine sensibilities, indeed. No doubt you'll wish me to make arrangements
for a house and a phaeton and four for her while I'm at
it."

Vera ignored his sarcasm. "You might mention that
you will expect him to be generous—we owe that much
to Ancilla, I suppose. And perhaps, if it goes well, arrange for a small allowance for her for pin money. She
won't want more if he is paying the bills."

"No," said George flatly. "I may have done more than
one thing in my time that I'd as soon not remember, but
selling my brother's wife is the thing I draw the line at."

"You are become very nice in your notions, George,"
Vera jeered. "You don't cavil at turning her over to
Robert to save your neck. She is going to go to Langley
anyway. I am certain of it. One has only to see them
together to see how it is between them, and his sort don't
offer marriage to poor country widows with no better
connections than the likes of us or that pompous bore
Crosby. You won't be selling her, dear brother, you

will simply be picking up the crumbs lying about the table she hasn't the sense herself to see."

George rubbed his chin thoughtfully. He was at no time overburdened with conscience, and the little piece of it that troubled him now wrestled unsuccessfully with his desire for five thousand pounds. "Robert will be in high dudgeon. He's not a man lightly crossed, you know," he said consideringly.

"I consider that the cream of it," said Vera with one of her rare, genuine smiles. "He may rage until he gives himself apoplexy. Once the thing is done, there's nothing he'll be able to do about it." She sat back in her chair and watched the battle clearly being fought in her brother's countenance, and never for a moment doubted the outcome.

12

George Martin walked past Langley House three times before he found the courage to go up the steps and ring the bell. Even then, when a footman opened the door and regarded him with polite inquiry, he found himself stammering his request to see Lord Langley. He pulled out his card case from an inner pocket of his coat to hand one of his cards to the footman, but it slipped through his unsteady fingers, and the contents scattered on the checkered marble floor, the result of which was that Devin, entering his front hall, was greeted by the sight of one of his servants and a caller crawling about on their knees.

The first notion George had that his host had entered the room was the sight of Devin's silver-tasseled Hessians coming toward him, shining so gloriously that they could almost have served as a mirror. Startled, George sat back on his haunches to find Devin staring at him in wry amusement.

"It seems you have suffered a minor catastrophe, Martin," Devin said in an amused drawl. He held out his hand to the other man to assist him in rising. "You needn't trouble yourself, though, my man will see to it."

Feeling supremely foolish and greatly at a disadvantage, George accepted the outstretched hand and stood. "Morning, Langley," he said gruffly to hide his embarrassment. "Just thought I'd come by to see if you were in."

"And so I am," said Devin, "but not for long. I was just on my way out. What can I do for you, George?"

George had a carefully prepared speech, but he could hardly deliver it in the middle of the entrance hall. "Well, actually, that is, I . . . I thought I might have a word with you," he said uncomfortably.

"By all means," said Devin amiably. He stood waiting expectantly.

George colored slightly, knowing that Devin was deliberately making it difficult for him. "It's of a personal nature," he said slowly, to keep any hesitation out of his voice. In spite of his longing for his share of the ten thousand pounds, which he had by now convinced himself was a sure thing, he knew a craven wish that Devin would put him off so that he might be well out of this unpleasant situation.

But Devin regarded him with curiosity. He didn't like George Martin and knew the feeling was mutual. He thought he knew what George had come to him for and was inclined to fob him off on Geoffrey, but he did not regard the particular piece of business that was between them as personal, and he began to wonder if it might have something to do with Ancilla. After a moment he suggested that they go into his bookroom and share a glass of wine.

George nodded and followed him across the hall toward the stairs, wishing, in spite of the early hour, that it was to be brandy instead.

In the bookroom he accepted a glass from his host and drank it off with such astonishing rapidity that Devin blinked at him in surprise and, without comment, refilled the glass. George now sipped more prudently and cast himself into one of the leather chairs without waiting to be asked. Devin seated himself across from him and waited for George to begin. Several silent minutes passed, and Devin decided that if he had any hope of keeping his other appointment, he had better prompt his guest. "You had something you wished to discuss with me, George?"

George, who had been staring into his glass and trying to make up his mind if the prepared speech was still appropriate, looked up, startled. "Oh, yes, well." He stopped to clear his throat and began again. "It concerns Ancilla."

"I thought it might."

George nodded absently. "It has occurred to me, that is to say, I couldn't help but notice that you are not without interest where she is concerned."

"You might say that," said Devin noncommittally. "But you must forgive me if I ask what concern that is of yours."

George sat up a bit straighter and squared his shoulders. "I am, after all, in a way of being her protector."

"Indeed?" said Devin, stiffness coming into his voice.

George hastened to reassure him. "Not in that sense, of course. I meant she was my brother's wife and, naturally, as she has so little kith and kin of her own, it is only right that I should exert myself to see that she is properly taken care of."

"I see," said Devin coolly, but with a return of his amusement. "can it be, George, that you are here to discover my intentions?"

George put his best man-of-the-town smile into place. Not a perceptive man, he heard the coolness in the other's voice but not the humor. Vera had assumed that the only thing Devin meant to offer Ancilla was a slip on the shoulder, and he accepted her judgment without question. "I hope I may claim more sophistication than that, Devin," he said in a confidential, man-to-man tone. "There is no need for us to wrap this thing in clean linen. Frankness at the outset will avoid any misunderstanding in the future, don't you agree?"

Devin gave him a long, expressionless stare, and nodded slowly.

Encouraged by this, George began to feel more at ease. "Like most gently bred females, Ancilla has very fine sensibilities, and the important thing is that we do nothing to disturb these."

"I shouldn't dream of doing so," concurred Devin blandly.

"Splendid," said George fulsomely. "Then I may speak plainly. You will be pleased to know that your regard in that quarter is not met with indifference."

"I had flattered myself that it might not be," Devin murmured, "but you greatly relieve my mind, George."

"Just so. Just so. Then I trust that nothing remains but for us to work out the arrangements."

"Just what arrangements are those?" Devin said silkily.

Well launched into his performance, and his nervousness at an end, George managed to look pained. "I've no wish to offend you, dear boy, but surely you cannot have imagined that your attractions alone—though no doubt Ancilla finds these considerable—would be sufficient for a young woman raised with the utmost respectability to give up her good name and all the virtues attendant on that."

An icy coldness settled itself inside Devin and nearly

made him shiver. "Did Cilla send you to speak to me?" he asked, keeping all emotion from his voice.

George gave him a brief smile that awakened in Devin a desire to wipe it off his face with his fist. "I am simply relieving her of an unhappy burden. Passion and negotiation have difficulty coexisting."

Devin managed a wry smile and said in a voice that he was pleased to discover was calm and normal-sounding, "Exchanging guineas in the bedchamber does have unsavory overtones."

Unaware of the irony, George nodded happy agreement. "I thought you might see it that way. Now, as I don't wish to keep you from your appointment, we'd best get down to it."

"That's very thoughtful of you, George," Devin said evenly. He sat well back in his chair, one leg crossed over the other; the picture of a man at his ease. "It will also save time, I think, if you just tell me what it is that you require."

George was mildly surprised. Like Vera, he had supposed that Devin would believe that the plum had been his for the plucking and would offer some resistance when he discovered that it had a price after all. "We," he began, careful to use the plural pronoun, "are sure that you would wish her to be properly placed in a setting that would not only complement her beauty but also have about it a certain convenience for both of you, if you take my meaning."

"Oh, I think so. A house in town."

"Yes, and you know how Ancilla loves to ride, and she has of late learned to drive as well."

"A hack and a carriage. Go on, George."

"Then there is the matter of expenses. She must do you credit in the eyes of the world—you would not wish it otherwise."

"Gowns, jewels, the usual trinkets, and no doubt sufficient pin money so she needn't come to me every time she loses at penny whist, I presume. Is there anything else?"

George was not only very happy at the way he had managed the thing, he had also assuaged any guilt he might feel by seeing first to the things that he believed would matter to Ancilla. But now it was time to get down to the real purpose of his visit. "There is, of course, the matter of a settlement. It is a sad fact that these arrangements, though delightful at first, do not have about them the nature of permanence, and in giving up so much, Ancilla must be adequately protected."

The iciness inside Devin had formed itself into a tight knot as they spoke, but it was gradually being melted by the heat of his rising anger. Anger that was beginning to shift away from his disliked guest and toward himself. "What figure did you have in mind?" he said baldly and with a definite edge to his voice.

The sudden sharpness in the other's tone, which until now had sounded perfectly easy to George, nearly caused him to lose heart and ask for only five thousand pounds, but the quick reflection that sharing that amount with Vera would not leave him sufficient funds to recover his debts from Sir Robert made him stick to his guns. "Ten thousand," he said with equal baldness.

Although his expression remained unperturbed, Devin raised his head slightly and his eyes narrowed. "I have been reliably informed that few of the desired things in life are without cost, but one had supposed there was a limit. She must be very sure of me—or of herself."

George swallowed the last of his wine and took a moment before speaking. He was uncertain whether success or failure was the closer, and he wished to step warily. "It is only a matter of practicality. You are a rich man and need not concern yourself beyond the present, but Ancilla has little and must look to the future."

"In other words, she is hedging her bets." Devin stood abruptly. "You must excuse me now, George, but I am already beyond my time."

George stood, too, though reluctantly. "We are agreed, then?" he said, trying to sound firm and not hopeful.

"I'll let you know." Very nearly turning on his heel, Devin strode purposefully out of the room and out of the house without so much as once glancing behind him. He knew that if he had stayed in that room one moment longer, he would have committed the unpardonable solecism of laying his guest out flat on the Aubusson carpet.

He did not keep his appointment, nor, in his present state, did he even think to send his excuses. The many things he had told Ancilla that he must see to were forgotten. He went directly to the mews and shocked his grooms by ordering his curricle and waiting there until it was ready for him.

He headed in the direction of the Great North Road and did not allow any thought to distract him from maneuvering as quickly and safely as possible through the traffic of the city until he had put it behind him and was on the open road. Once there, he lowered his hands and gave his horses their heads, thoughts tumbling over each other so rapidly and disturbingly in his head that he barely had room to keep some part of his mind on his driving, until he feathered one curve in the road so sharply that a wheel came off the ground. Certainly not intent on doing himself an injury, he reluctantly brought his spirited bays down to a more reasonable, safer pace.

With all of his being he did not wish to believe that he had judged Ancilla so wrongly. Love had at last come to him, not with the great thunderclap of the lyricists, but as the gradually and steadily maturing realization that she was entirely necessary to his happiness. Now that he had found his love, he longed to believe in her, but he did not believe in fantastical coincidence. For George to have come to him on such an errand at just this moment, and after Vera's fortuitous interruption the night before, would have smacked of just that kind of coincidence. That last night he should have declared his love to Ancilla; that George should have come to him today to set it out in contract form without her knowledge and consent passed credibility. He felt every kind of fool and it was not a sensation that sat easy with him; but it was not the wound to his pride that pained him most.

After her refusal to become his mistress he had pursued her with quiet earnestness, offering her his friendship, but in fact determined to win her regard for his own less-than-honorable purposes. Instead she had won his regard; and by the time he had spoken to her at Newmarket, he was rather ashamed that he had once stooped so low as to seduce so lovely and estimable a woman as he had come to believe Ancilla to be. He still wanted her as much as he ever had, but now it was love, not lust.

As he drove along the road, oblivious of the passing landscape, he consoled himself with the thought that at least the interruption had come before he had crowned his foolishness by asking her to be his wife. After her response to him it had seemed a superfluous question, but if for no other reason than to reassure himself, he would have asked it of her. And then there would have been no reason for George to have come to him today. She would have had it all, and his fear that he would find himself with a wife who cared more for his money than she did for him would be a reality.

He made no effort to calm his thoughts or to reason clearly, almost reveling in the self-flagellation of detailing how completely he had been taken in. Had everything between them been staged? Touch me, one minute; touch-me-not, the next? Whet his appetite and then move in for the kill? She would not take fifty pounds from him, but she would take ten thousand, thank you.

The obvious flagging of his horses finally brought him to an awareness of his surroundings and the time and distance he had gone, and he reluctantly turned them in the direction he had come. At a much more sedate pace, he returned home.

When he reached his house, he went directly to his study and paced about the room for the better part of an hour before coming to a decision. He pulled out a sheet of notepaper from his desk, mended a pen, and sat and wrote for several minutes. Disliking the result, he crumpled the paper and, taking another sheet, wrote again, much more briefly.

When the note arrived in Half-Moon Street, George was at home doing a bit of pacing himself. He snatched the paper off the tray and dismissed the servant summarily. He took a deep breath and broke the seal. An enclosed piece of paper floated to his feet. He read the message before retrieving it, and his face broke into a wide grin. He knew then what the other paper was before he stooped for it.

George consulted his watch and decided against taking Devin's draft to his banking house. There was an auction to be held at Tattersall's in half an hour, and he knew there would be a pair of gray carriage horses on the block that he had had his eye on for some time. With this bit of largess to pay off Purcell, the money he would have from the pending sale of Littlelands would be his to spend as he pleased, and he decided it was high time that he bought himself a sporting vehicle.

There was one other thing he had a mind to do. He put

Devin's note and the bank draft in his strongbox, where it would keep until he had more leisure, and then he sat down at his desk and found several pieces of clean paper. He wrote steadily for fifteen minutes, then folded the papers and sealed them together. He addressed them to Sir Robert Purcell.

He put the letter in his strongbox as well, intending that he would have the message delivered on Monday to Sir Robert after he was well on his way to Fairfeld. Feeling very pleased with himself, he left for the auction without even searching for his sister to tell her that her plan had carried the day.

When they arrived at Fairfeld, Lucina greeted Ancilla with as much warmth as if she were already a part of the family. Devin was at the stables, seeing to the final preparations for the racing, which would begin tomorrow, and he was not expected until dinner. Although disappointed that he was not there to meet her, Ancilla understood and saw no cause for concern.

She dressed with great care that night, choosing a gown of burnished gold silk because it was the closest thing she had in color to the amber silk she had worn that night at the White Hawk, a memory that she wished to evoke.

She went down to dinner early, as soon as she had finished dressing, in the hope that she would have a few minutes alone with Devin, but there were already a number of people in the formal grand saloon ahead of her. She was, though, rewarded by the sight of him as soon as she entered the saloon. He looked up when she came in, gave her a brief, impersonal smile, and then resumed his conversation with the man to whom he was speaking. Ancilla faltered a moment, then continued into the room, telling herself that of course he could show her no partiality while they were in public and she was foolish to feel hurt by his lack of attention to her.

She was not seated near Devin during dinner, but between her cousin Sir Waldo, who along with others of the local gentry had been invited to dinner, and a prosy man who had no conversation but horses. It was a dreadful dinner, for the latter bored her excessively with long, pointless hunting and racing stories, and Waldo, who had regarded her with cold censure ever since he had arrived, took the opportunity to deliver to her a lecture on the evils of becoming too attached to fripperies above one's station in life.

Finally, however, the ladies withdrew, leaving the gentlemen to their port and cigars. Ancilla spent an impatient half hour waiting for the men to join them before they finally began to drift, in twos and threes, into the room, joining the ladies of their choice. Devin came in with the last of them, and in the company of George. It was clear from his expression that he did not care for what George was saying to him, and Ancilla pursed her lips in annoyance. She wanted everything about her stay at Fairfeld to be perfect, and if George were involved in some disagreement with Devin, it was bound to cause some unpleasantness. She turned her eyes away from them to find Geoffrey regarding her with amusement. After a few awkward moments when they had first met at the ball at Langley House, their old friendliness had returned, if not, perhaps, with the ease of before.

"That is not the expression of someone who is enjoying herself," he warned. "You will ruin the Langley reputation for gracious hospitality if you go about with such a Friday face."

Ancilla's features relaxed into a smile. "I would not do so for the world. But I was not attempting to comment on the evening's entertainment. I was trying to work out a problem."

"Nothing serious, I hope?"

"No, I don't think so," Ancilla replied, and then turned the subject. "You are looking remarkably relaxed. I was certain you would be quite frazzled with all the preparations and details that must be seen to for tomorrow."

"Oh, I make a point of never becoming frazzled," he said, smiling. "I have learned the fine art of delegation, from which my cousin might prosper if he gave it study. Devin always takes too much on himself."

"I am glad you think so, coz." Devin said, coming up behind Ancilla. She turned her head to look at him, hoping that this time she would see more than cold politeness in his expression. He gave her a warm, intimate smile and linked her arm through his, drawing her closer to him.

"Alanetta Crosby is about to have a serious discussion with Tante Clothilde about why émigrés are actually a burden to English society," he said to Geoffrey, "and I need someone to mediate before an international incident occurs."

"And I am to volunteer?" Geoffrey asked.

"I thought you might," said Devin in a lazy drawl. "You are so good at being soothing."

"Am I?" said Geoffrey dryly. "It is the first I have heard of it. I suspect I am being routed," he said, addressing Ancilla.

"And so quick-witted," Devin said admiringly. "I just knew you were the right man for the job. You may safely leave Ancilla to my care, Geoff," he murmured, his voice deepening. "I think I can promise to look after her entertainment." He turned more to face her and brought his head so close to hers that for a moment she thought he was going to kiss her then and there.

Ancilla cast a quick, self-conscious glance at Geoffrey, wondering how he was taking Devin's blatant possessiveness, but though the laughter had gone from his eyes, he parted from them pleasantly enough.

"Really, Devin," she said with an embarrassed laugh, "that was rather obvious. What must he have thought?"

"The truth, I hope," Devin replied. "He has developed a habit I dislike of gravitating to your side the moment you two are in a room together. Now we will understand each other."

"I think he might have understood you without your going so far," Ancilla admonished, but with a loving smile. "I thought you were going to make love to me in front of everyone."

"I nearly did," he said very softly, looking at her with gratifying intentness. "There is no need for discretion now, though I suppose we must be circumspect for a bit."

Ancilla could hardly believe that such happiness was hers; if they were attracting attention, she neither knew nor cared.

"Everyone seems well settled now," he said, glancing about the room, "but it will be at least an hour before I can get away without causing comment. When it nears that time, you might plead a headache and go up to your room. I shall contrive to join you there as soon as I am able."

Ancilla was a littled startled by the boldness of his

suggestion that they meet in her room, but she readily agreed, castigating herself for being overly sensitive. They had already shared the greatest of intimacies and it was only natural that their love for each other, declared privately and soon to be made known to the world, should be consummated.

She went to sit beside Lucina for a time, and, having been separated from the *comtesse* by the peerless efforts of Geoffrey, Alanetta soon joined them. Lady Crosby questioned Ancilla closely on the time she had spent in town, wishing to know all the places she had been and the people she had met. She never missed an opportunity to insert an unfavorable comment or a barely veiled condemnation of Ancilla's behavior, and by the time Ancilla caught Devin's eye and saw him give her the briefest of nods, the pretended headache was not entirely a lie.

If her steps leaving the drawing room were weary, when she reached her room they had become as light as if she walked above the ground. She hoped with all her heart that Devin would not keep her waiting, for she felt that she had already passed too much of her time in that state. She sat down at her dressing table to be certain that every hair was in place, and imagined how it would be. Devin would come to her and they would reaffirm their love for each other, spending the rest of the night planning their future together. How glorious it would be. And of course it would be the supreme affirmation, the physical proof that they belonged to each other, and each other alone.

Sooner than she expected, there was a gentle tap at her door and Ancilla eagerly jumped up to let him in. He came in and, without saying a word, took her in his arms. She readily molded her body to his lean form, her desire rising quickly to match his. His lips left hers to travel hungrily down her throat to her breasts; his hands caressed her boldly and intimately.

Instead of being reassured by the tenderness of his embrace, Ancilla felt instinctively that something was wrong, that his caresses were more businesslike than loverlike. He kissed her again and began to undo the small hooks at the back of her gown.

"You are very impatient," she said tentatively.

"If I am, it is your fault," he murmured in her ear. "I have spent every day of the past two years wanting you."

Satisfying words to hear, but Ancilla could not shake her feeling of uneasiness. She moved back from him to look at him. "We might at least begin with a little conversation," she said lightly, searching his eyes for reassurance. "You go too fast for me."

His lids dropped over his eyes. "Do I, Cilla?" he said with an odd inflection to his voice. "this is not nearly fast enough for me." Having decided that he still wanted her—in some ways more than ever—and that he was willing to pay the price she demanded, he had determined that his manner toward her would be no different; that she would never know the tormenting emotion she had aroused in him.

But that had become increasingly difficult to do as the evening had progressed. Every time their eyes met, he felt as if he had been struck, and the self-command with which he prided himself was unequal to the task of keeping down his bile. "I can't be long from my guests," he said deliberately. "If you want pretty compliments, Cilla, you will have to wait until the others are in bed."

His words were meant to be degrading, and he was successful. "Is that why you have come to me?" she asked slowly. "Just for . . . this?"

"Why else?" he said with cool provocativeness.

Ancilla felt as if the floor had heaved beneath her feet; she could not believe that her ears had heard correctly. "You told me that you loved me," she said tightly. "Did you mean it?" A number of seconds ticked slowly by as she waited for his answer.

"I suppose," he admitted reluctantly, and, angry with himself for giving even that much of his feeling away, added, "It was what you wanted to hear, wasn't it?"

Angry hurt filled her eyes with unwanted tears. Blindly and roughly she freed herself from his arms and put half the distance of the room between them. "Is that what you thought?" she asked, her voice catching as she fought against the constriction of her throat. "Say the right words and I'd fall into your bed?"

He came toward her and she unconsciously retreated until she came up against the bed curtains. He stopped a few feet away and regarded her silently.

"I don't know what this is about, Ancilla," he said presently in a voice that was cold and hard, "but I am through playing your game. The 'proper little widow' role is rather out of place now, don't you think?"

"I don't know what *you* are about, Devin," she said as carefully and calmly as she could. "I don't know what I have done to make you believe that I have changed my mind about becoming your mistress, but I have not, and telling me what you think I wish to hear won't do it. Please leave me," she said, her voice starting to catch again. "I don't think we have anything else to say to each other." To emphasize her words, she moved toward the door to open it, but he caught her by the arm as she passed him and spun her about to face him.

"How much, Cilla?" he asked in a low, fierce voice. "Have you and George decided between you that I agreed too readily to the amount you set? Do you think a little more resistance might bring a few more thousands? Name your price, Cilla, while I am still in a generous mood, but be warned, I expect value for my money."

The astonishment in Ancilla's eyes was genuine, but he was too upset to see it. "You know I don't want your money," she said vehemently.

"Cut line," he advised her sharply. "I am not the besotted fool you think me."

"I *think* you have run mad."

He smiled caustically at this. "You have been so clever, Cilla, I find it hard to believe that you were ultimately so foolish," he said with deliberate quietness; his emotions were bare and he was no longer able to dissemble. "You might have had so much more of me than a mere ten thousand if you hadn't been so quick to play your cards. Remember the day we played piquet at the White Hawk? You were so anxious to take the trick that you pushed the play and lost the rubber.

"Was that when you began your scheme?" he went on contemptuously. "Just the right amount of resistance before complete surrender, designed to entice? Virtuous outrage over the fifty pounds, calculated to confuse? Whose careful planning took it from there? Was it George who told you to keep me at arm's length? Did that Cummings woman teach you to look at me with such wistful longing? Or do all the honors go to you?"

He saw the color leave her face and mistook its meaning. "You should have realized I'd come to understand you once you had sent George to me. I am sorry if my lovemaking has wounded your 'delicate sensibilities,' but extortion has the unhappy effect of dampening my finer passions and bringing the baser ones to the fore. You shall just have to take me as you find me."

Ancilla could scarcely believe what he was saying, but there was only one interpretation to put on his words; George had gone to him and asked for money in return for her compliance. No wonder he was saying these things to her; even she had trouble believing George could have done such a thing on his own, and at such a propitious time. "Please, Devin . . . you misunderstand," she began, but he cut her off.

"Do I?"

"Please listen to me." This couldn't be happening; her whole future could not be destroyed by the baseness and avarice of one man.

"I don't see any point in listening," he said flatly. "A woman like you isn't for talking—you were designed for another purpose. Undress and we'll get down to it," he added insultingly.

"*No*," she shouted, and it was a cry of pain.

"No?" he said with mock concern. "Perhaps you are right. The more I look at you, the more I am convinced that you are not worth ten thousand pounds. I doubt you are worth even ten." He made her a small, ironic bow and left her.

Given his choice, Devin would have abandoned his guests for the night and sought the solace of his study and a decanter of brandy, but breeding forbade the former and he had no real belief in the comfort to be found in the latter. He returned to his duties as host, and prided himself that his outward composure gave no hint of his inner distress. His guests from the neighborhood had all left before midnight, and there remained only those staying in the house to see to bed before his time and his thoughts were his own. He looked about for Geoffrey to assist him in hastening this process, but he was not to be found. The clock was just striking the first hour of the new day when he at last extricated himself from a conversation with Lord Pomfret, the last straggler, and, after having a few words with Newhouse, his butler, he started up the stairs for his own rooms.

"*Devin*," called a voice in an urgent whisper.

Devin turned, part way up the stairs, and looked over the railing. Cholly was standing below him, his face grim, his manner unnerved. "What is it?" Devin asked in an equally low voice.

"Trouble. In the training stables. You'd better come."

They went out through the back of the house, through the kitchens and the servants' hall, to save time. Cholbeck set a quick pace that did not allow of easy conversation as they walked.

They entered through the door of the main wing; it was lit by a single lantern in the center of the floor and standing around it were Geoffrey and Smitty, the head groom. Gathered at a respectful distance from them were a number of grooms, who had sleeping quarters at the end of the wing.

"What's happened?" Devin asked, addressing Geoffrey as soon as he came in.

"Trouble," Geoffrey replied, unconsciously echoing Cholly. "Someone tried to get to one of the horses."

"Nimbus?" Devin asked quickly.

"It looks that way. You'd better tell Lord Langley, Smitty."

Smitty licked at his lips uncomfortably. "I think it'd be best if the lads went back to bed first. Nothing for them to be up for now, and there's a powerful lot to be done tomorrow."

Devin nodded and, assigning one of them to stand guard, dismissed them, then suggested that Smitty and Geoffrey and Cholly join him in Mr. Bosley's office, which was next to the tackroom.

With the lantern Geoffrey lit a lamp on the desk and the others found chairs and settled in.

"Has anyone gone to fetch Bosley?" Devin asked.

Geoffrey shook his head. "His cottage is too far off for him to have heard the commotion, and now that you're here there's no point getting him out of bed. He'll need his rest for tomorrow."

"As will we all," Devin remarked. "How is it that you were here for the . . . commotion, as you call it?"

"I had some work I've been neglecting while preparing for the meeting," Geoffrey replied. "I went to my office to take care of it."

"And you heard a bother happening here from there?" queried Devin, raising his eyebrows. There was a large paddock area separating the two sets of stable buildings, and it would have required a great deal of shouting indeed for the sound of a disturbance to have traveled the distance.

"Actually I was taking a break from my work and I just happened to be looking out the window when I saw a man running across the fields with several others chasing him in the direction of the home wood," said Geoffrey.

"A most propitious coincidence," said Devin without inflection. He turned to Cholly. "And was it a coincidence that you were here as well?"

Cholbeck looked embarrassed. "Might say that. I know you laugh at me for caring so much, but I came out to have a look at Claret Cup before going to bed. He's got a match race tomorrow and I knew I'd sleep better if I went to bed knowing all was well with him."

"That wasn't a coincidence," Geoffrey said sarcastically, "that was to be expected."

Ignoring him, Cholly went on. "I was only a few yards from here when I heard someone yelling and I came in here on the run to find Smitty and the intruder rolling about on the floor. Didn't know who they were then, of course, but Smitty yelled out again and I recognized his voice and grabbed for the other fellow, but he got away."

Devin heard him out and then turned to his head groom. "Perhaps you'd better tell me what happened from the beginning, Smitty."

Smitty opened his eyes as if surprised that he'd been remembered, and looked as if he wished that he hadn't been. "After the last meeting and what happened at the Newmarket meeting, I wanted to be sure there'd be no more trouble this time, so I put Nimbus in the end stall near the hay box and made up a bed for myself in it so I'd be close by.

"I wasn't there long," he continued, "afore I dozed off for a bit. I came to all of a sudden, and lean' over the box, I see this tall, thin man standing just outside Nimbus's box. I started yellin' for the lads to come and give me a hand, and the next thing I know, Mr. Cholbeck comes runnin' in and he grabs for him, but the nobbler pushes him aside and runs out the door, and the lads gave him chase. They lost him in the woods, though.

Then Mr. Geoff, he comes running over from the stud and Mr. Cholbeck went to fetch you," he finished.

Geoffrey took a round white object from his pocket and proffered it to Devin. "I found this in the straw outside Nimbus's box while Cholly was gone to find you."

"Opium?" Devin asked, taking the object from him.

"I expect so." Geoffrey turned to Smitty and added, "You had better tell his lordship everything you told me. You know I'll have to if you do not."

Smitty looked more miserable than ever. Had any one of the company been in a pitying mood, the wretchedness of his countenance must have moved him to sympathy. But the faces that surrounded him were universally grim, and Smitty knew there was nothing for it but to tell the truth. "I meant to tell you tomorrow, my lord," he said uncomfortably, "after Nimbus ran the way he should, for my conscience had been troublin' me sore."

"Have you been concealing something from me, Smitty?" Devin said, not unkindly.

"Worse than that, my lord," answered the groom unhappily. "I lied to you outright. You asked me the day of the cup race if I thought it possible somebody could've nobbled Nimbus, and I said no."

"And this was the lie?"

Smitty nodded. "I had a bit of ale the night before with one of the lads—nothing I couldn't handle. But next morning, I felt like I'd got cast away, and this lad, he says to me, 'You just have a lie-down until things get under way and I'll see to your ponies same as mine.'

"You know I don't go neglectin' my duties, my lord," he said urgently. "But this one, Jemmy Stotten by name, a Colechester lad, he was a rare one with the ponies and a likable lad. I knew he'd care for them same as I would."

"Stotten," said Devin thoughtfully. He made it a point to know all of his many servants by name. "I don't recall him. Is he a new boy?"

"Was," said Smitty miserably. "That's the rub, my lord. After the race I went looking for him and he'd cleared off. Packed up all his things and left."

"I can see how that might have caused you concern," said Devin in a dry voice. He had the idle thought that his troubles always seemed to come in bunches. "Why didn't you tell me this that night when I questioned you?"

Smitty bowed his head. "I was scared, my lord. I was born to Fairfeld, it means everything to me. It was me that took the lad on, me that neglected my responsibilities, and me that gave him more place in the stable than he deserved."

"Why don't you tell me when he came to us," Devin said levelly, "and why you regarded him so highly."

Obviously he was not to be dismissed at once, and Smitty felt a glimmer of hope for the first time in two months. "He came a month or so before the meeting, from Pomfret's stud," he replied. "He said his mother'd been poorly lately and he wanted to be nearer her to give her a bit of support. His references from Pomfret were in his lordship's trainer's own hand and were the best."

"But unlike many stables," Devin put in, "we always keep a full complement of grooms and our turnover is small. How was it that there was an opening for him?"

"That was a bit of luck for him," Smitty allowed. "Just two days before he comes wanderin' in to the stable, Mr. Geoff had had to let one of the lads go, for suspected pilferin'."

"Yet another fortunate coincidence," Devin said, more to himself than to Smitty. "Go on."

"As I've said, my lord, Jemmy was a rare hand for the ponies. Made me notice him, it did. I got to talkin' with him and it turned out we thought alike in most things and we just got on together."

"How very convenient," said Devin very quietly. He sighed and stood up. "I think we'd better get to our beds if we aren't all to feel like the devil tomorrow."

"You're not just going to leave it at this?" said Geoffrey incredulously.

"No, I suppose not," Devin said, sounding weary. He looked to his groom again. "You have been very remiss in your duties, Smitty, but the worst of it was that you *lied* to me. I begin to think that a great deal of trouble might have been saved if you had just told me the truth that night. However, I do not believe in dismissing one's best employees without giving them a chance to redeem themselves. You are on warning, though, and I shall have more to say to you after the meeting is over." He turned to Geoffrey and added, "Is that sufficient for you?"

"You needn't be caustic with me," said Geoffrey indignantly.

"I know. I'm sorry," Devin apologized. "I've other things on my mind tonight. Thank you, Geoff, Cholly, for your diligence on my behalf." With that he quitted the room and returned to the house, leaving the three men still in the office to stare at each other.

13

Ancilla was aroused the next morning by the sound of a crash in the hall outside her room. She wondered vaguely if she should shake herself out of her lethargy to see what was happening, but then, remembering that it was the first day of the meeting, assumed that it was the normal bustle of the servants preparing their masters and mistresses for the event. She turned on her side and tried to shut out the sounds so that she could return to the numbness of sleep, but after a while she gave it up as useless.

She opened her eyes, which felt swollen and sandy, and sat up. Still only half awake, she got out of bed, stumbled over to her dressing table and sat down on the stool, resting her elbows on the surface of the table and her head on her hands. She sat there, somewhere between sleep and wakefulness, for some time until she realized that if she did not soon ring for Sally, the maid would come of her own accord and find her in this state, still in her evening dress, her hair half down and matted in tangles.

Ancilla got up and went to open the draperies, hoping that the light would increase her wakefulness. It was a glorious day for racing, but instead of reviving her, the brilliant sunlight made her wince. She turned her back on the sun-sparkled panes of glass, unfastened her gown, stepped out of it, and kicked it away from her with distaste, finding a blue wrapper in her wardrobe and putting this on over her petticoats. She sat down again at the dressing table and saw that her reflection presented an even more woebegone appearance in the light. But how she looked was nothing to how she felt inside: tattered, hollow, and numb.

It was difficult for her to grasp that the events of just one night could have shattered every hope she had had for her future. She removed the remaining pins from her hair and shook it out, combing out the worst of the tangles with her fingers before applying a brush to it. A single, silent tear fell down her cheek and she brushed at it impatiently. She would not cry again for a man who could not believe in her and would not listen to her explanations.

There was a sharp rap at her door, and, assuming it was Sally, Ancilla gave permission to enter. George strode impatiently into the room, slamming the door behind him. He put a rough hand on her shoulder to turn her toward him. "What the devil are you about, you little fool?" he said furiously.

His evident rage did not frighten her; it only fed her own anger. "How dare you, George?" she said with icy rage. "How could you do such a thing to me? Have you no feeling? No sense of honor or decency?"

But George, having just come from a very unpleasant private conversation with his host, was too upset to mind what she was saying to him. "I've had enough of your damned miss-ish ways. I set you up with a veritable honey pot and you throw it away. I didn't go seeking you—you're the one who came to me with your hand out. Well, the dibs are being called in, Cilla, and it's damn well time you proved worthy of your keep."

"I came to you asking for nothing that was not mine," she said, pulling out of his grasp and rising. "I knew you were selfish and unprincipled, but I wouldn't have believed that even you could have used me in such a way. It is obvious to me now that you never meant to do as you promised. The legalities that prevented the deed from the cottage being drawn up at once were just inventions, weren't they, George?"

"Well, you've learned some sense from your time in the world," he said nastily. "If it had been left to me, you would have gone to that prosy cousin of yours or slept in a ditch if you preferred. It was Robert's idea to placate you and keep you in town by dangling treats and trinkets before you. He paid for 'em as well.

"But you," he continued as Ancilla stared at him in shocked silence, "with all your fine friends, decided you were too good for him. Well, you've had your chance to go to the one you wanted. It isn't my fault you botched that. As far as I'm concerned, you can either make it up with

Langley or you can just make up your mind to go to Purcell as originally planned."

Ancilla was stunned by the depth of George's perfidy. Sir Robert had paid for her time in town and the things she had bought. No *wonder* he was so possessive of her. She was his kept woman; it hardly seemed to matter that she herself had been unaware of it. She looked at George, and for the first time in her life she felt genuine hatred for another human being. "Get out," she said in a low and deadly voice.

"We'll all be getting out if you don't come to your senses," George said, unperturbed. "He wants us out of here by the end of the day. I don't think you really want Purcell, Cilla, so you'd best do the right thing and make it up with Langley. Otherwise, the minute we get back to town Purcell will have you." He turned on his heel and left the room, slamming the door forcefully.

Ancilla closed her eyes and swayed slightly, though she did not feel faint. She remembered again the high spirits and hope that had animated her at the start of her journey to London. Never had she supposed they would bring her to this. And the irony of it was that she was far worse off than she had been before; had she simply bowed to George's treachery and accepted the command of Mr. Grogan to vacate the cottage, she would at least have a little money left now.

The man she loved had no faith in her and thought her a whore; the man to whom she had gone for assistance and protection had betrayed and used her, and now she had nothing but pretty dresses and other fripperies from a man who would use her the worst of all. She had only one choice now. She would have to swallow her pride, give up the last vestiges of her independence, and go begging to her cousin to take her in.

But it would not be forever, she determined as she went to the bellpull to ring for Sally. Nor would she give in to Waldo's wishes to marry her off to his friend, should he start on that again. That, in its way, was nearly as bad as what George had wished for her. There must be some employment for which she was suited, and she would find it as soon as she possibly could.

She sat down on the bed to wait for her maid. For the first time in her life she wished that she had listened to the long-suffering governess who had tried to instill in her all the proper accomplishments, instead of spending so much of her time in the stables.

It was not easy for Ancilla to keep from becoming entangled for the day with Lucina and her other friends, and what they must have thought of the excuses that she gave them for not joining them in the Langley box in the grandstand she neither knew nor cared. Devin had gone to the stables early, before she had come down to breakfast, so at least she was spared having to meet him that morning. It was a small blessing to count, but she felt she had so few of these at the moment she could not afford to overlook the least of them. But another piece of good fortune awaited her.

Coming around the back of the grandstand, Ancilla nearly collided with Lady Crosby. "You must not rush about so, Ancilla," Alanetta said in her lecturing way. "I am sure I have told you a hundred times that it becomes a lady to walk with careful grace. I must say that you do not look any better for having retired early last night, and really, Ancilla, that color blue is too washed out for your complexion. I wish you might have consulted me in the choosing of your wardrobe."

Ancilla did not even bother to reply to these remarks; her purpose today was the only thing that mattered. "Isn't Waldo with you?" she asked quickly. "Surely you haven't come alone?"

"No, of course not," Alanetta responded in the tone of someone trying to be patient with an especially dull-witted child. "I am not even sure I consider horseracing a proper setting for a lady of birth even when properly protected, but one must not give offense to one's neighbors. Lord Langley counts on us all for our support."

"Where is Waldo?" Ancilla persisted.

"He stopped to have a word with Mr. Sedgewick, whom we met getting out of our carriage," she said, and began to explain that Maria Sedgewick and her two daughters were saving a place for them in the stands.

But Ancilla had no time to waste on Alanetta. Thanking her hurriedly, she went at once to find Waldo. There were a great number of carriages—curricles, phaetons, gigs, barouches, landaus—some placed in neat rows, others milling about as horses were walked by grooms, but Ancilla had no difficulty finding the one that the Crosbys had come in. Sir Waldo had decided that Ancilla's father's old traveling carriage, though twenty years out of date, was serviceable enough, the old-fashioned lines of his carriage were easy to pick out. Ancilla's luck held, for he was still beside it, talking to Mr. Sedgewick.

The latter greeted her with warmth, accentuating all the more her cousin's cool nod to her, and Ancilla prayed that the incautious letter and her coolness to him last night had not given him a permanent disgust of her.

After a few minutes' conversation with both men, Ancilla turned to Waldo and said, "May I please have a private word with you, Waldo, before the racing begins? It is most important."

Sir Waldo, a man of below-average height and above-average girth, and balding as well, was always mildly irritated by having to look up to talk to his taller cousin. "I hope it is no unpleasantness," he said discouragingly. "I am here for a day of pleasurable occupation, and if there is some difficulty, you will find me at home tomorrow, for though I would not offend Lord Langley by staying away from his meeting altogether, and I am sure his money is his to do with as he likes, I cannot approve of wasting time on such frivolities as watching horses race against each other for more than a day at a time."

"Please, Waldo," Ancilla pleaded. "It is most important or I would not have bothered you."

"Are you in some sort of difficulty, Mrs. Martin?" Mr. Sedgewick asked with evident concern. "Perhaps I can be of assistance if Sir Waldo cannot spare you the time."

Ancilla could have hugged him. Like most people in the neighborhood, Mr. Sedgewick tolerated rather than liked Sir Waldo, and she knew he had said this to make Waldo appear neglectful of his responsibility to her as head of her family. Waldo would never be able to resist such bait and, in fact, he did not.

"If you are in some sort of scrape," he said crossly, "of course I can spare you the time. Be so good, John, as to tell Lady Crosby that I have some business to attend to and will join her shortly." He then turned to Ancilla and added, "I do not know what this is about, but I believe that I warned you in my letter to you in town that the course you were on was marked out for trouble. So it always is with you, though. My advice goes unheeded and then you come to me for assistance when you have nowhere else to turn."

Looking embarrassed, Mr. Sedgewick quickly took his leave of them. Ancilla swallowed the constricting anger that Waldo's words aroused in her. She longed to be able to remind him that after the dreadful six months she had lived with him and Alanetta, she had never gone to them for advice or anything else. But she desperately needed Waldo now, and if the price she had to pay was the silent endurance of his spiteful remarks, then she would manage to hold her tongue. She led him a little away from the carriage to a spot where they would not be overheard.

"Very well, Ancilla," he said with a show of patient resignation. "What is it? And kindly begin at the beginning. You know I dislike a hodgepodge in speech. It is the sign of a disorderly mind."

Ancilla drew a breath and collected her thoughts, then plunged into her story. She had thought this morning of various things to tell him that might make him more sympathetic to her plight, but now that the time was at hand, she decided that she could not improve upon the truth. So she began with the time she had received the letter from George's man of business and went straight through to her unhappy scene with George this morning, leaving out little except her meeting with Devin at the White Hawk.

Waldo heard her with a faint, disapproving frown that deepened as he listened. Not certain whether it was directed at her or at those who had victimized her, she began to rush her words for fear that he would stop her before she could finish. "So you see," she concluded, almost stringing her words together, "I cannot return to town with George and it is obvious that he will never acknowledge my right to the cottage now. I would fight him legally if I could, but you know I haven't the means for that. I know I am not faultless in this, for I was naive and placed my trust blindly, but if you don't help me now, cousin, I honestly don't know where I shall turn."

Waldo said nothing for several agonizing minutes. He stood, staring at her, thoughtfully running a forefinger alongside his rather long nose. "I find it hard to believe that even George Martin, of whom I have never approved, could be capable of such villainy against the wife of his own brother, or that you could have been living under his roof these past weeks and had no notion of his character until now."

Ancilla recognized the signs of an impending lecture and, knowing there was nothing she could do to prevent it, composed herself to see it patiently to the end.

"I am appalled at the conduct of Lord Langley," Waldo went on. "I have always thought of him as an exemplary gentleman and I cannot but think that you must have in some way—however unwittingly—encouraged him. As for Sir Robert Purcell, I cannot say I know anything of him, but he sounds to me just the sort of man that any person of sense would have studiously avoided. If he is the manner of man with whom George Martin associates, then you should have seen at once that you were in improper company. Alanetta and I have always had a deep concern for your happiness and comfort, but if you will go on in your headstrong way you will never learn to profit by our advice."

Ancilla meekly listened to his strictures, though at another time his sermonizing tone and the pious look of rebuke in his eyes would have evoked a retort from her. She said nothing not just because she dared not risk offending him but because she believed that at least in part, Waldo was right. She had seen in both George and Devin what she had wanted to see, and had deliberately shut her eyes to the rest.

"You know I believed that Jack Martin, with neither family nor fortune to offer you, was a poor choice for a husband, and after his untimely demise I did my best to settle your future for you, but you willfully insisted on going on in your own way, and now you see where it has brought you."

His words gave her no encouragement and she said as calmly as she could, "Does this mean that you won't help me, cousin?"

"Do you deserve that I should?" he asked self-righteously. "Still, since the death of my dear uncle, your father, it has been my honor to assume the position of head of our family, and I must make it my duty to see to the needs of even its most recalcitrant and least-deserving members. You may come to us, Ancilla, and I only hope that you have learned from bitter experience what you would not from my counsel."

"Thank you very much, Waldo," Ancilla said sincerely.

"You need not fear that I mean to be a burden to you for the rest of my days. As soon as possible, I shall begin to seek some employment for which I am suited."

"That is a very sound course, Ancilla. I am sure *something* may be found for you. An idle mind leads to idle hands, which I needn't tell you are the playthings of the devil." He began walking in the direction of the grandstand and Ancilla meekly followed him.

"Will Alanetta mind very much, do you think, Waldo?" she asked.

"You may trust that she will know her Christian duty, as I do," he said loftily, and then stopped and turned to Ancilla. "Perhaps it would be best, though, if I spoke to her alone. Go to the house, cousin, and pack your things, and we will bring the carriage around to collect you within the hour."

"I did not wish to spoil your pleasure in the day," said Ancilla, startled by his haste. "I don't mind waiting until you are ready to leave."

"After the way Lord Langley has behaved toward you, it is not fitting that you should remain under his roof," Waldo informed her. "Though, of course, I do not intend to cut the acquaintance, for in most other things I believe Langley to be a just and right-thinking man, and one whom it would not be wise to offend. But I would be derelict in my duty toward you if I did not protect you at once from his importunings."

Although Ancilla knew that being hastened away from one of the prime social events of the neighborhood would not contribute toward putting her in Alanetta's good books, her own desire to be away from Fairfeld made her protests no more than token.

Ancilla returned to the house at once and rang for Sally. She gave her maid an abbreviated account of the things she had told her cousin, and Sally exclaimed her amazement and dismay throughout the whole of their packing. The worse part of it for Sally was the knowledge that she and Ancilla would eventually be parted when her mistress was herself forced to seek employment, but she was philosophical. "Kitchen maid I began," Sally said, "and kitchen maid I'll be again, but I'll miss you, Miss Cilla."

While Sally finished packing and rang for a footman to take their baggage to the front hall, Ancilla composed a brief letter to Lucina, begging her pardon for leaving so abruptly and stating only that it was necessary for her to go to Waldo for family reasons. To Devin she wrote nothing: it was hardly necessary. As for George, he could think what he pleased.

Though she did not like Ancilla any more than Ancilla liked her, Alanetta accepted her return to Crosby Hall— not, however, with good grace. Her first act was the predictable one of informing Ancilla that she saw no point in supporting a lady's maid for her when her own dresser could see to them both, and she consigned Sally to the kitchen just as the maid had predicted she would.

Ancilla actually slept well that night, though the small back bedchamber allotted to her was stuffy and warm, for the events of the past two days and the fact that she had had so little sleep the previous night had completely worn her out. In the morning she was reassured that her letter to Lucina had answered, and that both Devin and George had understood what she had done, for she had no word from Fairfeld.

After breakfast Alanetta informed her that it was only fitting that she should put herself to good use about the house, and Ancilla readily and resignedly assented to the tasks given her. The first of these was to remove the breakfast tray so as not to disturb the housemaids at their work.

Ancilla took the tray down to the kitchen, carefully negotiating the poorly lit stairs. She knew that Alanetta's wish for her to do so was designed solely to put her in her place.

Sally saw her enter the kitchen and hastened to relieve her of her burden. "Here, Miss Cilla, I'll take it," she said as she expertly eased it onto her hip and carried it to the sink. "You shouldn't be doin' such a thing, it isn't fittin' for a lady. Her grand ladyship could've rung for me or one of the other girls, and so she knows."

"I don't mind, Sally. It is little enough to do in exchange for a roof over our heads," Ancilla replied, "though I must admit I hope I won't have to remain here very long."

"It's not right, Miss Cilla, and that's a fact," Sally said severely. "Time was when you were mistress in this house."

"But not any longer," Ancilla reminded her.

The chime of the front door sounded and Higgins, the butler, broke off his conversation with the cook, donned his best coat, and left to answer the door. He was new, the man who had held that post during Ancilla's and her father's tenure having been pensioned off shortly after Ancilla's marriage, and he passed Ancilla without a word or a glance, his attitude being that if his master and mistress thought she was fit to do the chores of a servant, it was not his place to gainsay them.

Several minutes later, Ancilla was surprised to meet Higgins returning to the kitchen as she was coming out of it, and even more surprised when he informed her that the caller was for her. When she heard that her caller was George, her face set in grim lines. She had hoped never to speak to him again, and since he had been requested to leave Fairfeld, she had supposed that he was well on his way back to town. She might have guessed, though, that he would not give up so easily; there was no doubt that he would lose the settlement he had extorted from Devin, and it was likely that he was in equally bad odor with Sir Robert.

But she decided she would have to see him, if for no other reason than to convince him that no amount of persuasion or threats would have the least effect on her future behavior.

"It took a great deal of bottom for you to come here, George," she said coldly as soon as she entered the salon, where he was waiting for her. "You must realize that I have told Waldo everything. You are very fortunate that he is at the home farm today and that Alanetta has gone to visit Maria Sedgewick, or you would not have been admitted. Or did you make certain that they would not be here?"

George attempted a menacing smile, but there was about him an air of distraction, perhaps anxiety, that spoiled the effect. "You would be wise never to underestimate me," he warned. "This little diversion of yours was clever and certainly inconvenient to me, but it does not affect the outcome of events. Have your maid get your things together, Cilla. Vera has returned to town in the carriage, but I was able to rent the trap from the Green Man. Robert has a room there and you may stay there until he is ready to collect you."

Ancilla stared at him with astonishment. "Have you lost your senses, George?" she asked incredulously. "You must realize why I have come to Crosby Hall. I own it was not a thing I would have chosen to do, but you left me little choice."

"I don't care why you have come here," he said, "but

you are not staying. It's obvious you have made up your mind against Langley—though it's a great pity, for we would both have profited handsomely—so Robert Purcell it must be. Frankly, that is the *only* choice you have."

"You *are* mad."

"Not mad, desperate," he admitted, and his air of bravado slipped away from him. "I stupidly burned my bridges behind me when I thought it was a sure thing that you would accept the carte blanche from Langley. I wrote to Purcell and told him that he had been cut out, but he followed us here and he's more than furious, Cilla—he's dangerous. It will go poorly for both of us if I don't deliver you to him at the Green Man by five this afternoon. That is the time he has allotted us to come to heel."

"Sir Robert cannot possibly harm me, and don't expect me to feel sorry for you, George," Ancilla told him roundly. "After the way you have used me, I have no interest in what becomes of you. I not only find the person of Sir Robert disgusting, I know that he is a wicked man and was involved in the crimes that Henry Lippcott is assumed to have committed." She saw George's eyes open at this, and added, "And I now know that you are not innocent in that matter. What is more to the point, it is only a matter of time before the stewards of the Jockey Club discover the truth, so you would be wise to concern yourself with that and leave me in peace."

"That is precisely my concern," George said with urgent intensity. "Robert told me yesterday he has had another visit from Brisbane in town, and he is certain they are suspicious of him. If you know what has been going on, it is all the more reason for you to take proper heed of my words. This is a very dangerous situation and we are all at a very great risk."

"*I* had no part in it."

"Nor did I, except peripherally," he said defensively. "But Robert has the wind up and he thinks it would be prudent for him to leave the country for a time. He wants companionship for the journey and he's decided on you. If I don't bring you to him, he'll have information laid against me involving me in things that were none of my doing, and he'll see to it that my debts are called in as well. These were the least of his threats, so make up your mind to it, Ancilla, you're coming with me," he concluded, the portentousness returning to his voice. "I'm damned if I'll be brought to ruin by a damned chit like you."

"I don't care what happens to you, George. I can't even make myself feel very sorry for you, for the mess you are in is quite your own fault. I am not going anywhere with you and that is final." She turned to leave the room, but George moved quickly and placed himself between her and the door.

"I think you had better hear me out before you make up your mind."

"I have made it up," she said without hesitation.

"I was serious when I said you had no choice," he said. "I wasn't bluffing, Cilla. I have in my pocket a number of receipts for gowns paid for by Sir Robert Purcell. Suppose I were to take them to your holier-than-thou cousin. What do you think he would make of them? No doubt those very dresses are at this moment in your wardrobe upstairs."

Ancilla felt a chill of fear touch the base of her spine, but she said calmly, "It might distress him, but I have told him everything, George, and he would not credit any lies you might tell him."

"No? Don't be too sure, Cilla. I can be very convincing if necessary, and believe me it is necessary." He rested his back and shoulders against the door to give himself the appearance of negligent ease. "I would tell him that you were Purcell's mistress and stayed with me only for appearances. Reprehensible of me to permit it, of course, but I condoned it only until I discovered that you were playing my friend false by taking up with Langley as well. When I told you I would have none of that, you laughed at me and said it didn't matter because you could just as well live at the cottage and be near to your lover at Fairfeld. Then, in a fit of moral indignation, I said you should not have the cottage, but you were unperturbed. You told me that Waldo was an old fool and could be duped into taking you in if you could convince him that you needed his protection, and you would still be near enough to Fairfeld to carry on your liaison with Langley. The true facts should fit in nicely with the lie, don't you agree?"

Ancilla did agree, but she refused to let George see her fear. "He'll never believe you. He knows what you are, and I have never given him reason to think that I would behave in such a way."

"Oh, I don't know about that," said George with an unpleasant smile. "Even I know there was a bit of gossip going about the neighborhood about you and Langley before Jack died, and Waldo was pretty quick to attack you for going to town and giving yourself over to the frivolities of town life. But even if he don't credit my story, I'll wager anything you like that his good lady will. She's jealous of you, Cilla. She hates you like poison and would be glad of the chance to see you fall."

Ancilla stared at her brother-in-law and was not deceived by his poise. He was indeed desperate, for he was as cornered as she now felt herself to be. He would get Waldo to listen to him, and probably Alanetta as well. She tried hard to convince herself that Waldo would stand by her, but she could not stretch her faith in his sense of duty that far. The Crosbys did not want her here any more than she wished to be here. If he gave credit to George's lies, he would be able to wash his hands of her and self-righteously proclaim that he was justified in doing so at the same time.

So she would receive no mercy from Jack's brother and probably none from her cousin either. In that case she had no idea where or to whom she might turn. The prospect genuinely frightened her; she would need to think what she could do, but there was no time for that now. She had to get rid of George somehow and without giving him cause to search out Waldo at once.

"I admit that you hold very good cards," she said in a controlled voice, hoping that he would not be suspicious of her sudden capitulation. "Alanetta would certainly listen to your lies, and most likely do all she could to convince Waldo of them as well."

"A sensible conclusion." He smiled with self-satisfaction. "I take it you are beginning to see things my way?"

"I see that you have backed me into a hopeless position," she retorted angrily and truthfully. "If it is not Sir Robert, then it will probably be the workhouse, though I hold that place in only a little more disgust than I do your friend."

"But if you are as clever as I think you are," said George, "you will not tell him so. You won't find him ungenerous if you play your part well." He moved away from the door. "You'd best get your things. I have to take the trap back to the Green Man, as it's bespoken for the afternoon. They let me have it only because I promised not to keep it out above an hour."

Ancilla saw in this her opportunity. "In that case, you had better take it back at once and come for me later. I can't possibly be ready in so little time."

George frowned. "I wouldn't have any means of collecting your things later, and I don't fancy lugging them to the village on foot."

"You could have the Green Man send a cart over for my trunk, and you and I could walk there together. I am a country girl, George. The distance is nothing to me."

"Is this some sort of trick, Ancilla?" He regarded her suspiciously. "I'll go straight to Waldo, I promise you."

"As if I didn't know that," she said caustically. "You know nothing of female matters. Do as I say and I promise I shall be ready for you when you return."

George pondered for a moment. "I have business to attend to at the cottage after I take the trap back," he said, more to himself than to her. "I could walk here from there, I suppose."

"Business at the cottage?" asked Ancilla, curious about what could take him there. "But it is completely empty. Why would you go there?"

"Never you mind," George said crossly. "It is a nuisance that I have to take care of, but it is no concern of yours. I'll have the Green Man come for your things when they can, and I should be back here no later than four. See that you are ready, Cilla, and no games, I'm warning you."

"No games, George," she said innocently. "You may rely on me to do as I ought."

Concerned with his own problems, George looked for no hidden meanings in her words. He nodded a curt farewell and let himself out.

_____ *14* _____

Ancilla sank into a wing chair near the window and
watched George drive away in the trap. Her first inclina-
tion was to go to Waldo at once and tell him of George's
blackmailing scheme and thus effectively foil George's
hand, but she was not sure enough of Waldo to believe
that this would be in her best interests. It would be
infinitely better if she could find some means of disarm-
ing George and Robert Purcell without involving Waldo.

She wasted a whole precious hour sitting and thinking
before the solution came to her. If the stewards were to
learn of Sir Robert's plan to escape, they might be made
to act at once against him. George could not make her go
to Sir Robert if Sir Robert were taken in charge, and she
did not believe that he personally wished her any harm.
She was only the means of saving his own neck. Even if
George still found himself caught up in the mess, he
would have far too much on his mind to concern himself
with being vindictive toward her.

She went up to her room to change. Lord Brisbane, as
was his custom, was once again at Fairfeld for the meeting.
She felt too awkward about the lie she had told Brisbane
at Rockhill to go to him herself, but she could find Geoffrey at the course, avoid Devin or any of the others, and
use Geoffrey as her intermediary. She put on her brown
velvet riding habit as hastily as she could and went at
once to the stables, grateful that neither Waldo nor
Alanetta was about to question her activities.

Ancilla rode directly to the course, picking her way
among the crowd of race goers, not even stopping to reply
to greetings sent her way. She headed for the stables,
knowing that Geoffrey spent most of his time there during the meeting. She asked several grooms if they knew
his whereabouts, but none did. She had almost decided to
dismount and go to the grandstand, though this she did

not at all wish to do, when she saw Devin's trainer coming toward her. He was in conversation with a rider dressed in the Fairfeld colors, but he came over to her obediently when she called to him.

"Do you know where I might find Mr. Drake?" she asked. "I must speak to him at once on an important matter."

"He isn't here," Bosley told her. "He was called away on an errand a while ago. He didn't say when he'd be back."

Ancilla bit back an exclamation of dismay. She certainly did not wish to wait about Fairfeld until he returned. "Do you know where he has gone? Perhaps I could meet up with him."

"Can't say that I do," said Bosley. "He was headed for the short way to the village through the Littlelands property, but I can't say for certain that it was to the village he was bound." Though there was much for him to do on such a day, he could not resist the opportunity to vent his grievances to an ear he knew would be sympathetic. "It's a pity it wouldn't keep, though. With his lordship meaning to go to Colechester on a matter of his own, and Mr. Cholbeck gone up to the house with that lady that fainted dead away when a horse stepped on her foot, and not yet returned, there's more here as needs doing than there are people to do it. It'll be raining soon, too, if you ask me," he said, looking up at the sky, which had been overcast since early morning, "and that won't help."

Ancilla murmured sympathetically but barely heard his complaints. She was thinking rapidly. There was no point in going after Geoffrey when she had no idea where he might be. If Cholly were still at the house, she might take her problem to him, but her reasons for not wishing to confide in him were as valid now as they had been before.

She came at last to the solution she had been avoiding. Devin. She knew that he would handle the matter expeditiously if she went to him, and his lack of objectivity no longer mattered, for there could be no doubt now about the culpability of Sir Robert and George. She dreaded seeing him, but there was no other solution to her problem and she knew it. With her whole future at stake, this was no time to let personal matters interfere.

"Has Lord Langley actually left for Colechester yet?" she asked.

"That he has, Mrs. Martin," Bosley replied. "He was meaning to wait until after the last of the races, but with the weather so threatening, he thought he'd better do the thing at once, as he said it wasn't a thing he could put off."

Ancilla nearly groaned aloud. Her luck was certainly not in this day. "Is it long since he left? Will he be back soon, do you think?"

Bosley shook his head slowly. "I don't know the nature of his business, but I know it's something to do with some trouble we had here the night before last. I expect it will take a while before he's back, as he's only just left. I took leave of him just before I came out of the stables."

Ancilla' spirits, which had been downcast, suddenly rose. This was the first bit of good news she had had. She quickly thanked the trainer and turned the mare in the direction of the drive.

If Devin had only just started out, she still had hope of catching him up. It was likely that he was driving his curricle with his favorite bays between the shafts, but if he had not traveled too great a distance, she would at least have a chance of intercepting him. Ancilla had already discovered that Waldo's hack was no slug. She had speed and spirit, and now Ancilla meant to test her heart as well.

Ancilla realized that taking the conventional way, by the drive, to the carriage house would only waste time, for it would be far faster to cut through the pastures. She turned the mare again and retraced her steps past the stables and to the pasture gate, which was always left open during a meeting for easy access to all wings of the stable. She passed through and dug her heel into Cassandra's flank, and the mare sprung into a canter that quickly lengthened to a full gallop.

The carriage house was soon ahead of her, and, to her dismay, she also saw the strip of whitewashed fencing that separated her from her goal. There was a gate, no doubt, but she did not know its location and she had only a moment to think what she would do when she reached the fence, for at almost the same moment she saw and recognized Devin's curricle pulling out of the yard. She felt exhilarated that she had not missed him, but the emotion was fleeting, for Cassandra's gait was fully extended and the barrier was nearly before them. It was not an especially high fence, perhaps no more than five feet, no great challenge for a trained hunter, but the mare was only a hack and had not been trained to fences, and this was certainly not one to put a green horse at.

The fence loomed closer, seeming to grow in inches as she approached it, and Ancilla realized that the time for decision had passed. She used the reins to even out the mare's pace and pointed her at the fence, grabbing a handful of mane to give herself some support to stay in the saddle should the mare balk.

With relief, Ancilla felt the mare gather herself beneath her. They sailed over the fence with room to spare, landing neatly on the other side amid a shower of gravel and several startled grooms. Ancilla continued across the yard and onto the drive without pausing for breath. This portion of the drive was flat and straight, and Devin had put his horses along it at a brisk canter.

Ancilla could feel the gallant mare flagging. She had no whip, but with the judicious use of her heel and words of encouragement, Cassandra renewed her effort and soon the distance between them and the carriage narrowed and they at last came up alongside it.

Devin was startled when he saw Ancilla beside him, for the sound of his own horses had masked her approach. It was clear that she had ridden hard and that something was wrong, and he pulled up at once. Ancilla reduced her speed as well, but circled the mare at a walk for a few moments before speaking to give them both an opportunity to catch their breath.

"What is it, Cilla?" he asked brusquely. His thoughts about her had cost him a deal of needed sleep for the past two nights, and the only result was that he still did not understand her or what had happened between them. He was no longer convinced that she was George's conspirator, but neither was he positive that she was her brother-in-law's victim. He now regarded her warily.

"I know you have important business in Colechester," she said, still a bit breathless, "but could we speak for a few minutes first?" She saw from his expression that he was about to refuse, and after their last meeting she was not surprised. She quickly hit on the one thing that would make him listen. "It concerns Nimbus and those who did not wish him to win his race."

He gave her a long, measuring look, as if he half suspected a ruse of some sort, and then turned to the groom seated beside him and told him to help Ancilla into the carriage and to walk her horse on the grass a little away from them.

"What do you know about the events of the other night?" he asked as soon as she was in the carriage and the groom had moved away.

"The other night?" she asked, not understanding.

"You said you knew about the attempt to give opium to Nimbus the night before last," he said, suspicion creeping into his tone.

Ancilla realized that they were talking at cross purposes. "I was speaking of the time when he was disgraced in the cup race. Has it happened again? I left so early yesterday that I heard nothing of it. Was he able to run against Peerless as you'd planned?"

"Yes, and he won, despite the efforts of someone to the contrary," he replied, watching her face for her reaction. There was nothing to be seen but interest and surprise and perhaps a bit of diffidence, but that was easily accounted for. "What do you know about the first time?"

"Well, it does not concern Nimbus precisely, though it may," she admitted, and then told him what she had told Geoffrey at George's house, adding what George had told her of Sir Robert's plans to flee the country. She left out the part that contained George's threats to her and his plans for taking her to Sir Robert. This made her story a bit choppy, but she still managed to convey to him that it mattered very much to her that Sir Robert did not escape the consequences of his acts.

He digested what she had told him for a few moments before speaking. "So George has confirmed the suspicions you had when you overheard his conversation with Purcell," he said at last. "You have obviously taken trouble and ridden hard to make this known to me. May I ask why?"

"Sir Robert is an unscrupulous man," she said. "If he is permitted to go free for these crimes, I don't doubt his intention is to return when he thinks it is forgotten, and he will most likely then involve himself in some other wickedness."

Though this was not the answer he wished to evoke, he did not press the matter. "Neither do I doubt that," he said dryly. "What you've told me makes it all the more urgent that I go to Colechester at once. Since you do not care to go to Brisbane yourself, I'll send my man with a message to him, informing him of Purcell's intentions and whereabouts, and request him to have him watched. If the weather doesn't hold, I may be delayed longer than the time Purcell means to be away." He took out his card case and a pencil from his pocket and scribbled on the back of one of his cards in a close hand.

"Why is it more urgent for you to go to Colechester?" she asked. She had hoped that he would turn his carriage about and return to the course to find Lord Brisbane as soon as he had heard her story. "Surely it would be best if you were to go to Brisbane at once and tell him what I have told you?"

"What you have told me is very interesting, but it is not evidence. A man cannot be convicted of crimes on suspicion." He paused to signal to his groom. "I hope to be able to find that evidence in Colechester today, and to do so before it can be warned away and in time for it to be of use against Purcell."

Ancilla understood its importance, but she still needed a solution to her own problems. If Sir Robert was not taken in charge by the time George came to Crosby Hall for her, she would find herself trapped. It was still quite early and if the weather did hold, Devin could easily return before George came for her, but from the look of the sky she was afraid that the weather would once again prove no friend to her.

She hated the prospect of returning to Crosby Hall to wait helplessly for what fate would visit upon her. She toyed with the idea of not returning there, of letting George find her gone when he arrived. She knew that she was grasping at straws, but she had an idea that George might not immediately go to Waldo. He would not be certain, after all, that she had tipped him the double, at least not at first. As she knew it was her person that was more important to him than ruining her with Waldo, she thought he might hold his peace at least till he was certain of what she was about. This might give her, and Devin, another hour of grace. Whether she returned to Crosby Hall or not, she saw before her an afternoon of anxious solitude, and the idea was daunting. "May I go with you?" she asked Devin abruptly.

"Why should you wish to go with me?" he asked as he finished his instructions to his groom.

Ancilla thought quickly and came up with an answer that was not far from the truth. "I feel I have a personal stake in this. After all, George is my brother-in-law, and if I have to spend the afternoon by myself with no other occupation than to wonder what, if anything, will happen, I should probably end up having the vapors."

His eyes searched her face again. Ancilla knew her reason for wishing to accompany him was lame, and she could not hope that he would any longer simply wish for her company. She was certain he meant to refuse her, but he nodded curt acquiescence and instructed his groom to stable the mare at Fairfeld until their return.

He gave his horses the office to start and they began their journey in silence. They were no more than a mile or so from Fairfeld when the rain began. The hood of the carriage was already up, but they were driving into the rain and could not avoid becoming wet. The good thing about the rain was that the heavy drops soon ceased; the bad thing was that they were replaced by a foggy mizzle that in its way was as uncomfortable to bear as the rain had been.

The roads had not suffered from the brief rain, and they were soon nearly halfway to Colechester. Their conversation had been only desultory during that time; the mind of each harbored thoughts that neither chose to share with the other.

"When I asked why you had come to me now," Devin said after a lengthy silence, "I meant, why have you come to *me?* You told me you went to Geoff with your confidences last time." He did not sound displeased by this, but as though simply stating a fact.

"I went to Geoff because I knew how strongly you felt and how upset you were about the cup race," she replied truthfully. "I was afraid you would not be objective."

"And this time you think I shall be? Or perhaps it doesn't matter to you any longer if I am or not."

"This time it is more than just suspicion," she replied. "I was afraid then that you would pursue it too earnestly and that George might get caught up along with Sir Robert. I felt I had to protect him if he were not as responsible as Sir Robert was for what had occurred."

He turned to look at her. "Have you and George come to a parting of the ways? I thought you might have when you left Fairfeld to go to Crosby Hall."

Ancilla looked down at her gloved hands. This was the perfect opportunity for her to explain to him that she had merely been a pawn for George's greed; indeed, a part of her wanted to plead her innocence, to beg him to believe that she truly loved him and cared nothing for his money, but another part of her clung to the last vestige of pride that she had before him, and this part forbade her to speak.

Though Devin had been perfectly civil to her, his manner was cool and businesslike. If his original profession of love for her had been sincere, it had not been of a strength to withstand George's plotting. If he had so easily believed so badly of her, she doubted her ability to turn his mind again, and feared that he would think her words just another scheme to win him back again.

Keeping her voice steady, she said instead, "When I went to George in London, I foolishly placed myself entirely in his hands. I thought that he would behave properly toward me, but I was mistaken."

There was no response to this and Ancilla looked up at him. His eyes were directly on the road ahead, his clearcut features as set as stone. Aware that she was skirting too close to the untouchable subject, she thought it best to change it. "May I ask what the evidence is that you hope to find in Colechester?"

"A groom named Stotten, who worked in my training stable at the time of the first meeting," he replied readily. He gave her a brief account of what had occurred that night after he had left her, and the story Smitty had told him. "Obviously the thing was well planned, from creating an opening in the stable for Stotten to fill, to discovering the interests of Smitty so that he could be used as well. Even I was gotten out of the way with that story about Hoby wishing to sell Spanish Coin, though I am still not sure why. I don't think Stotten was put in my stable for just that one meeting. There was too much trouble involved. I think the boy was probably green and took fright. If he is frightened, all the better. It will probably be easier to make him talk to me.

"He came to us from Pomfret, you know," Devin added

as he skillfully eased his team around a slow-moving cart without checking his pace. "In the course of their inquiry, the stewards have discovered that Lippcott had a half-brother who until very recently was employed by Purcell as a training groom at Rockhill, which you know is near to Pomfret's. Despite Purcell's claim that his acquaintance with Lippcott was only casual and of a business nature, it is well known in the neighborhood that Lippcott was a frequent visitor to Rockhill."

"So there is a definite connection between Stotten and Sir Robert," Ancilla concluded.

"A likely one, let us say," Devin corrected. "That is what I am hoping to discover. If Stotten's recruitment came from Rockhill, then Purcell is definitely implicated."

Their conversation came to an end as they neared the outskirts of town. The mizzle had given way to a vapory mist that spiraled about the legs of the horses and in places took the form of a low, patchy fog. Ancilla hoped they would find Stotten quickly, before the fog had the opportunity to thicken and slow their return to Fairfeld.

Colechester was not an overly large town, but neither was it so small that all the residents were well known to each other; nor, in such inclement weather, was there a superfluity of people about to ask for Stotten's direction. However, playing in a pitiful patch of dank grass, and oblivious of the weather, was a young boy, with a thin and hollow look, who might have been any age from nine to sixteen.

When Devin asked him if he could direct them to the Stotten cottage, the boy looked at him blankly for a moment and then said simply, "They be gone."

Devin swore under his breath and asked if he knew where they had gone.

The boy shook his head. "Up north, I hear tell."

Devin thanked the boy and tossed him a coin. "I might have expected this," he said tersely, "but I'd hoped against it."

"He's run away," Ancilla said dully.

"Or has been paid off to leave. 'Up north' is very telling. He could take his references from Pomfret and find work in Yorkshire or Scotland without a blemish to his character or the fear that he would be recognized by one of my grooms."

Ancilla felt defeated. All this precious time wasted and for nothing. She was certain that it would soon be time for George to come for her at Crosby Hall, and she doubted their ability to return before he would make up his mind to go to Waldo about her, for as they drove out of the town she saw that her fears had been realized and the fog had thickened. A few miles farther on, Devin was forced to reduce his team to a trot.

She turned to look at Devin and saw that he was again staring intently at the road, but this time she knew it was in concentration. Every mile passed brought them deeper into impenetrable fog, as they came nearer to the sea. Once, for a few moments, they had even gone off the road, and branches of trees that could barely be seen in passing scraped at the paint of the curricle.

Until now most of her thoughts had centered on the immediate problem of drawing off George and the purpose they had hoped to achieve in Colechester, but the one was now almost hopeless and the other a complete failure. It was a consciousness of the man beside her and the memory of their last encounter that filled her mind, thoughts no more propitious to her peace of mind than the other thoughts had been. They did nothing but add to her sense of hopelessness about her future. Though it would not have changed her untenable position one whit, she wished with all her heart that she had not come with Devin.

Devin, his own thoughts running in a similar vein, kept his horses moving along at a brisk trot, though he knew the wise and cautious thing to do would be to slow the horses to a walk. He was becoming afraid that the fog would soon reach that density not uncommon to the area, which could cause a man to walk into a tree before seeing it; he feared that if they did not soon reach Fairfeld, they might not be able to reach it at all before nightfall.

The fog had not yet reached that dangerous stage, but as they rounded a sharp corner the horses again went off the road. This time the foliage was thicker than the last, and a great branch, fortunately supple, struck Ancilla full in the face.

Ancilla gasped and instinctively grasped at his arm to maintain her balance in the carriage. He pulled up his horses at once.

"Are you hurt?" he asked, quickly turning to her.

Ancilla shook her head, her breath quite taken away. "I-I don't think so," she managed to stammer after a few moments.

Her beaver hat was knocked off and her hair was coming down on one side. Devin reached out with a finger to touch her cheek, and as he did so, a current of sensation went through Ancilla. She closed her eyes to shut it out.

He mistook her expression for pain, which of a sort it was. "You are hurt," he said, his tone accusing.

Ancilla opened her eyes and shook her head again. "Truly I am not."

But he was not listening to her. "That settles it, I suppose," he said in a resigned voice, and gave the reins into her hands. "Keep them up on their bits," he advised. "They're worn, but skittish in this weather."

Before Ancilla could speak, he had jumped down from the carriage. "Where are you going?" she called after him urgently, craning her neck to look beyond the hood as he walked away from her. He did not respond and in a few moments his figure was lost in the fog. He was gone for only a few minutes, but they were very long ones for Ancilla.

"I thought those were the gates to Littlelands that we passed before," he exclaimed as he climbed back into the carriage. "I wanted to make certain of it."

"Then we are not very far from Fairfeld," Ancilla said, her spirits rising a little.

"But we are still too far," he said, taking the reins from her. "I don't wish to alarm you, Cilla, but I'm afraid the rest of the way is too dangerous for us to go on. You know there are a number of sharp curves and twists in the road between here and Fairfeld, and if we did go on in this damned fog, you might well be able to accuse me of deliberately landing you in the ditch," he added dryly.

"But what can we do but go?" she asked, feeling prickles of anxiety.

"The turn off for the road to the cottage should be only a little way ahead. Look out for it."

Ancilla thought she knew his intention and was puzzled. "But you know the lane that connects the Littlelands and the Fairfeld stables is too narrow for a carriage. There aren't any ditches or curves, but we would surely come to grief if we tried it."

"We won't," he replied. "The cottage itself is our goal. We'll have to stay there until the fog lifts and we can safely go on again."

"That might not be until morning," said Ancilla with alarm.

"I know. But I have no intention of risking our necks or those of my horses."

He spoke with finality, and Ancilla gave up her argument. She knew he had made up his mind and would not listen to her, and she was also, by now, almost too dispirited to care. Being forced to spend the night alone in the cottage with the man she at once most and least wished to be with was all of a piece to her on this wretched day.

Halting frequently to stare into the fog beside them, he at last found the turning and safely negotiated it. The cottage soon appeared before them, spectrally shrouded in fog. He turned the curricle off the road and pulled up his horses beside the house.

"I'll undo the traces and tie the horses up at the back," he said. "I'll need some old towels or rags to rub them down and old sheets, if you have them, to use as makeshift blankets."

Ancilla nodded. "I think I have a bucket in the kitchen that you can use to water them."

Devin jumped down, knotted the reins over a low branch, and came around the other side to assist Ancilla out of the carriage. "I suppose it is completely locked up and we shall have to force our way in," he said, sounding tired.

"No. The latch on the dining-room window does not work properly and I was not able to lock it." She led the way and he opened the window with a minimum of effort. He stepped through it first and then helped her with her skirts as she climbed over the low sill.

The cottage had a musty, closed-up smell of stale air, and a thin layer of dust was everywhere. It seemed silent and alien to her and she had no sense of homecoming. She felt a tiny shiver of apprehension as she stood in the center of the dining room, but she ignored it, assuming that her sensations were due to the eerie, feeble light coming in through the windows, and the emotional exhaustion of the day itself.

She walked wordlessly past Devin into a small passageway to the kitchen, where the linen closet was situated.

Devin followed her, and sorting through several sheets, she pulled out two and handed them to him. "There are rags and the bucket in the kitchen. I'll put them outside the back door for you. I'm afraid there won't be anything here for us to eat or for the horses either," she added apologetically.

"I didn't expect there would be," he said matter-of-factly. "It's enough that we have a roof over our heads. We'll make do." He left the house by the more conventional means of the front door and Ancilla went into the kitchen.

He was reaching for the handle of the door when he heard her call his name. It was such a small sound that he was not sure he had not imagined it, but then she called him again and there was a strange note in her voice. Before he could reach her she called out a third time, and this time it was nearly a scream.

He found her almost where he had left her, facing the linen closet. She was leaning against it, and her hands, which grasped the shelf at shoulder level, showed white at the knuckles. Instinctively he took her by the shoulders and turned her into his arms. Ancilla clutched at him like a frightened child. She did her best to compose herself. "H-He's dead," she began, and broke off as the bile rising in to her throat choked her.

"*Dead?* Who?"

Ancilla managed to swallow uncomfortably and tried again. "Sir Robert. At least, I think it is. His head and face are all covered with blood." She shuddered at the memory.

"Are you going to be sick?" he asked gently.

"No," Ancilla managed to say, though she wasn't sure it was the truth. "I don't think so."

He led her into the front parlor to a sofa. He held her tightly against him to comfort her until her tremors began to dissipate.

"Where is he, Cilla? The kitchen?" he asked after a while.

"On the floor," said Ancilla, nodding.

"Will you be all right if I leave you for a moment to see for myself?"

Ancilla merely nodded again. She lay against the back of the sofa and let the waves of nausea wash over her.

When Devin returned to her from the kitchen, he looked

far from well himself. He sat down beside Ancilla again. "I don't think we need waste any time looking about for his killer. I think he has been dead for some time."

Ancilla put her hands together and brought them to her face. She was not the sort of woman to whom tears came easily, but this was a day that would have brought them to a stoic. Devin gathered her into his arms and she wept against his shoulder in great, gulping sobs. "He couldn't have done such a thing," she said through her tears. "I know he is weak and selfish, but he isn't a murderer—it can't be true."

"Of whom are you speaking?" Devin asked quietly.

"George."

"Why would you think George killed him?" Devin asked levelly.

Ancilla raised her head and moved a little away from him. She accepted the handkerchief he offered her before speaking.

"When I saw George today he told me he had to meet someone here. I wondered at it, but he wouldn't tell me what it was about, only that it was a nuisance that he had to take care of. But he couldn't have meant this. I *won't* believe it of him."

"Why not?"

"Do *you* think it?" she asked unhappily.

"I don't think anything yet," he replied, then stood up. "I suppose we should leave things as they are until we can notify the authorities tomorrow, but I don't much relish spending the night here with that in the kitchen. I'll move him out to the shed in back."

"*No*," Ancilla exclaimed quickly, standing as well and grabbing his arm. "We can't stay here now."

"What do you suggest we do?" he said tartly. "We are here only because we had no other choice. Nothing has changed."

"Please, Devin. I couldn't," she said. "I'm sorry. You know I don't usually suffer from an excess of sensibility, but I just couldn't spend the night here now. The Littlelands stables are just a little up the road from here. We could make it there."

"I suppose we could," he admitted, "but where would we sleep?"

"There was straw left behind in the loft," she replied. "I know because George told me I might have it for mulch in the kitchen garden if I wished, but I never used it."

"It's probably moldering by now."

"Then we will make do with blankets that we take from here," she insisted. "Please, Devin," she said again, "if you do not come with me I will go alone. I truly can't and won't stay in this house."

Devin thought her wish to leave the cottage absurd and fanciful, but he saw that she was genuinely upset and to spare her any further distress, he capitulated. "Very well," he said, and went into the dining room again, returning with several blankets beneath his arm. He picked up his hat and whip from a chair and walked out of the house, leaving Ancilla to follow him.

The quarter mile to the Littleland stables was accomplished without incident. After much muscular effort and verbal abuse, Devin was able to persuade the wide carriage door to roll along the rusted track. He advised Ancilla to bend down, and he led the carriage into the stable. Ancilla raised her head, peering into the shapeless twilight inside, and then closed her eyes to give them a moment to adjust. She heard Devin sliding the door closed and alighted from the carriage without assistance. The voluminous skirt of her habit, meant to drape a lady's legs properly while she was astride, was signally unsuited to carriage riding. After first nearly tripping her as she reached the stone of the stable floor, it caught between the wheel and the hub as it dragged behind her. She gave the material a sharp tug, and succeeded in making a jagged tear in the hem, but she was beyond caring about her appearance. The coffee-colored velvet was hopelessly crushed, her face was smudged with dirt, and her mist-dampened hair had fallen to her shoulders in a tangled riot of curls.

She pushed it behind her ears impatiently and began to undo the traces. Devin soon joined her, and when the horses were as properly seen to as could be managed, he went up into the loft for the straw, which, though dry and brittle, turned out to be free of any discernible mold or parasites. He distributed some of it in the loose boxes where they had placed the horses, and the rest he carried to an open space between the last box and the tackroom. He spread the straw there in a thick, flat layer.

"It's a poor sort of bed," he said over his shoulder when

he had finished, "but if we spread the bedding we have brought over it, it will do." He sounded as weary as Ancilla felt.

He went to the carriage to fetch the blankets and Ancilla stood staring at the straw bed he had made for them. The area it covered was barely ample for their needs, not much larger than the small bed they had shared that night at the White Hawk. This was not a fortuitous thought. It seemed to her, in her dispirited state, that from that night on she had stumbled from one misadventure to another, and every time she had convinced herself that at least matters could not be worse, fate had smiled on her sardonically and dealt her another blow. Tears again stung at her eyes but these were from anger and self-pity at the injustice of things in general. She sat down in a heap on the straw and gave in to them.

Returning with the bedding, Devin saw her and dropped the blankets over the closed half of the nearest box door. "Oh, the devil," he said, sounding tired and exasperated. "Why are you crying now? If it's for George again, I suggest you save your tears until you know the extent of his crime."

Ancilla did not regard him and, sighing, he sat down on the straw beside her. "We neither of us know how involved George is in all of this, but if he isn't responsible for what we found in the cottage today, I promise I'll do what I can for him."

Ancilla swallowed a sob and raised her tearstained face to look at him. "Why?" she asked. "You know you dislike him. Why should you wish to help George?"

"Isn't that what you would wish me to do?"

"George may go to the devil for all I care," she said vehemently.

Devin looked stunned. "Then what is this about? Damn it, Ancilla, what are you about? Exactly what is George Martin to you?"

"He is my brother-in-law," she said, puzzled by his question, "however much I might wish that he were not."

"And nothing more?"

After a moment Ancilla understood him. "You can't think that," she gasped.

"I don't know what to think about you," he said, as if the words were forced from him. "For two years I have been trying to understand you, and sometimes wondering why it should matter so much to me that I should," he went on in a dull voice. "Every time I think that I do, you begin chopping and changing and I don't know what is the reality and what is only my faulty judgment."

"You had no trouble deciding what to believe when George came to you after Lucy's ball," she said bitterly.

"What was I to think? What *am* I to think?" he said in a tone that matched her own.

"If you had meant what you said to me the night of the ball, you would at least have given me the chance to explain."

"If I had cared less, I might have," he said very quietly.

She stared at his bowed head for a moment and then stood up to lean over the edge of the box next to them. "It doesn't matter now, does it?" she said, sounding as defeated as she felt. "Do you still want me for your mistress, or have you taken too great a disgust of me even for that? If you do, I suggest that you look for me in the workhouse in a month or so. I think by then I shall find the loss of my honor a very good bargain."

"What is that supposed to mean?" he asked.

"By now I am sure that Waldo has thrown all of my things onto the front lawn of Crosby Hall and has probably washed his sullied hands with strong soap," she said flatly. "I don't doubt that he is now convinced that I am a hopelessly fallen woman and unworthy of his assistance, and when I don't return tonight, he will no doubt be confirmed in his belief."

No longer caring for her pride or whether he believed her or not, and needing to unburden herself of her troubles, she told him of her interview with George on the morning of the first day of the meeting and the threats he had made to her this day. Devin let her speak without interruption. Gradually the uncertainty that had racked him since his temper had cooled began to evaporate into hope, and then into belief, that what she was telling him was the truth. He rose and stood beside her. "Why didn't you tell me this before?"

Ancilla laughed scornfully. "Would you have believed me? Wouldn't you have wondered what new game I was playing? Thought it was more chopping and changing?" she jeered. She turned to him. "I wish you might see yourself now. You *still* don't know what to think. You are no gamester, Devin Langley, at least not at this sort of play."

"I never dissemble when I am in earnest," he said with quiet fervor, "and you are mistaken. I know precisely what I think." He caught his finger under her chin and raised her face to kiss her. She did not resist him, even when he pulled her down with him onto the straw. His lips moved down her throat to the swell of her breasts, and she felt the exhaustion in her muscles begin to give way to the tautness of desire. She closed her eyes and allowed it to happen.

His lovemaking had a curious intensity, but she did not question it, she merely responded, letting her body, with its heat that demanded fulfillment, completely envelop her mind. When they were at last at peace in each other's arms, she did let herself think again, but her thoughts were no longer a torment. One thought she found particularly ironic came to her and she laughed a little to herself.

Devin raised himself on one arm and looked down at her. "What are you thinking?" he asked softly.

Ancilla smiled. "I was thinking that for once Waldo will be imagining the worst of me and he will be quite right.

"Would it please you if, also for once, Waldo were made to eat his self-righteousness?" Devin asked, kissing the tip of her nose.

"I should love it," she said positively. "How will you manage that?"

"By presenting him to you the next time we meet as the future Lady Langley."

Ancilla caught her breath. "Because I shall be hopelessly compromised? Or is it pity because you know I have nowhere to go?"

"Reasons as good as any for becoming leg-shackled," he said with pretended seriousness. "But I think my reason has more to do with the fact that I love you to distraction. You know that now, don't you?" he added with a hint of anxiety in his voice.

Ancilla nodded, her eyes misting with joy.

"You aren't going to cry again, are you?" he asked suspiciously. "If you are going to develop into a watering pot I may be forced to revoke my offer."

"I might," she admitted with choked laughter, "but it won't be from sadness."

He kissed her and then lay down again beside her, cradling her in his arms.

She was just drifting off to sleep when she heard him speaking. "Do you forgive me, Cilla?"

"For what?" she asked, opening her eyes only a little.

"For having so little faith in you. For being a damned fool."

"I expect I shall, in ten years or so," she teased. "Though if you are going to develop into the sort of man who keeps his wife awake half the night by talking, so that she wakes in the morning looking hagged, I may be forced to revoke my consent."

15

Ancilla awoke sometime later, with a start. She sat up quickly, feeling as though someone had touched her, and looked about. The whiteness of the fog had given a lighter shading to the dark of the stable, but it seemed much brighter to her now, and she realized that it must be dawn. She listened intently, but the silence, the muffled quality that fog usually brings, was complete; not even the horses seemed to stir. Still, she knew that something had awakened her, and she knew that it was not her dreams, for these now were only happy. Devin lay peacefully beside her, undisturbed, but she was unconvinced that it was her imagination. She stood up and, taking care to be quiet, stepped out into the aisle. She stood there for several minutes, but there was no movement or sound.

Deciding that she must have been mistaken after all, she was about to lie down again when the quiet of the stable was shattered by a loud clatter coming from the tackroom. Devin was awake in a moment and on his feet the next. He looked about him for some manner of weapon and found a broken piece of broomstick that was not very large, but better than nothing at all. He moved quietly and cautiously toward the door of the tackroom and with a sudden movement kicked it open.

"Don't hurt me, please. I swear I know nothing," a voice said in a terrified falsetto.

Devin advanced into the room, and Ancilla, curiosity overcoming caution, followed him. George Martin was on his knees on the floor; a small overturned table, an empty bucket, and several used-up tins of saddle soap testified to the cause of the noise.

"*You*," said George in dramatic accents, looking at Devin. "I never thought *you* were a part of it."

"Very likely I am not," said Devin caustically. He held

out his hand. "Get up, George, you have a bit of explaining to do."

George took his hand and rose, pausing to rub his knee before straightening completely. When he had done so, he looked directly at Ancilla for the first time. "The *devil*," he said, thunderstruck. "So you've made your own deal with him, have you? To think your principal attraction for Robert was that he thought you an innocent."

Devin's hands clenched into fists at his side. "I would with pleasure put you on the floor again, Martin, for the merest trifle," he told George tightly. "Don't give me more excuse than I need."

George's emotions were in his face to be read: fear, puzzlement, and even a bit of bravado. "Why are *you* here?" he asked, his voice heavy with suspicion.

"On the merest mischance," Devin said. "Before you think to begin with the lies that come so easily to you, it might be well for you to know that I know all about you and Purcell and the connection with Lippcott. And," he added, allowing menace to come into his voice, "we have been to the cottage and found Purcell. You might begin by explaining that. If you can."

"Explain it?"

"You told me you had to meet someone at the cottage, to rid yourself of a nuisance," Ancilla reminded him.

"You mean you think that I . . ." George blanched. "Good God! I found him that way, too. I went there to meet Drake. About Littlelands."

"*Littlelands*," exclaimed Ancilla. "Why should you meet Geoff about that?"

George turned to Devin. "He must have told you he was meeting me. I sent him word today that if he'd meet me there I'd be willing to discuss your offer for the place. I thought that would be best because of the short way between these stables and yours."

Ancilla looked at Devin. She had had no idea that he had offered to purchase Littlelands, but he was not looking at her, and explanation could wait for later.

"And did you meet him?" Devin asked coolly.

"No," George replied, shaking his head. "The place was deserted when I got there, but I saw from the tracks in the dirt that a horse had been taken around back, so I thought I'd find him there. I didn't, but the back door was open a bit so I went into the kitchen." He paused, swallowing uncomfortably at the memory. "I found Purcell that way, I *swear* it. If I was the one who killed him, do you think I'd be fool enough to still be about?"

"Foolishness in you would not particularly amaze me," Devin said sardonically. "Why *are* you still about, George?"

"After finding Purcell like that I was afraid to go back to his room at the Green Man," George said candidly. "I don't know why Purcell was killed, and I'd a small enough part in his doings, but first it was Lippcott and then him . . ." His voice trailed off.

"And you fancied you might be next?"

"It isn't any fancy," George said positively. "Why do you think I was so terrified when you kicked open that door? I thought he'd caught up with me at last."

"Who'd caught up with you?" Ancilla interjected.

"I don't know, but someone's been following me," George said. "At first I thought it was just my nerves, but I'm sure of it now. After I found Robert, I thought I'd take the short way to Fairfeld and mingle with the crowd there, leave with them in numbers so I wouldn't stand out. I meant to get my things at the Green Man and leave on the mail this morning.

"But I hadn't got much past here," he continued, "when I thought I heard something behind me. I admit I was getting a bit vaporish. I went into the woods to a path I know that goes to the manor through thick brush. By the time I got there I felt a bit silly about having taken fright, but it was as good a place as any to stay out of sight for a bit."

"Then why didn't you stay there, George?" asked Devin. "What made you come crawling in here through the window?"

"There was someone in the house with me." He saw a contemptuous smile touch Devin's lips, and said defensively, "There *was*. I heard footsteps plain and clear, and you know how quiet a house is in fog."

Small wisps of suspicion began to creep into Ancilla's mind, and although she wished them away, they remained. If Geoffrey had gone to the cottage to meet George, it was not unreasonable to suppose that he, too, would have found Sir Robert's body. He would surely have hastened back to Fairfeld at once for assistance, but it was a long while since he had left on his errand.

The thought she had next was ugly, but it could not be

entirely dismissed. She knew how strongly Geoffrey felt about his lack of position; she remembered his bitter words, and she forced herself to admit that it was not out of the realm of possibility that Geoffrey had become impatient with waiting for the honest means of gaining what he most desired. Geoffrey's unassailable position in racing circles would have presented him with every opportunity to give to Purcell and Lippcott any information they might need to carry out their crimes.

If she had not wanted to believe that George could do murder, even less did she wish to believe it of Geoffrey. It was a dreadful thing to think of a man for whom she had a genuine regard, and she was almost ashamed of her thoughts.

She was still standing just inside the doorway of the tackroom, but, wishing to have the solitude to think things through, she turned to leave. Out of the corner of her eye she caught a slight movement in the box directly across from them. Instinct made her jump back from the doorway. Both men stared at her, and in the next moment there was a loud retort and George suddenly crumpled and fell heavily to the floor. In one movement Devin pushed the door shut and grabbed Ancilla, drawing her into a corner near the door. They crouched there like trapped animals, waiting for the hunter to ferret them out.

Devin spotted his carriage whip leaning against the wall and reached for it. "I carry a pistol in the carriage, but it's still there. I never thought we'd need it," he said with bitter self-condemnation. "This," he added, indicating the whip, "is the only defense we have. We can only wait and see what his next move will be."

They waited. The time seemed interminable to Ancilla as the seconds became minutes. It was so quiet in the tackroom that she could hear Devin breathing beside her. Her calves and thighs began to ache, and the leather harnessing hanging behind her pressed into her back. She wondered why it was necessary to stoop and thought of standing, but a motion of the whip past the window in the door brought an instant result. There was another retort and fragments of glass showered into the room.

The door to the tackroom began to swing open, an arm became visible, and the hand held a pistol. Devin moved quickly. He stood and cast the whip, and the point, slightly barbed, caught the man at the wrist. He gave a sharp cry and dropped the pistol on the floor. Devin did not go after it but threw himself at the intruder, catching him at the wrist and pulling him headlong into the tackroom. Ancilla had the wits to stoop for the gun, but was knocked over as their bodies crashed onto the floor.

Devin blocked the face of the man he was fighting from her view. All she could see was his dark blue coat, form-fitting buckskin breeches, and white-topped hunting boots, the correct costume for any gentleman of leisure in the country. Then their positions shifted, and her heart sank as she caught a glimpse of fair hair.

She got to her feet, gingerly picking up the pistol and aiming it at them. "Move away from him, Devin," she said, raising her voice. "I have his pistol."

Devin quickly scrambled to his feet, barely eluding the grasping hands of his opponent. Ancilla caught her breath as the man came into view. She stared into the intent, contorted features of Cholly Cholbeck. Devin took the pistol from her and she let it go, hardly aware of doing so.

Cholbeck wiped blood from his cut lip and slowly stood. "Damn it, Dev," he said feelingly. "Why the devil are you here? Couldn't you have stayed out of it?"

"When you involved my horses and my stables, *you* involved me," Devin said, glad there was to be no pretense. "Though I admit I am in it at this point only through my own misfortunes. This at least is one coincidence that is genuine."

Cholly shrugged in resignation. "I know that involving Fairfeld was a piece of arrogance and a bit of a risk, but I am a gamester, after all. I thought I had that solved, though, by getting you out of the way for the meeting. Thought that by the time you reached Fairfeld the cup race would be history and the events hearsay. Still might have pulled it off if I hadn't been surrounded by a pack of fools. Knew it was me, did you? Or are you as surprised as Cilla looks?"

"The night before last I knew, or rather guessed," Devin replied. "What Smitty told us, combined with the knowledge that it was necessary to keep me from Fairfeld for the first meeting, made it inevitable that someone was involved who had more than a nodding acquaintance with me and the operation of my stables. It had to be you or Geoff, and one does not put the whole of the management of one's principal seat into the hands of a man who has not already demonstrated his integrity. That left you, Cholly. I did not suspect it readily, and probably never would have suspected you if you had left Fairfeld out of it. That was not cleverly done of you. Even the meanest dog knows better than to soil his own bed."

Cholly sighed. "It was just too much of a temptation, I suppose. Having my own man right at hand. But I never meant to involve your horses. I just wanted someone about for the meetings at Fairfeld and for when we went to other meetings. Only gave the word to nobble Nimbus because his training gallops were too good. You were right about the Blue, of course. He isn't what he was, and he *had* to win that race. I'd put almost everything I had on him to win. But the boy was only to give Nimbus water, not opium. The damn fool gave him almost enough to drown the horse and then, when the thing looked obvious, he took fright and bolted. Then that idiot, Lippcott, goes and pops some balls into the feed of the Blue the night before the Newmarket meeting. Had Robert tell him it wasn't necessary—Claret Cup *would* have taken it. But this time *he* had a big stake on the race and he took it on himself to do the thing."

"And so you killed him," Ancilla said in quiet horror, speaking for the first time. She was almost awed by the discovery that Cholly, with his cheerful patience and philosophical bent, could be capable of such deliberate evil.

But Cholbeck did not admit casually to this crime, as he had to the others. He turned ashen. "Good God *no*," he said forcefully. "My uncle Purcell did that. Lippcott was getting altogether too cocksure and taking too much on himself. He went to Rockhill and began making demands, and then, when the thing happened with the Blue, my uncle decided he was expendable. Shouldn't have done it. Makes me sick to think of it." And he did indeed look unwell.

"Yet you rallied sufficiently to take care of Purcell when, I gather, he too became expendable," Devin said dryly, "and we, too, were apparently fair targets."

"I don't know why I went after George and shot at you," Cholly said, sounding miserable. "I panicked, I suppose. Self-preservation. Gods knows I'd never want to hurt you or Cilla." For the first time he glanced down at the prone figure of George on the floor to the right of him. "Did I ..." he asked with a feeble nod toward George.

"I don't know," said Devin. Advising her that the pistol was cocked, Devin returned it to Ancilla's unwilling hands and knelt beside George. He turned him over on his back and after a brief examination said, "I think you missed him entirely. He has a lump on the side of his head and I suspect he just fainted from fright and struck his head on the saddle peg as he fell. He'll come to in time."

"Thank God," Cholly said sincerely.

"However, I don't believe that that mess we found in Littlelands Cottage was the result of any accident," Devin said bluntly as he rose.

"Beg you won't speak of it," Cholly said, sounding distressed. "I can't bear to think of it. It was an accident in a way. I never meant it to happen." He paused, looking as if he might be ill. "That wasn't an attempt to nobble Nimbus the other night," he said to Devin when he could safely speak again. "I saw Purcell that morning but we couldn't talk, and he said to meet him outside the stables sometime after midnight so that we could. Didn't want to do it, but he left me no choice. Still, I thought it would be safe enough. Supposed everyone would be in bed by then, with the meeting starting in the morning. But he went into the stable for some reason and Smitty saw him and you know the rest.

"I dropped that opium ball outside Nimbus's stall," Cholly admitted, "to make it look like just another piece of the same trouble. Knew my uncle wouldn't dare to come to Fairfeld again, so I sent him word at the Green Man to meet me at the cottage. I hit on there because I thought it was one place that we would be undisturbed. Couldn't have been more wrong about that, could I?" Cholly added ironically. "Place had all the attraction of a water hole in the desert yesterday."

"Why was it so important for you and Purcell to meet yesterday?" Devin asked.

"It wasn't to me. He insisted on it," Cholly replied. "Said he'd make a stink if I didn't. When we met I could see why. He was sure it was only a matter of time before his part in the nobbling was discovered—damn fool shouldn't have lied to Brisbane and made him suspicious.

He told me the interest was past due on all he'd done for me and he was calling in the principal. He wanted me to give him every cent I could get my hands on, as he meant to leave the country, and he wanted me to give Brisbane the hint about George. Meant to put the whole thing on him so he could come back when it all blew over.

"Couldn't do it, of course," said Cholbeck, sighing. "In the first place most of what I won on the Blue at Fairfield went for my gaming debts and to get the cent-per-cents off my back, and in the second, whatever you may think of me, I couldn't say the words that could mean the hanging of an innocent man. George is just a flat who was useful to my uncle. Probably didn't know the half of what he was into."

"So you saw that justice was done," said Devin grimly.

"*No.* At least, it was, but I didn't intend it. I told him I wouldn't do the thing and he got pretty heated. Said if he was to be ruined anyway he'd take me with him. He meant to send a letter to Brisbane confessing the whole as soon as he got away. Never could abide my uncle, always knew he was bad *ton.* Perhaps I was the fool for getting involved with him, but I needed the ready, you see.

"Scared me white to think of what would become of me if he did," Cholly went on. "I didn't mean to kill him, but I think I wanted to. I hit at him with my cane. Didn't hurt him, but it infuriated him. He grabbed at me and tore at my neckcloth, and I just reached out for the nearest thing at hand, a flatiron left on the table, as it happened. I shut my eyes and struck at him a couple of times, and when I heard him fall, I looked and I saw . . . saw what I had done." He stopped speaking and very slowly sank to a sitting position on the floor. His shoulders began to shake, and Ancilla, who was still standing by the door and aiming the pistol at him, realized he was crying. She and Devin exchanged glances, and Devin, with a grimace of disgust, turned away to stare out of the tackroom window.

Ancilla lowered the pistol, aware that her arm was aching from holding it steady. She felt utterly drained and exhausted, and from the weary set of Devin's shoulders, she knew that he was feeling the same. She saw Cholbeck raise his head and she quickly pointed the pistol toward him again; but he was not looking at her.

"Let me go, Devin," he pleaded in a pitiful voice. "You're the best friend I've ever had. Never had a claim to your notice, but you took me up, let me make Fairfeld my home, and made me feel a part of the family. Couldn't love you more if you were my brother. Do this one last thing for me, Dev," he begged.

Devin didn't look at him. "You know that I can't," he said evenly. "If it were just the horses . . . but it isn't."

"Don't mean it that way," Cholly said, grabbing a saddle peg and pulling himself upright. "Don't want to run away. Where would I go? This is the only life I know, the only place I have friends, and I hate being alone. I couldn't go through it, Dev—I'd die a hundred times before they took me to Tyburn. Please, Dev, the carriage and the pistol. You may trust me to do the thing right."

Devin stared at the fog-shrouded panes of glass as intently as if the vista of the world lay before him. Ancilla, not entirely sure she understood the demand Cholly was making of Devin's friendship, watched as Cholbeck went over to Devin and laid his hand on his friend's shoulder. He said something very softly to Devin. His words escaped her ears, but she thought she caught her name. Devin looked at Cholly in silence for a moment and then turned away from him, bowing his head over his arm, which leaned on the sill. "Give him the pistol, Cilla," he said quietly but firmly.

Ancilla hesitated, but Cholbeck moved quickly and snatched the pistol from her fingers. Alarmed, she stepped back from him, hugging the doorframe, but there was nothing threatening about him. He only smiled at her sadly, then, taking the harnessing off the hook on the wall, he walked past her out of the tackroom.

"Devin?" said Ancilla uncertainly.

He turned. "It's all right, Cilla," he said in a flat voice, and, not looking at her, he followed Cholly out of the room.

Ancilla started to go after them but thought better of it. She picked up the table that George had knocked over when he had come in through the window, and, righting it, she sat down on it. She glanced dispassionately at her brother-in-law, who had not stirred since Devin had turned him over. and then she put her hands to her face and sat very still, just content to rest her weight, exhaustion depriving her even of thought.

She heard the sounds of the horses being put to the carriage, but if there was conversation, it was too quiet to be heard in the tackroom. After a time there was the sound of the carriage doors opening, the clatter of the horses' hooves on the cobbled face of the stableyard, and then the doors were drawn closed again.

Devin came back to the tackroom. "I suppose we'd better make up some sort of a compress for George," he said without emotion. "He probably has a concussion."

Assuming the chore to be hers, and acting more on reflex than on will, Ancilla stood and started to leave the tackroom, but when she came abreast of Devin she stopped and looked up at him. "Why did you let him go?" she asked in as toneless a voice as he had used.

"I had to—it was more than the claim of friendship."

"What did he say to you before he left?"

"He reminded me that through George you are involved, even if only superficially," Devin replied, "and if it came to a public trial there would be a scandal that could not help but touch all of us,"

"You let him go for my sake?" Ancilla said, shocked.

"No. That just added weight to the other things. It's done, Cilla."

But she was not ready to let it go. "What does he mean to do? I am not sure that I understood."

"What, in his mind, is the honorable thing to do," said Devin. "If he can find the courage, and I expect he will. This way will be much easier for him, you know. Cholly was very proud of the position he had in the world. His reputation for good *ton* is important to him. I know that sounds odd, given the dishonorable things he has done, but in his mind taking his life with his own hand will right the balance and give his honor back to him. It truly would have been a form of death for him if he'd had to live through his disgrace."

"So you have played Pilate."

"Yes," he admitted. "I'm sorry if I've disappointed you."

Ancilla shook her head slowly and embraced him. He held her quietly for some time as the brightness in the room became more and more prevalent.

"The fog is lifting," he said presently. "We'll have to walk back to Fairfeld. I think we'll take the road instead of going the shorter way. I suppose there were many at the meeting who were caught by the fog as we were, and we may meet up with someone leaving Fairfeld and have them fetch someone to attend to George. Even after he wakes up, I doubt he'll be steady on his pins for a time."

"What will we say when we do meet someone?" she asked.

"That will depend on whom we meet. There are a few people we shall have to tell everything, but for the time, at least, we'll say as little as possible until I can meet with the stewards and decide the proper way to handle it."

Ancilla agreed that this would be the best way to go on, and then attended to her brother-in-law. She used his neckcloth and water from the pump outside the stable to make up a compress, binding it in place with strips torn from her petticoat. George groaned once or twice, but still did not awaken as she and Devin made him as comfortable as they could with the bedding they had brought from the cottage.

They waited until most of the fog had been burned off by the risen sun, and then they began their trek toward Fairfeld. They had gone perhaps a quarter mile along the main road when they at last heard the sound of an approaching vehicle. When the carriage came into view, Ancilla was surprised to see its occupants, Geoffrey Drake and her cousin Sir Waldo; it seemed odd that they should be together in the latter's gig.

The countenances of both men looked grim and set, but when Geoffrey saw them, the relief that spread over his face was almost comical. Waldo, who was driving, saw them as well and halted the carriage, no such expression in his features. He looked down upon Devin and Ancilla with a glare that was no doubt meant to leave them quaking, but with nothing to fear from her cousin now, Ancilla favored him with her sunniest smile.

"What the deuce has been going on?" Waldo demanded, and launched into a spate of questions. But the rest of his words were lost as Geoff jumped down from the gig and ran over to hug each of them in turn.

"Thank God," he said with feeling. "I've been half demented with worry since we found your carriage about a half hour ago."

"Where did you find it?" Devin asked quickly.

"Just outside the village on the path that leads to the sea." Geoffrey's smile faded and his expression sobered again. "The horses were tied to a tree and the carriage was empty save for a cocked and loaded pistol left on the seat. Some of our lads are still there searching about the place, but we came on to look further in case you'd been robbed or some such thing. We just didn't know what to think. Is that what happened?"

"Not exactly," Devin replied. "Has Brisbane left Fairfeld yet?" he asked, and, when Geoffrey replied in the negative, said, "Good. As soon as we get to the house and I've changed, we'll meet in my study and I'll tell you everything."

The three on the ground had all but forgotten Waldo, who was still seated in the carriage. "I think an explanation is in order at once," he said haughtily, recalling to them his presence.

But Waldo had to content himself to wait a bit longer before he was answered. They heard a horse coming toward them, being ridden hard, and soon Smitty appeared around the bend. His reaction when he saw them was similar to Drake's. "God be praised," he exclaimed with emotion. "I feared the worst, I did, my lord," he said to Devin. He picked up a small pile of folded material lying across the pommel of the saddle and handed it to Geoffrey. "We found this under a rock just out of reach of the tide."

Geoffrey unfolded the top piece, which proved to be a dark blue coat, smudged in several places with the dust that had lain in an unused stable for a number of years. Ancilla saw it and, with a muffled cry, buried her head against Devin's shoulder. The reality of Cholly's death was much harder to view unemotionally than the theory of it.

Devin put his arm about her and drew her close. "That will have an explanation as well," he told Geoff.

"And we'll have that explanation right now," said Waldo commandingly, furious at being so long ignored. "I hope I know my duty to my family, Ancilla, but your behavior this time is outside of enough. When Higgins told me that you'd received Martin after the things you'd told me about him, and that no one had seen you since, I wondered what devilry you were about now. Then I discovered that you'd stolen a horse from my stable."

"I didn't steal your mare, Waldo," Ancilla said quickly and patiently. "If it hadn't been for the fog, I should have been back before I was missed."

"I have given you every benefit of the doubt, Ancilla," he said piously, "but I cannot but think I have been sadly deceived in you. You needn't think to look to the weather for an excuse for the way you have conducted yourself. Alanetta is most deeply disturbed by all of this and, frankly, she won't have it. This time I must say I concur. You have behaved shamelessly."

"I wouldn't be too hasty in my condemnations, Waldo," Devin advised him. "I predict that Lady Crosby will not object to Ancilla remaining with you, at least for as long as it is necessary for her to do so."

Waldo turned his frosty gaze to Devin. "You needn't think, my lord, because you are the principal person in these parts that you have the dictating of the behavior of others."

Devin laughed with genuine amusement. "Well done, Waldo. That is the first time you have dared to disapprove of me openly. Perhaps you have some bottom after all."

Ancilla, too, was smiling and Waldo did not look kindly upon their mirth. "It may be amusing to the two of you—I cannot say that that surprises me. I hope it will also amuse you, my lord, to know that I wash my hands of you both. If you are to Ancilla's taste, then she may look to you for her keeping."

"I intend just that, cousin," Ancilla told him, smiling broadly.

Expecting contrite pleading from her, Waldo almost gasped at her brazenness, but Geoffrey and Smitty, who had stood a little apart as interested spectators, exchanged glances, and Geoffrey, grinning his delight, said, "Damme, Cilla, I *will* dance at your wedding and be proud to do it. I only hope I have Devin's luck one day, though I fear you are an original." He embraced her and kissed her chastely, as was his prerogative as the future groom's cousin.

Waldo stared at them dumbfounded, but he was not a stupid man and the truth became a distinct suspicion. "However," he said hastily, "I am not unwilling to hear your explanations, but they had better be very, very good."

"It won't fadge, Waldo," said Devin. "We know you are onto us. But your strategic retreat does confirm my newfound opinion of your sense. I hope you may convince Lady Crosby to equal charity. I doubt she would wish to be on ill terms with the mistress of Fairfeld."

Waldo found no insult in these words. He merely nodded and, suggesting that they might wish to return to Fairfeld in some comfort, offered them the use of his gig, saying that he and Geoffrey would gladly return on foot. Devin did not give him the chance to rethink his offer but handed Ancilla into the carriage at once. As he took up the reins he called to Geoffrey, who had already started up the road with Waldo and Smitty.

"I had almost forgotten," Devin said when Geoffrey approached him. "We left George Martin at the Littlelands stables. He suffered a blow to the head and I think you should send one or two of our men to see to him. He was not conscious for our little dénouement, and if he awakens and finds himself alone there, he may have a bad time of it. Have the men tell him that all is well, and have him brought to Fairfeld."

"Devin, what the devil *has* been going on?"

"Later. I promise I shall satisfy all your curiosity," he replied and as an afterthought added, "There is one little piece of curiosity on my part that you may satisfy. Did you go to the cottage to meet George yesterday?"

"Yes," said Geoffrey. George sent me a note saying that you could have your price for Littlelands if I met him there to discuss it. I never did meet him though. My damn horse threw a shoe, and by the time I got there the place was deserted. Will George still be agreeable?"

"I should think so," said Devin smiling, "but it doesn't matter as much now." He brought the horse onto his bit and Geoffrey stepped back with a wave and walked off after Waldo.

"But you will satisfy *my* curiosity now," said Ancilla. "I could hardly believe it when I heard George say that you wished to purchase Littlelands. I know it marches with Fairfeld, but surely you do not need the land."

Devin cast her a sidelong glance. "I wonder if I should tell you. You might not like it, and may yet revoke your promise to marry me."

"If it is as bad as that," Ancilla said severely, "I had

better know the whole at once, else it will be twenty years before I deign to forgive you."

Devin smiled and turned the horse toward Fairfeld before answering. "I wished it for you, when I had the arrogant hope of a quite different relationship for us. I hadn't worked out how I was going to present it to you when you wouldn't even take a loan of fifty pounds from me, but I should have thought of something."

"I suppose I should be flattered," Ancilla said, pursing her lips with mock severity. "It cannot be every doxy who has an estate purchased in her honor. Not even you are that odiously rich."

"Yes, I am," he assured her. "And if you do not promise to forgive me at once, I shall purchase every estate in Essex and torment you with wondering how I mean to dispose of them."

Ancilla made as if to strike him and he pulled the gig up abruptly. He enfolded her in his arms, and for several minutes they were a shocking sight to any possible onlookers.

At last he gave the horse the office to start again and Ancilla rested happily against his shoulder, still exhausted but utterly content, knowing that dreams could come true.

About the Author

Originally from Pennsylvania, Elizabeth Hewitt lives in New Jersey with her husband and cat. She enjoys reading and history and is a fervent Anglophile. Her first Signet Regency Romance was BROKEN VOWS.